CHRONOSCAPE

Roger Ley

For Tony and Madeleine

"Time is nature's way of keeping everything from happening at the same time."

JOHN ARCHIBALD WHEELER

"Who controls the Past controls the Future."

GEORGE ORWELL

"The future is flexible, we can change it."

MARTIN RILEY

Prologue

A few miles further down the road, the Woodrow Wilson Bridge soared majestically on concrete stilts high above the water. Riley drove onto it but, as he reached the central span, an explosion under his car flipped it upside-down and flung it over the low parapet. Strapped in his seat, gripping the steering wheel, he began the long screaming fall to oblivion, but the fall became slower, as if the car was plunging into treacle. At first, he thought that his mind was working faster than events, that in a moment his whole life would flash before his eyes, an upload to the CosmicCloud. Still clutching the steering wheel, he watched as airbags slowly inflated all around him, obscuring his vision. He realized that time was running more and more slowly until finally it stopped all together and the car was suspended in space. Panting he looked at the Potomac River forty meters below him, there was no movement in the water, everything was still. He realized that he was weightless in his seat belt.

"Sorry to have to leave it until the last moment, Dr Riley," a female voice said from behind him. "If you could just unbuckle and make your way back here to the portal."

He looked in the driving mirror of his inverted car and saw that a flexible, multi colored membrane had replaced the whole of its rear section. It looked like a soap bubble, strange polychromatic patterns shifting over its surface. A woman of indeterminate age sat on the other side in what appeared to be another vehicle which he did not recognize. She wore a close fitting overall of pastel colors which changed and sparkled in the dimly lit interior.

"We can't hold this configuration indefinitely, Martin, so let's get moving." He sat motionless; her voice became more urgent. "If you don't come right now I'll have to disengage and leave you falling."

Realizing that he had no choice, Riley unbuckled his seat belt and pulled himself towards the rear. He was disappointed that the Colonel and his masters would think they'd won. *Fuck them all anyway,* he thought, as he slid through the membrane and into the future.

Part One

Martin Riley — The Scientist

Roger Ley

Chapter One

England the 1990s

Not another one of these bloody things thought Riley, looking at the computer screen. It was the third hoax email to arrive in his inbox that week. He called Estella over from the other side of the lab. She was his senior research assistant, although their relationship had started to overlap working hours recently.

"Another email from my future self," he said.

"Somebody's taking the piss," she said looking over his shoulder. "Perhaps a post grad has found a back door into the system. You never know what these geniuses will get up to next."

"Well if I find out who's responsible," he said loudly, "they'll be off the system and doing their calculations on an abacus for the foreseeable."

If the culprit was among his team working on one of the nearby computers, it wasn't apparent. Nobody in the room took more than cursory notice, they all had their heads down writing, typing or plotting graphs.

Estella pointed at the screen.

"It's dated 2009, almost twenty years in the future and the sender's address is 'martinriley@osti.gov', an American Government website by the look of it. So apparently, you've emailed yourself from a time when you'll be nearly fifty years old," she chuckled. "Why don't you answer it and ask for a picture of your middle-aged self? We could all have a laugh."

Riley ignored her and read the title out loud.

"Number three -You ought to act on this one, Martin." His finger hovered over the delete key.

"Surely you're going to open it," said Estella. She was enjoying his discomfiture.

"Well, as the first two emails were racing tips, I expect this will be the same." He spoke quietly to her, "I can't see how it's being done. Those last two were winners and it wouldn't surprise me if this is another."

"Well that's not likely, is it?" she said. "Come on, I know you're only a physicist but you must understand a bit about probabilities. Nobody can predict racing results with one hundred percent accuracy. The first two wins must have been flukes."

"Yes, all right, I know you're a mathematician and good at arithmetic. So how do you explain it then?" he asked.

"Maybe somebody's trying to manipulate the odds? I don't know much about horse racing but I've heard of doping and odds fixing. I grant you the date on the email is a mystery but that might be one of the young geniuses showing off. Anyway, what does it say?"

Riley clicked his mouse, and they both read, "Darkling Spy–Aintree two o'clock."

"I need to think about this," he said as he stood and walked towards his office.

"So, what are you going to do?" Estella had followed him.

"Go down to the bookies tomorrow morning and put a fiver on 'Darkling Spy' to win at Aintree." He braced himself for her reaction.

"You are joking, surely you're not going along with this?"

"Go back to your sums."

The first hoax email had arrived on Wednesday and he'd deleted it as soon as he'd read it. When the second arrived on Thursday afternoon he'd checked into it at his local newsagent's. Mr Singh had told Riley which paper to buy and shown him the racing pages.

"Nobody wins but the bookies," he'd muttered, his turban emphasizing the wobbly sideways headshake, that didn't have a European body language equivalent. Riley had agreed with him, folded the paper and taken it home. Sure enough, the second tip, "Midnight Swimmer" had won at Yarmouth on the previous day. A little investigation and a quick search of his deleted emails folder had revealed that the first tip, "Hoarse in the Morning" had also been a winner.

The next morning was a Saturday and despite the memory of Estella's gentle derision, he went ahead with his plan. He didn't want to risk other members of the physics faculty seeing him go into a betting shop, so he wore a hat and scarf by way of disguise. The bookie's shop was near his Cambridge flat. He walked along the rainy street and stopped outside it, hoping to appear casual, as he looked around to see that no one he knew was on the street. Feeling awkward and unsure he pushed open the door and went in. The scarf was itchy on his neck, the hat felt unnatural, he smelt the sweaty tension in the air. He'd never been inside a betting shop before, illogically he'd expected all the other punters to be bigger than him, but they seemed to be an average lot. Riley was not a big man, and he felt self-conscious about his bitten fingernails and nervy disposition, but nobody took any notice of him as he approached the counter and put a tenner to win on his horse. The race wouldn't start for half an hour so he bought a coffee from the machine and sat reading a paper and keeping his head down, trying not to call attention to himself.

Riley soon forgot the nasty lukewarm coffee in its paper cup as the race was announced on the TV above his head. He'd never had a bet on before, the personal involvement made such a difference, he was instantly transfixed as the starting gates opened and the horses and their riders exploded out and onto the track. The horses galloped bunched together at first, but as they began to separate he started shouting along with the other customers, his heart racing in his chest. Darkling Spy came into the home straight and broke away from the leaders. The other punters around him were urging their horses on, but Riley's was ahead and he was screaming louder than the rest as it finished first, at four to one. He was stunned at the excitement and the exhilaration he felt at winning, he stood panting and staring, this was nearly as good as sex. He'd had no idea what he'd been missing. How would he explain it to Estella? Should he even try?

Around him the losers, muttering, tore up their betting slips. They turned their backs on the screen and returned to their racing pages. This could become addictive, he thought as he took a deep breath and mopped his face with a handkerchief.

He was surprised and pleased by the result but now the emails puzzled him even more, three wins couldn't be a coincidence. Two maybe, but not three, the sender was either predicting the future or knobbling the horses.

He stepped up to the counter, handed his betting slip through the grill and took the small bundle of notes from the assistant.

"There you are dear; first time lucky, don't spend it all at once." She smiled to herself as she picked up her knitting.

Riley counted the money as he moved over to the side of the shop. He hated that it was so obvious he was a betting virgin? He put the notes into his wallet, making sure that they were in the right order, all the same way up and all the same way around, with no folded over corners. The other, older punters, sat and rustled their newspapers, cigarettes dangling from their mouths as they squinted at the tiny lettering of the racing pages. Riley coughed as their tobacco smoke caught in his throat and, still feeling conspicuous, he adjusted his unfamiliar hat and scarf before leaving the shop and walking home.

In their flat on Pound Hill he made tea and held the mug to warm his hands. He stared out of the kitchen window and thought about the emails. An indistinct reflection looked back at him and he tried to imagine lines on its face and grey hair. Martin Riley aged fifty. Surely he wasn't really sending emails to himself from the future?

When Estella got home from the gym, he took out his wallet and, with a flourish, placed his winnings on the kitchen table.

"Ta-dah, another winner," he said.

"No, really?" she looked perplexed. "This is getting mysterious, what do you think's happening? Perhaps it's a doping ring, but why would they want you to put bets on and why would they pretend to send emails from the future? Surely they'd just approach you in the street or the pub?"

"Well, what was it Sherlock Holmes said? Something like, 'When you have eliminated all the impossibilities then whatever's left must be the truth, however improbable.' For the sake of argument, we could assume that my future self really is sending messages back, and see where that leads us? We should consider the means, the motivation and the opportunity."

"Well the motivations a cinch," said Estella. "He wants you to make him rich by betting on the gee-gees. Having the means implies access to equipment that can send messages twenty years into the past, perhaps you'll invent it. The opportunity would only present itself if he could do it secretly or with the approval of whoever owns the Time Machine unless he owns it."

"Or else something criminal is going on." They stared at each other for a few moments.

"Let's talk about it in the pub, I'm famished," she said.

In the bedroom, hours later, he lay staring at the Victorian plasterwork around the ceiling rose high above their bed. Their clothes were scattered over the floor but he was losing the plot as far as lovemaking was concerned. Estella was blonde, voluptuous and intelligent; well-rounded in all respects with well-developed physical appetites.

"I can tell you're not concentrating," she said. She sat back. "You're still thinking about the emails, aren't you?" she was slightly breathless. There was a sheen of sweat on her forehead, she pushed her hair back from where it was sticking.

"What, you mean the emails from the future that are predicting the results of horse races, and might make me a millionaire? No, not really, I was wondering what to have for breakfast! Of course, I'm thinking about the emails, I can't think about anything else."

She flopped down on her front next to him.

"So, let's talk about it," she said.

"Well, assuming this isn't a hoax of some sort, it all makes sense. The racing tips have certainly got my attention; they're a quick, simple and legal way of getting rich. At the same time, they prove their own authenticity. It's very logical. I feel quite proud of my future self for being so imaginative."

"Something tells me you need to be careful, Martin. We should keep this to ourselves. If you get any more tips, save the winnings and don't flash the money around."

"The trouble is that temporal messaging must lead to problems with causality," he said. "What if I killed my grandfather and all those other paradoxes?"

"Temporal Messaging, I like the sound of that, it rolls off the tongue, TM, very good," she said.

"But interfering with the past will alter the future," he insisted.

"Well, as long as it makes us rich, why worry about it? What was it Mae West said? 'I've tried rich and I've tried poor. Rich is better.' " She closed her eyes and her breathing began to slow and deepen. They'd made quite a night of it at the Cricketers.

Us, rich, he thought as he drifted off to sleep. He dreamed of horses galloping backwards towards the starting grid with smiling, high kicking dancing girls throwing handfuls of bank notes into the air.

The next morning, they sat in a local café, nursing headaches over a late breakfast.

"If TM is real then how is it being done?" he asked. "I mean, there's a Nobel Prize in it if we can work that out."

"Tachyons," said Estella poking at her Eggs Benedict. "Don't they travel faster than light? They could carry information back through time just like photons and electrons do through space."

"Tachyons are hypothetical particles that have never been observed," said Riley primly. "What about wormholes?"

"Another hypothetical concept," she said. "Anyway, they connect different points in space."

"No, they connect different points in space-time, so they might connect different points in space or time or both. So, you can connect the same point to itself in the past or the future if you only have a wormhole."

"A Time Tunnel," said Estella pulling a theatrical expression and waggling the fingers of both her hands in his face. "What about sending people through it?" she said, sitting back.

"No, the energies needed to control one that big would be astronomical. It might be possible to find one at microscopic level and then send information through it, using short wave radiation."

"It sounds as far-fetched as tachyons," she said as she lifted a forkful of egg.

"Not really, wormholes are allowed by general relativity and there has been serious talk of them existing at the quantum scale, they might connect everywhere to everywhen. Infinite numbers of the little buggers, our problem would be to detect them as, they're so small, if they exist at all."

"Well perhaps you'll send yourself a message explaining how to catch one and control it," said Estella, taking a sip of tea.

"That interferes with causality, where would the knowledge have originated? I think he wants me to work it out for myself. But knowing it's possible makes a problem much easier to solve."

Over the next week he waited to see if anybody he worked with mentioned horse racing but no one did, and every few days another TM arrived in his email account.

He entered a double life. During working hours he was Dr Martin Riley, respected high energy physics researcher, leader of a team of scientists at Cambridge University, analyzing data from the low Energy Antiproton Ring accelerator at CERN. At lunch times, he became a furtive punter driving around Cambridge, spreading bets in different bookmakers. He had to involve Estella because it doubled the number they could place without repeating visits.

"What are we going to do with it all?" asked Estella a month later. They had pulled the suitcase out from under the bed and tipped the bundles of notes out onto the floor just for the fun of looking at them.

"Let's buy a house, we've enough for the down payment." He had been reasonably happy as a bachelor but Estella had brought something into his life he hadn't known was missing. He was a workaholic and could get absent minded when he was fully engaged with a research problem. It was Estella who reminded him to shower and shave, who made him eat properly, made him change his clothes and tried to stop him biting his fingernails. She cared for him. She also took the piss a lot, but he didn't mind that. He loved her and she seemed to love him. "We could even think about getting married."

"Was that your idea of a proposal?" she asked after a short pause. "You're going to have to do better than that, Martin."

They opened bank accounts in the Channel Islands and made occasional trips to St Peter Port to deposit their winnings. They kept their bets moderate and began travelling to betting shops outside their area, they wore different clothes and even used different accents. The money kept rolling in.

Secretly, Riley still worried that this was a scam operated by a gang of horse dopers. He half expected that one night there would be a knock at his front door and imagined himself peering, through the curtains of the upstairs flat, at shady characters waiting on the doorstep below, come to claim their money. He bought a cricket bat in a charity shop and kept it by his bed.

Chapter Two

England the 1990s

"Ah, Dr Riley thanks for coming," Riley stepped into his faculty head's office. The memo summoning him had been left in his pigeon hole. He supposed that it was too late for an oldster like Middleton to get to grips with the new technology and send emails like everybody else.

"Not at all Professor Middleton, how can I help?" He coughed. He hated the smell of the small cigars that his boss smoked, the air in the room was blue and he never opened any windows.

Riley was unimpressed with Middleton as a scientist. Even though he led the physics faculty he hadn't published a paper in living memory. He had only two years to go before he enjoyed his index linked retirement. Riley had noticed that he was careful not to cause administrative ripples, he was probably hoping to get an honor for "outstanding contributions to education" or something similar. The framed display of hand tied fishing flies, on the wall above his boss's head said it all, thought Riley. He might as well put up a notice saying, "I'd rather be fishing than doing science." Riley wanted to be sitting in this office, leading the department, pushing the envelope, getting recognition from his peers. He secretly dreamed of a Nobel Prize and wondered if the emails were the route to one. The money he was accruing was all right but what he wanted more was recognition. He pulled up a chair, sat down and tried to look attentive.

"Have you heard of John Oakwood?" asked Middleton as he leaned back in his swivel chair and puffed his noxious smoke at the ceiling.

"Dr John Oakwood, the Chief Scientific Adviser to the Government?"

"Yes. Well, he's coming here to discuss a new contract we will be bidding for. We'll be in competition with the particle physics people at Warwick but I think we can confidently assume that the light blues will have it. Why he wants to get involved at this level I don't know, but there it is, politics." Middleton made a gesture of helplessness, gave a wry smile and took another puff on his cheroot. Riley imagined that he must be secretly thrilled to be hosting a VIP of this caliber; the bragging rights would be enormous at management meetings. The best way to magnify them was to pretend indifference, and Middleton obviously knew that.

"He wants to keep things low key, no fuss. He likes to speak to the people at the chalk face doing the research, not old war horses like me, so I'll need you to be at the meeting."

Riley felt a frisson of excitement. "Fine" he said evenly, "no problem, I'll make sure my team wear clean lab coats, in case he wants to go walkabout."

"Good, good, that's one problem solved then." Middleton looked down and placed a tick on the list that lay on his desk. "I'll send you details of the contract, so you can prepare the proposal." He looked up and smiled, "Don't let me keep you, Dr Riley." He returned his attention to his paperwork.

Riley left the office barely able to hide his excitement; shutting the door he silently punched the air as he walked down the corridor to his section. Back in his office, he paced the carpet, unable to settle, he couldn't believe his luck. He went and found Estella in the laboratory and, holding her by the elbow, hurried her back with him, closed the door and leaned against it.

"I say, Martin, not before coffee surely?" she laughed.

In the early days of their relationship, Riley and Estella had consummated it over his office desk several times, after working hours. These days they were more sensible, although there had recently been an incident in a bus shelter one night, while they were waiting for the last bus.

"You'll never believe this," he said. "The Government's chief scientist is visiting here next week. He wants to discuss a high energy physics contract."

"Marvelous," she said, "and what's that got to do with the price of fish?"

"I'm going to ask him to fund the TM project."

Estella sat on a chair and looked thoughtful. "How are you going to get him alone?" she asked, "and when you do, how are you going to convince him? 'Messages from the future,' you'll sound completely bonkers. You might find yourself looking for another job."

"Yes, well, I can always fall back on my modelling career."

She laughed, rather unkindly he thought.

"I'll have to play it by ear," he said.

A week later, Riley sat in a conference room listening to his head of faculty, various other section heads, the Government's chief scientist and his civil servants, discussing the research project. As they broke for coffee, Oakwood announced his wish to visit the gents and Riley quickly offered to show him the way. Fortunately, the place was empty and their footsteps echoed off the hard, shiny surfaces as they walked in and the door swung closed behind them.

The two men stood at the urinals, leaving one vacant between them as convention required.

"So, no sign of the Higgs Boson yet, Dr Riley?" asked Oakwood.

"I understood that you were a biologist, Dr Oakwood." During the meeting the breadth of Oakwood's knowledge had surprised Riley.

"I'm usually well briefed by my team before I come on these expeditions," he said. "No scientist could fail to be fascinated by the new discoveries in your area though. Quantum fields, elementary particles, gravity waves, so many exciting things for you young Turks to explore."

Riley stopped pretending to piss, he would have been far too nervous, even if he'd needed to. He zipped up his fly and turned towards the other man.

"Sorry, Dr Oakwood, but this will be the only opportunity I have to speak to you alone," he said, interrupting the other man's musings. "I need a few minutes to make my 'elevator pitch,' I've a proposal I believe will lead to the most important scientific breakthrough of the century."

Oakwood turned to look at him, his face expressionless.

"Really," he said, as if it was something he heard every day.

Riley paused for a second then continued, "For several months now I've been receiving messages from the future."

Oakwood stared straight ahead, Riley knew he couldn't walk away in mid-stream.

"And what form do these messages take, Dr Riley?" he asked. "Voices in your head or something more concrete, Tarot cards perhaps, tea leaves, chicken giblets?"

Riley sighed; he knew this was going to be the most difficult part.

"No, racing tips, actually."

"Racing tips," said Oakwood as he shook, zipped and stepped back from the urinal. "Racing tips. Winning racing tips?"

"Yes."

"How many?"

"Well, twenty-seven so far."

"All winners, no losers?"

Riley nodded. Oakwood moved to the hand basins on the opposite wall and spoke to Riley's reflection in the mirror above, as he rinsed his hands.

"And can you prove any of this?" he asked as he turned to pull paper towels from the dispenser.

"I realize how this sounds, Dr Oakwood, but I have records of all the bets I've laid. I'd be happy to show you my bank statements, you can see the deposits. In the meantime, I wanted to give you this." He tucked a card into the top pocket of the older man's suit. "I've written the winners of three races at different racecourses tomorrow on the back of that Doctor. You might like to have a flutter on them, I can guarantee the results."

Oakwood dropped his paper towels in a bin and removed the note from his pocket. He examined it as they walked to the door and Riley pulled it open to let him pass. He made no comment as they re-joined the meeting. Oakwood left at lunchtime with his entourage.

"Very nice to meet you, Doctor," said Riley. He gave a wan smile as they shook hands, Oakwood's expression was unreadable, as he nodded his goodbye.

The next evening, as Riley arrived home on his new racing cycle, he noticed a black Range Rover parked in the street outside. He leaned the bike against the hedge and, as he went to open his front gate, the driver's door opened. A man in his early forties stepped out and approached. He wore a grey suit and had flecks of grey in his hair, he moved with confidence and had a characterful nose; Riley guessed, from his build, that he might have broken it playing rugby or possibly boxing.

"Good evening, Dr Riley, my name is Paul Burnley." He held up an identity card for a moment and Riley caught the letters "SIS" printed on it as it passed by his line of sight. "Dr Oakwood has asked me to escort you to a meeting with him, if you could just get into the car sir." He moved to the rear door and reached to open it.

Riley stepped back, "I'm not going anywhere until you tell me what this is about." His voice quavered slightly and was higher pitched than he meant it to be. He cleared his throat.

Burnley tapped on the roof of the car and the other doors opened. Three athletic-looking younger men dressed in dark suits climbed out and walked over to Riley. They surrounded him, standing closer than he liked.

"I want to speak to my lawyer if I'm under arrest." Riley noticed that his voice had quavered again. He felt little trickles of sweat running from his armpits and across his ribcage. He realized that he didn't know any lawyers.

The older man sighed. "Look sir, there's no need to excite yourself, I'm not arresting you, I only want to take you to a meeting with Dr Oakwood." He spoke deliberately as if to a child. "So, it would save us both a lot of trouble if you could just get in the car, please."

Riley made a move towards the safety of his front gate. With startling efficiency, two of the younger men grabbed his arms while the third slid a cable tie over his wrists. They bundled him into the back of the car, with one man sitting on either side of him. The third walked back and got into the driving seat.

"There now, that wasn't too difficult was it sir?" said Burnley as he got into the front and slammed the door. He sighed and muttered something to the driver. As they set off, Riley looked back and saw a flash of light from his front garden. It was hidden from view as the car rounded a bend. He looked forward as they drove off through Cambridge and then South on the M11 motorway. He hoped Estella was all right, she'd gone to the supermarket and wasn't due home yet.

Riley's emotions were in turmoil. He hadn't had a fight since he was a child. Burnley and his agents scared him, he was trembling and had no idea what would happen next. Would they torture him? Murder him? Imprison him under the Official Secrets act? What powers did these people have, official or otherwise?

"Where are you taking me? Estella's expecting me, when will I get back? What about my bicycle?" He realized that he was gibbering.

"Now don't worry," said Burnley. "You won't be away for long, Dr Oakwood just wants a little chat with you, and then we'll get you home safe and sound. I'm sure your bicycle will come to no harm."

The other agents chuckled quietly and the rest of the journey passed in silence, Burnley ignored him, and the agents stared out of the windows. What with the exertions of his bike ride home and now all this stress, Riley realized that he was beginning to smell rank. Nobody commented, he assumed that they were used to the smell of fear. Other people's unpleasant body odors, just another, seldom mentioned aspect of the exciting life of a secret agent. He felt calmer as he thought the situation through, Oakwood must be taking his pitch seriously. If he'd written Riley off as just another nutty scientist, then he wouldn't be sitting in the back of a car full of secret agents, speeding towards a meeting with the British Government's chief scientific adviser. Things might not be as bad as they seemed.

Their destination was a detached house in a residential street in Bishop's Stortford. It was set back from the road, Riley guessed that it had been built in the nineteen twenties.

"This is one of our safe houses, Dr Riley," said Burnley. "Dr Oakwood is waiting for you inside." They helped him out of the car and then stood in the porch while one of the agents knocked and spoke into an intercom. A man in shirtsleeves opened the door and as they entered Riley saw the he was wearing a shoulder holster, with a nasty looking black automatic pistol in it. His confidence took a downturn. He stumbled over the sill and realized that he was sweating again. With an agent on either side of him, he followed Burnley through the hall and into the lounge where Oakwood was standing with his back to the electric fire. The room felt warm and welcoming, a piece of classical music that Riley couldn't identify was playing in the background. The furnishings were bland and tasteless but looked unused.

"Ah, Riley, how nice to see you again. I say, remove those restraints at once," he said harshly and Burnley produced a pair of wire cutters and briskly cut through the cable ties. Riley wondered what other uses they had been put to.

"Good for pulling out fingernails, are they?" he asked as he massaged his wrists.

"No sir, we use pliers for that," said Burnley, he put his other hand in his jacket pocket and brought a pair out, "but only if it's necessary." He looked into Riley's eyes for a moment unsmiling, and Riley shuddered at his lack of emotion. He dropped his tool kit, and the broken cable ties, back into his pocket and walked out of the room to join his unobtrusive colleagues.

"I am so sorry," said Oakwood. "I gave orders they should treat you with the utmost respect. Can I offer you one of these?" Oakwood held out a tumbler with a generous measure of amber liquid in it. Behind him, on a coffee table, Riley noticed a bottle of fifty-year-old

Macallan and another tumbler. Oakwood turned and poured himself a small one. "Your tipple I believe," he said smiling and holding up the bottle. "Sit here by the fire. We can have our talk in comfort." Riley sat, and knocked back his whiskey.

"I don't usually do that," he said and looked at the glass as it trembled in his hand.

"No, no, of course. My dear fellow, you've had a terrible shock." Oakwood leaned across and poured him another measure. "It wasn't supposed to happen like this, it has all been an unfortunate misunderstanding." Riley didn't believe a word, he was convinced that they'd scared him on purpose, as a way of establishing dominance.

He sat and waited, rubbing his wrists, more from nerves than discomfort. His bonds hadn't been tight, there was no point in complaining, in fact he was pleased they were taking him so seriously. He looked around at the insipid decor and noticed the slight squeaking from the electric fire's flame effect mechanism.

"We watch our scientists carefully you know, depending on the work they're doing and its implications for national security," said Oakwood. "Your work has not had a high enough priority to merit more than routine scrutiny. After our conversation yesterday, I put in a query about you." He passed Riley a note which showed the account numbers and balances of all of his and Estella's bank accounts, including the one in the Channel Islands which his bank had assured him was safe from inspection by the Inland Revenue.

"Please understand, Dr Riley, that I am not a spy, I am a scientist, or perhaps a civil servant, but I need to know everything about this, er, Temporal Messaging. It has enormous political potential, but I do not want to go off half-cocked at a cabinet meeting if it comes to nothing."

Now that the intimidating agents were no longer present, and as the alcohol hit his blood stream, Riley began to relax. He felt better; he noticed that the tremor had disappeared from his hands.

"There isn't much to tell," he said, "I've been receiving, what appear to be emails from the future, for about a year. I have copies of them."

"Yes, so do we now," said Oakwood. His smile had a hint of self-satisfaction. He had the habit of steepling his fingers in front of his face, thumbs under his chin and slowly rubbing his lips with his forefingers. It reminded Riley of an irritating personal tutor from his early student years. "So how do you suppose it's being done, Dr Riley?" he asked

"I'm not sure how Temporal Messaging operates yet, but I assume I'll work it out once somebody underwrites the research." Riley smiled at his own faultlessly circular logic. Oakwood reached forward to top up his glass. Riley noticed that Oakwood was barely drinking from his own. "There's no need for coercion," he said. "I can't afford to fund this project; it has to be financed by the Government."

Oakwood sat back, "You must have conjectured how you can achieve it though, surely you've thought about it," said Oakwood.

"I've thought of little else for months now. I think we need to use wormholes at the quantum matrix level; we might be able to send information back through them using high frequency electromagnetic radiation, X rays or gamma rays, I'm just not sure yet."

"If we can send information back through time, Dr Riley, then we would have control of the future. The idea is extraordinary; we could change the course of history. Have you discussed it with anybody, apart from your partner, Ms Pearson?"

"Talking about 'messages from the future' in the senior common room wouldn't do me any good professionally, would it?"

"No, I don't suppose it would," said Oakwood, "but a discovery like this would largely obviate the need for intelligence work. Normally, the spooks are trying to get information so they can prevent unpleasant things from happening. Foreknowledge would change everything, prevention would be relatively easy."

"Yes," said Riley, "but don't you see how dangerous that would be. Changing the future would have unpredictable consequences further down the line."

"Yes, well we'd have to put on our thinking caps wouldn't we, Dr Riley? But first we need to see if we can do it, then cross our bridges as we come to them."

Riley leaned forward, "Yes but remember it's my idea and I want to be in charge of it."

Burnley drove Riley back to Cambridge alone.

"Not bothering to tie me up this time?" asked Riley as they turned out of the driveway.

"People only make a fuss when we collar them, Doctor. They're usually relieved when we take them home." Riley wasn't sure if he had heard a slight chuckle.

During the rest of the journey Burnley was as taciturn as ever, but when they stopped outside Riley's flat he spoke again. "Apologies about before, Dr Riley, I expect we'll be seeing more of each other, so I'm sorry if we've got off on the wrong foot." He reached across to open the passenger door and Riley thought he wanted to shake hands, after a clumsy moment he climbed out.

"Mind how you go," said Burnley, as Riley slammed the door. The Range Rover drove away; its rear lights disappeared as it rounded the corner at the end of the road.

Riley's expensive new bicycle had disappeared. He found it leaning against the shed in the back garden and assumed that Estella had moved it. As he let himself into the flat, she came out of the lounge to meet him.

"Bloody hell, Martin, you look terrible. Where have you been?"

He walked past her and sat in an armchair. "I think I may have solved the funding problem," he said, massaging his wrists absentmindedly.

"Well, you don't look thrilled about it."

"No, it was all a bit sudden, I need a cup of tea."

"I'll get you one," she said, "and then you can tell me all about it."

The speed of events, after Oakwood became involved, surprised Riley. He was given an immediate leave of absence from his faculty at Cambridge University. Called to an office in Whitehall two days later, Riley watched a jacketless Dr Oakwood make hurried calls as he walked back and forth, his movements limited by the length of his telephone cord. Riley sat, making notes as he picked a team of scientists and listed equipment he needed to start the project.

"My name will be mud or worse at Cambridge," he said. "I'm denuding my former department of most of its mathematical and scientific talent."

"And that bothers you?" asked Oakwood, pausing with his hand over the mouthpiece.

"No, this project is too important to worry about details like that. You do realize that if I'm successful, this discovery would be worth a Nobel Prize?" said Riley.

"You won't be publishing scientific papers, Doctor, the ramifications are far too sensitive," said Oakwood. "I advise you to get used to the idea, it's quite normal with Government scientific work. Academically speaking you will drop out of sight like a stage magician through a trap door."

Riley knew that he had no choice, he wanted that Nobel Prize but needed Government funding. If he made TM work, perhaps they would eventually release the technology to the United Nations, and then he would get the recognition he deserved.

Chapter Three

England the 1990s

A week later Oakwood rang Riley at his flat.

"I've found a suitable venue for the project," he said. Riley heard the satisfaction in his voice. "The Martlesham Heath research station in Suffolk has spare capacity, it's part of the Government's signals intelligence network, and very secure. There are useful facilities, computers, telecommunications, all that sort of thing, and it's an easy run up the A12 from London."

They met outside the Martlesham facility a week later. Oakwood had clearances that got them through the main gate. They walked through the complex to the recently vacated building that was to be the home of the new project.

"It's standard Government construction, built in the sixties, rather stark I'm afraid, economy block work," said Oakwood. He produced a set of keys from his raincoat pocket and unlocked the entrance doors. They walked along a corridor with small individual offices leading off on either side.

"I'm disguising Temporal Messaging as a communications project, for funding purposes, and hoping the accountants don't ask me for too many details," said Oakwood.

"Tell them it's all done with laser beams, that's what I do," said Riley trying and failing to get a laugh out of his new boss.

"Good idea, I'll call it a 'Laser Communication Project.' Anyway, I will avoid explaining TM to my masters until we've proved the theory. We'll need something convincing to show them."

"I'm surprised that you're taking such a risk, Dr Oakwood," said Riley as they continued along the corridor towards a second pair of double doors. "I've always assumed you civil servants were conservative in your habits."

"This will house the main research lab," said Oakwood, making an expansive gesture as they stepped through into a large empty workshop with a high, framed roof. He stopped and turned to face Riley, his expression intent. "You don't get to be Chief Scientific Adviser to the British Government without taking a few professional risks along the way, Dr Riley. It's a matter of picking the winners, to use a metaphor close to your heart. You were right when you said this technology might be the discovery of the century."

Oakwood's commitment impressed Riley, but he felt exposed, knowing failure would leave him unemployable as a research scientist. He had committed professional suicide by poaching so much talent from his previous employer. If he didn't succeed, he could end up as a school science teacher. There was nothing for it, he had to make TM work.

He walked over to the electrical breaker board and peered up at it. "Three phase power," he said, "we'll need plenty of that."

In the two months that followed, Riley assembled his team and their equipment. There was the irksome business of identity cards, barber wire fences and guard dogs patrolling the Martlesham facility. When Riley delivered his welcome speech and pep talk Estella had been standing at the front smiling encouragingly. His explanation of the project up until that point had been as nonspecific as he could make it, and he was pleased at the number of his workmates that had still been willing to sign up with him.

In the center of their large laboratory space the team put together the jury-rigged collection of racked hard drives, digital computers, scanners and most important of all, the cyclotron particle accelerator. They jokingly called the arrangement the "Transmogrifier". Nobody remembered who had come up with the name.

"I'm surprised that you haven't thought of a more, er, aptronymic title, something more accurately descriptive," Oakwood said, as he stood looking at it on the second of his monthly visits.

"It's good security," said Riley. "The name gives no clue to the machine's function."

"Ah, yes, I suppose you're right," said Oakwood. "Like 'tanks' in the first world war. The fewer clues to our activities here the better." He surveyed the team working at their benches and computers. "So, Martin, any progress yet?"

"Yes, there is. When we bombard a thin gold specimen and raise its charged state instantaneously, we've been able to detect a raised charge in parts of the crystal structure a short time before we initialize."

"What is the time interval?"

"About a nanosecond. We appear to be detecting the ends of charged wormholes with one end in the present and the other a nanosecond in the past. Frankly I'm surprised that they haven't been detected before now. I can only assume that nobody's been looking for them."

"Being able to send information a nanosecond into the past isn't very useful, Martin. It could even be an experimental error. Why can't you detect wormholes that are further displaced in time?"

"We're not sure yet, we might need to use higher energies, different frequencies or possibly different materials."

Riley escorted Oakwood to the staff car park where his uniformed driver, standing next to his car, was hastily stepping on a cigarette. The scientists shook hands.

"I have a lot riding on this, Martin," Oakwood said, his expression serious. Riley couldn't think of a suitable reply. There was a slight pause before Oakwood got into his car and was driven away.

That evening Riley and Estella sat in the local McDonald's.

"You certainly know how to spoil a girl," said Estella as she bit into her burger.

Riley felt slightly sick and toyed with his. "Oakwood is already pressing me," he said. "He can only continue funding us unofficially for a limited time. We need to make progress, show some useful results."

"Get the team together and have a brainstorming session," she suggested. "You never know what the young geniuses will come up with."

They finished their meal and went back to the laboratory for another late session.

Riley became more edgy as the end of the month and Oakwood's next visit approached.

"I need something to show him," he told Estella. "We'll all be out on our fucking ears if we're not careful."

Oakwood phoned the next day. "I'm travelling down the A12, Martin so I thought it would be economical to make this month's visit a few days early. I hope it's not inconvenient?"

"Not at all, Dr Oakwood, when can we expect you?" Riley's felt the beginnings of panic, his mouth felt dry.

"We're approaching the car park now; I'll be with you in a few minutes."

Riley made frantic phone calls. The visit was not a success. They had made little progress and, although Oakwood was polite, he was less patient than before as Riley escorted him to his car.

"Martin, this experiment is costing a lot of money and currently we have nothing to show. The Government will be happy to fund it once we have some results, but you really must come up with something soon." Riley noticed that he left without shaking hands this time.

Later, Estella walked into Riley's office to find him sitting with his head in his hands.

"We'll never get it to work. I feel as if I'm committing career suicide here."

"We all understand how important this is, Martin," she said. "The team have been working twelve-hour shifts but we need better detectors. We're pretty sure we're on the right track but the wormholes become more difficult to find as we move further along the time axis."

Riley worked longer and longer hours; his moods developed a monthly cycle synchronized with the imminence of Oakwood's next visit. When he shaved in the morning, he could see that he was looking gaunt. He needed to pull in his belt by an extra notch. His anxiety wasn't helping his relationship with Estella; he was too tired for sex.

Four months later, he was in his office examining columns of figures on a stack of computer printout when Estella breezed in.

"Good news," she said, "one of the geniuses had the idea of trying spent Uranium as the medium, and lowering the excitation frequency. Apparently, it's not just a question of higher energies, there seems to be an element of tuning. Different materials need different frequencies for us to detect wormholes at varying temporal displacements."

He looked up, his expression resigned.

"So, what's the time shift now, two nanoseconds, three?"

"A second," she said.

"A second, a whole second? Bugger me, that can't be experimental error, I need to see this." He moved rapidly out into the laboratory. "Which display are we talking about?" Estella pointed, he stood behind the operator and read the column of figures over his shoulder.

"Show that graphically and give me a printout," he ordered as he picked up a nearby phone and rang Dr Oakwood.

Oakwood arrived the next day, a measure of his level of anxiety thought Riley. They looked at a series of sheets that Estella had pinned to the notice board in Riley's office. They showed a three-dimensional graph with peaks and valleys scattered, seemingly randomly.

Riley pointed to it, "Were beginning to get a grip on the situation, we've been working all night in shifts, you can see the relationships appearing. The major factors seem to be the density of the medium, the charge levels, and most importantly the excitation frequencies. If we can get hold of a bigger cyclotron with say, double the power, I'm sure we can make significant progress."

"What sort of temporal displacement would you be able to achieve?" asked Oakwood.

"I'm confident we can make the signal jump back a day." Riley's hands were resting openly on his desk but mentally they were behind his back with their fingers crossed.

"That would justify much more serious funding, Martin. I'll go back to London and see if I can call in some favors."

A new cyclotron arrived from ALCEN Technologies, its manufacturer in France, a month later.

"It's on loan," Riley told Estella as they watched it being craned into the space they had made for it, next to its smaller cousin. The rest of the team were waiting impatiently for their opportunity to start wiring it up. "You can't buy these things off the shelf, but ALCEN's client has a delay in their building project, and won't be able to take possession for two months. We've got six weeks to nail this."

"What do you mean by nail it?" asked Estella.

"I mean, produce a significant temporal displacement. I promised Oakwood a day. He needs something to show the Cabinet Secretary before he can hope to start funding us officially."

Estella pulled a wry face. "Let's get on with it then."

The team worked over the weekend to connect and calibrate the new machine. Oakwood called Riley two days later.

"How is the project progressing, Dr Riley?" he asked.

"It's not progressing, the bloody things broken down. I've been on to ALCEN, they can't send a tech rep to fix it for weeks. All their people are busy working on other machines in different parts of the world."

"Leave this to me."

A technician arrived two days later, and the machine was on line within twenty-four hours. He left, but the lab smelled strongly of Gauloises afterwards. They had to hunt out all the flattened cigarette butts and bin them.

The new results came quickly. Riley was leaning over Estella's shoulder, looking at her computer monitor.

"The graphs extend very nicely, Martin. As we get the tuning more exact, we find wormholes with greater temporal displacement."

"What's the maximum displacement now?" he asked.

"About four thousand seconds, a little over an hour. The problem is that the charged wormholes are more and more difficult to find as the temporal separation of the ends increases. We think we're detecting clusters but as we increase the separation, the numbers of individual wormholes in a cluster reduces. It's a law of diminishing returns. I've done some statistical work, there will be an upper limit of about two weeks and we'll need a much bigger cyclotron to achieve it."

"What's the limiting factor?"

"Well, at a displacement of two weeks, we'll be at the theoretical limit of our ability to detect the cluster. It'll also give us a limited bandwidth for sending digital information through it."

"Okay, when can we show a one-day separation?"

"Probably next week, but don't go phoning Oakwood until we've got it all sorted."

It took a little longer than a week. Oakwood and the Cabinet Secretary, Robin Buckley, arrived at Martlesham ten days later. Riley met them in the car park. Buckley seemed too young to be the most senior civil servant in the land, he was shorter than average and dark haired, Riley thought he had a mid-European look. He appeared relaxed as he shook Riley's hand, smiled and nodded as Oakwood introduced him. The three men walked through the building to the main laboratory.

"I've brought Mr Buckley here by himself because the security implications of the TM project are so critical," said Oakwood. "I'll leave the demonstration to you, Dr Riley."

Riley knew that despite the veneer of good manners and mutual deference this meeting would be the most important of his career so far. His chest felt tight, and he'd already given the visitors noticeably sweaty handshakes.

The three men stood beside a bulky monitor and keyboard. Riley hoped that his voice wouldn't quaver as he began an explanation of the equipment and process. He'd worked on his presentation for hours the previous evening, trying to simplify the science, but Buckley interrupted soon after he'd started.

"Excuse me, Dr Riley, but I really don't need to know the technical side of this, although Dr Oakwood has attempted to explain it all in the car on the way up." He laughed. "Of course, I did Greats up at Oxford and thoroughly enjoyed it, but I'm afraid I'm not the most practical of types when it comes to science or engineering, all that sort of thing. All I need to see is that you can send information back in time. If you can do that, then the world is your oyster, 'the crustacean of your choice,' so to speak. Funding will be showered upon you in biblical proportions." He laughed. "But you have to convince me, all this equipment could be smoke and mirrors for all I know. How are you proposing to send this message?"

"I'm going to ask you to send it now," said Riley. He picked up an envelope which was lying on the desk beside the keyboard. "This envelope contains the message you're about to send. It arrived on the hard drive yesterday at about this time. Please don't open it, put it in your pocket, then type anything you like on this keyboard."

Buckley took the envelope, placed it in the inside pocket of his jacket and, after a glance at Oakwood, he began to type. The words "Horas non numero nisi serenas" appeared on the screen. Riley took over the keyboard and copied the phrase into the first line of a screenful of computer code he had called up. He pressed the enter key.

"I've just sent your message back to myself. I didn't have to do it straight away, I could have left it until you'd gone, but I like to keep things tidy," said Riley. "You can look in the envelope now, Mr Buckley."

Buckley tore it open, drew out a piece of paper and read the same message out loud. One of the geniuses had written underneath "Only count the happy hours."

"Yes, very clever, Dr Riley but I've seen conjurers perform a similar trick." Buckley smiled engagingly. "You must do better than that, if you want me to recommend to the Prime Minister that the Government stump up millions of pounds to support your pet project."

Despite his friendly demeanor, an image of a smiling great white shark swam through Riley's mind. He looked at his watch and turned on the television arranged next to the computer monitor.

"How about the winner of the three-thirty at Beverly, Mr Buckley?" Riley took a sheet of paper from his pocket and handed it to the Cabinet Secretary smiling confidently. "I also received this message yesterday."

The civil servant read out loud, "The winner will be 'River in May,' at six to one on the nose. Oh, I say," said Buckley suddenly becoming animated. "Now you're talking Riley, now you're talking. What a shame it's too late to put on a small wager." He turned to look at Oakwood, grinning, his eyes bright. Oakwood gave a wan smile, Riley thought he was doing his best to appear enthusiastic.

Riley laughed inwardly and said, "Actually, Mr. Buckley I did place a small wager, and I took the liberty of putting a tenner on for you." Riley handed Buckley a betting slip and the three men pulled up seats and sat down to watch the race.

After the civil servants had gone, Estella brought in two cups of tea, she sat at the desk next to Riley. He was feeling slightly dreamy as the stress leaked out of him. He tapped slowly at his keyboard.

"How did it go?" she asked. "They both seemed pleased as they left, chatting away to one another ten to the dozen. Buckley was rubbing his hands together. He looked positively gleeful."

Riley finished typing and swiveled to face her. "I got Buckley to send himself a message."

"The one we received yesterday?"

"Yes, he wasn't impressed, virtually accused me of sleight of hand. I knew I had to come up with something more convincing, so I fell back on our old friends, the gee-gees. I didn't tell you but I also got a message from myself yesterday, I've just sent it. It gave the winner of the three-thirty at Beverley. I heard on the grape vine that Buckley's a betting man; in the most civilized way of course. The first message didn't convince him but the second one certainly did. I even arranged for him to win sixty quid. You should have seen Oakwood's face. You know he's a lay preacher, he hates betting, but as they say, 'Needs must when the Devil drives.' " They both laughed out loud and Riley managed to spill tea over the front of his trousers.

"Let's leave early," said Estella. "I'll help you get those off. We can open a bottle of Prosecco to celebrate."

The research continued, sometimes problems held them up for weeks or even months before they overcame them, but as time passed the team made progress. Oakwood's visits became more routine and, for Riley, less stressful. Now that funding was no longer a problem, they had commissioned a new cyclotron from ALCEN. It was built to their own specifications, and customized for the excitation amplitudes and frequencies they needed. It proved to be a turning point in the project.

One evening, soon after its final commissioning, Riley and Estella were working late together. They were both scrutinizing a monitor on a bench in the deserted laboratory. At intervals of a few seconds, filenames were appearing on screen, eventually seven were listed.

"I'll print them," said Estella, who was standing nearest to the keyboard. She tapped some keys and went off to the nearby large format laser printer. Returning a few minutes later she laid seven large sheets out along an empty bench.

"So, this is a scan of the back page of tomorrow's Guardian newspaper," said Riley, scrutinizing the date and heading at the top of the first page. He pointed it out to Estella. The image was less than perfect, grey and fuzzy but just readable. He stared at Estella. "Fuck me, I can't believe it, we've done it," he stared at her unblinking. "We've done it," he shouted, "the bloody thing works, we're vindicated," he grabbed her hands and jumped up and down, dancing with delight.

His enthusiasm puzzled Estella at first but then the realization flooded over her and she joined in. "If we can send a page of newsprint back a day, then the sky's the limit. We've done it," she shouted.

They stopped dancing to take another, longer look at the printout. "Is that your thumb in the picture?" asked Riley.

"It looks like mine but I haven't got a broken nail."

"Not yet," he said.

Estella checked her thumb nail to be sure, but it was intact.

"So tomorrow I'll scan that day's newspaper and send it back twenty-four hours to us now, and the file will have appeared on the hard drive the day before we sent it. It's difficult to get used to the effect coming before the cause. What would happen if I decided not to send it?" she asked.

"But you will, or if you don't then somebody else will, somebody with a broken thumb nail."

"I must remember to pick up a copy of The Guardian on my way in to work, although I've always been a Telegraph reader myself."

"Yes," he said, "and we'll scan the day's newspaper and send the file back up the Timestream every day this week. We need to designate one of the geniuses to do this from now on." He gestured at the bench. They looked at the first sheet again.

"I can just read it," said Estella. "What a pity that the sports news is so boring, why can't we scan the business pages and see what the share prices are doing? We could make money."

"Because we don't understand the ramifications of making even tiny changes in the present yet, if we fiddle about with the present we'll change our future. Anything could happen. There might be horrifying

43

consequences, we might blink out of existence; we have to be very careful. Why am I the only one who can see this?"

"Alright, calm down, Martin; don't get your knickers in a twist."

He calmed himself with an effort and looked at the print out again.

"I see the West Indies are sixty-five for four, or at least they will be tomorrow. Let's look at the printout from the next day."

Riley and Estella looked at the next sheet, it was less clear.

"So, we'll send this one the day after tomorrow. I can't read it. Perhaps it's noise in the receiver," said Estella. They walked along beside the bench looking at each of the pages. "As we go further forward the quality reduces even more. The ones from over four days ahead are just a mass of grey. We have to find a means of sharpening the transmission; we could filter it or perhaps increase the resolution of the scan head?"

"That'll make the files larger and slow their transmission rate. We need more bandwidth if we want to send files back from further down the Timestream., we'll need more power as well."

Riley and Estella were sitting in a quiet corner of their local six weeks later, they were both on their second pint.

"It doesn't matter how much power we use," said Estella, "information sent from two weeks downstream seems to be the limit, if we try to send it further it doesn't arrive. I told you, the numbers don't lie, if there are wormholes that stretch more than two weeks then we haven't found any. Perhaps they exist in a different form. It's probably a quantum effect we don't understand."

"You're right," Riley agreed, "the further downstream we try to go, the more difficult it gets to detect the wormhole clusters and the more the bandwidth for transmissions reduces." He thought that if he was still working in academia, scientists would call this the "Riley Effect." With his name permanently linked to the new field of study he would be the "Father of Time Travel."

"Well, if we've established the limitations then it's time to try something practical," said Estella.

"Practical, what do you mean?" said Riley. He had a sudden hollow feeling in his guts.

"Well, we could make a small intervention, a Temporal Adjustment. We might stop something bad happening. That's what you want to use this technology for isn't it. You've said so enough times, after a glass or three."

"I don't think we're ready," he said, "we need to gather more data, do more experiments." He realized how pathetic he sounded, and that Estella knew he was playing for time.

"Oh, grow a pair, Martin; we have to try it sooner or later, Her Majesty's Government won't fund us forever and Oakwood's no fool, he knows how much progress we've made."

Riley felt a terrible emptiness flow over him. He realized she was right, but the prospect of making even the smallest change to the future petrified him.

Next day, back at his office, Riley spoke to Oakwood using the encrypted phone. "I want to try something new, Dr Oakwood, I want to try making a small intervention. We call the idea a Temporal Adjustment, a TA."

"Yes, I suppose it's the logical next step," said Oakwood, "given that the whole purpose of this technology is to control or possibly to steer the future. What do you have in mind?"

"I'm not sure yet, it depends what we get from our scans of the newspapers. Something important enough to appear in print but the less significant the better."

"Do nothing without consulting me," said Oakwood. "Call me if you find anything suitable and I'll be there post haste."

Riley spent days reading future news stories as they arrived on the hard disks each day. Eventually, after much soul searching, he made his choice. He, Estella, and Oakwood met in Riley's office. Oakwood punched "999" into his brick like, government issue, mobile phone. They wanted to avoid any chance that the call could be traced.

"Hello, is that the police? I want to report a disturbance at 19, Moorefield Street, High Barnet," he said.

It was the address of a house where a drug addict would murder his partner in about an hour's time, according to the newspaper story that had arrived almost two weeks earlier. The copy had lain on Riley's desk for over a week while he overcame his uncertainties. They had chosen this episode carefully.

"I think I heard a gunshot," said Oakwood, thus triggering the attendance of an armed response unit. He hung up giving no further details. Riley sat quite still, shoulders raised, he didn't speak, he half expected oblivion. They had finally interfered with the Timestream. He waited to see if there were any discernible changes.

"Well everything appears to be normal," said Oakwood brusquely after about a minute. "If there were to be any ramifications, they probably wouldn't be immediately apparent." He got up from his chair. "Congratulations, Martin, I'll be on my way. Let's talk next week." He left and as nothing untoward appeared to have happened, Riley and Estella went home for the weekend as usual.

Riley's worry that they had caused the Timestream to branch or change in some way nagged at him. He suspected that Oakwood wasn't interested in the consequences of Temporal Messaging, as long as it worked, and its success reflected on him.

The next day was Saturday, early that morning Riley got up, threw on a pair of jeans and quietly let himself out of their house in Ipswich, they'd moved there to be closer to the lab. He walked around the corner to the tobacconist and bought a copy of the Guardian. Back home, in the kitchen, he made two mugs of tea and took them upstairs. Estella grunted, sat up, pushed her hair back, and reached for her tea.

"Thanks," she said. "Well, what's the news?"

Riley opened the paper to the story of the police raid and placed it on the bed. He unfolded a copy of the printout of the page from the future and laid it next to it. They looked very similar, except that the original story's headline was, "DRUG ADDICT MURDERS WIFE," while the newer one was, "POLICE STORM CRACK HOUSE." While the stories differed, the layout of the rest of the page was unchanged.

"Well," said Riley, "now we know."

"We saved a life," said Estella smiling.

Riley nodded, "Yes, yes we did," he said, although he was far less sanguine than he appeared. Why was it that everybody around him was oblivious to the cliff edge they were sleep walking towards, he wondered?

Chapter Four

England the 1990s

"Well, they've finally done it," said Estella. She'd walked into Riley's office and was sitting on the edge of his desk.

Riley was working on the end-of-year report. "Who?" he asked without looking up.

"Charles and Diana of course."

He carried on typing. "Done what? Look, I have to get this finished before the end of the day, before we break up for Christmas. Can we talk about it tonight?"

"It's the Queen I feel sorry for," she said, ignoring his objections. "It's just one thing after another. Those photos of the Duchess of York, disporting herself topless with that Texan millionaire. I've never had my toes sucked," she said wistfully. "And that biography of Princess Di that came out earlier in the year, that was a slap in the face for the Royals, but Charles and Diana separating, well it must be the last straw for her."

"You've forgotten income tax," muttered Riley, peering at the computer screen.

"Income tax?"

"The Queen has to start paying tax, like the rest of her subjects," said Riley. He couldn't keep the satisfaction out of his voice.

"But she isn't like the rest of her subjects," said Estella. "You're so cynical, I don't expect she cares about the tax."

"Well, it would've been a much worse year for her if we hadn't put a stop to the fire at Windsor Castle, remember? The original pictures of that were almost apocalyptic, Windsor Castle in flames, what a sight. And all it took to prevent it, was for a man with a fire extinguisher to be in the right place at the right time. Just a quick squirt of carbon dioxide, child's play for Paul Burnley to arrange. We didn't save any lives, but we did something important there, I still believe in our national heritage."

"Yes," said Estella, "I was so glad we could do that for her. It would have broken her heart to see Windsor Castle burning, on top of all her other problems. It's been a difficult year for her."

There was a knock on the door and Paul Burnley, now head of internal security for the project, came into the office. *Still wearing the same grey suit, he had on when he arrested me*, thought Riley.

"I thought you'd like to know," he said, "we've had a story come in about a bombing in Manchester. Two bombs, one near the city center and another near the Cathedral, sixty-five injured. I expect we'll be able to stop them but I knew you'd want to include it in the report. I wouldn't publish it yet."

Riley, Oakwood and Burnley were well aware that their funding depended on results. Unfortunately, their results were invisible to the general public and most politicians. The unpleasant events they predicted didn't happen, because of the Temporal Adjustments made by the security services. It was crucial that they reported their interventions to the Cabinet, along with prints of the newspaper as evidence of the original incidents.

"Well, I'll leave you to it then." Burnley withdrew, closing the door.

Riley sat back. "You know, we've accomplished a lot this year. We couldn't stop all the IRA bombs without risking giving the game away, but we stopped the biggest ones."

"How many people do you think we've saved?" asked Estella.

"There was the big one in September, that would have injured twenty people and damaged seven hundred houses. The one at the Baltic Exchange was bigger, about a ton of fertilizer. There would've been about ninety people injured, but the damage was going to be enormous, hundreds of millions of pounds worth."

"So, are you still worrying about interfering with the Timestream?"

"I realize that people change the Timestream every time they make a decision or do anything, but I'm still uncomfortable about what we're doing. I mean, we've always made changes for the better, to save lives or prevent crime. We've done nothing for personal gain."

"What about the betting? We took a lot of money off the bookies with our little scam," she said.

"Well, we had no choice, we had to prove the theory."

"We didn't need to place the bets, just knowing the tips were right would have been enough."

"Yes, but apart from that, since the project started, the Government hasn't stepped out of line. They've always worked for the public interest and disadvantaged nobody," he said.

"I don't think the IRA would agree with you."

"But they're terrorists," he said.

"One man's terrorist, Martin...."

He didn't rise to the bait.

"Anyway, its five o'clock, and I'm going home. I fancy a nice long bath and a glass of Chardonnay, then off to bed, all snuggled up warm under the duvet waiting for you. Don't be too late or I might be asleep." She left, leaving the door open to annoy him.

"Stuff this for a game of soldiers," he said as he quickly logged out. "Wait for me," he called.

Chapter Five

England the 1990s

Over the next two years, the Temporal Messaging team developed an administrative framework. Riley was head of science and administration. Estella led the mathematics team. Paul Burnley was in charge of internal security and he brought in two teams of agents. The "Gleaners" gathered information, mainly newspaper stories, and then fed them into the Transmogrifier using large format scanners. Their data appeared on the hard drives two weeks back upstream in their past. Riley suspected that they were not the sharpest knives in the SIS drawer, although they were all young, enthusiastic and cheerful, with private school accents and impeccable manners.

The "Scrutineers" analyzed the files, sent by the Gleaners, from two weeks in their future. They were a different type of agent, intelligent, quiet, intense, very pleasant but they never socialized outside their group. The teams had separate offices on opposite sides of the building and were discouraged from talking to one another. Burnley chaired occasional meetings between them but he held them behind closed doors. Two technicians would arrive from London and sweep the room for bugs beforehand. Riley didn't know what they discussed, even Estella hadn't been able to penetrate Burley's security bubble using her, surprisingly successful, water cooler gossip technique.

"I wonder what they're talking about in there?" said Estella one morning. She was sitting on Riley's desk again, swinging her legs and eating a piece of fruit cake. The coffee she had bought from the machine in the corridor was beside her. Riley's cake and coffee were at his elbow but so far, he had ignored them.

He looked up from his paperwork. "What, are they having another one of their bloody meetings? I expect it's all very mundane. The Scrutineers are probably complaining about something the Gleaners will do in two weeks" time. You can imagine the protestations of innocence. 'We can't be blamed for something we haven't done yet?' "

"Yes, but you will do it darling, you will," he said in an effeminate posh accent.

"They're not all gay, Martin," objected Estella.

Secretly, Riley was self-conscious about his own Estuary accent, but had decided that it was too late to do anything about it. "I don't envy Burnley," he said, "he's a field man, not a bureaucrat. I expect he feels that it's time to come in from the cold, but he won't find office politics easy."

"Drink your coffee, Martin, and if you don't eat that cake I will," said Estella as she knocked crumbs from her hands and reached for her coffee. "Have you heard about the 'Mull of Kintyre' incident?"

Riley's team was still in charge of the hard drives and so they had first access to incoming information. He expected this to change soon as the security noose continued to tighten.

"No, I haven't, what's the story?" he asked, mildly interested.

"Well," said Estella, taking a breath and obviously anticipating the delicious pleasure of disclosing new gossip, "a report's just come in, front page in all the papers in two weeks" time. Apparently, this RAF helicopter was flying most of the security experts from Northern Ireland, thirty of them, to Glasgow, and it crashed into the cliffs at the Mull of Kintyre. There were no survivors."

"Bloody hell," said Riley looking up at her. "That'll cause a stink. Was it the IRA?"

"Don't know yet, we've only seen the first reports, we have to wait twenty-four hours for the next scans to arrive. By the way, I heard," she lowered her voice and leaned forward towards him, "that there's a new feed on the hard drives. One of the programmers, Wendy, told me they're encrypted files that even she can't open. We think it's something to do with Paul Burnley sending himself secure information from two weeks ahead."

Riley knew of the new SIS secure feed and saw it as further evidence he was being squeezed out. "It doesn't really matter what caused the crash, the Government won't sit by and lose their advantage over the IRA," he said. "They'll prevent it and bollocks to the consequences."

"What consequences, surely if they can save all those lives then that's a good thing?" said Estella.

Riley stood up and paced around the office, his fists bunched. "Why am I the only person in this organization who understands that altering the present will inevitably change things further down the line?" He was speaking through clenched teeth. "If that helicopter was going to crash and we prevent it, what will be the effects in Northern Ireland and the rest of the UK? We don't know, but we can be sure that we're deflecting the Timestream, either that or we'll be taking a different path, a spur that divides from the main path and where will it lead?"

"Well the main path might be leading us towards nuclear oblivion, Martin, so what's the difference?" Estella stood up and left.

He knew she'd heard it all before. He cleared up the paper cup and other debris she'd left on his desk, threw them in the bin and picked up his phone.

That afternoon he sat at a table in the conference room, the room where Burnley held his security meetings. Burnley sat opposite him and at the top of the table was a personal computer with the monitor turned through one hundred and eighty degrees so it faced towards them. A technician was fiddling with the keyboard. The screen cleared and Oakwood's face appeared. The technician adjusted the camera mounted on a tripod nearby and left.

"Good morning gentlemen," said Dr Oakwood. "We have convened at the request of Dr Riley so I think we should let him kick off, so to speak. Martin?"

"Yes, er, it's about the Mull of Kintyre thing that happens in a week and a half. I want an assurance you will not make alterations to prevent it. The consequences would be unpredictable."

"I believe some of your colleagues will be passengers Paul," said Oakwood.

"Yes sir, there will be people on board who I've worked with over the years. People with valuable knowledge and experience we can't afford to lose." He sat impassively, looking at the screen.

"Friends of yours?" asked Riley. Burnley turned towards him, his face expressionless, he said nothing. Riley shivered, he thought back to the incident with the wire cutters and wished he'd kept silent. He was afraid of Burnley and wasn't ashamed to admit it to himself.

"I understand your position, Martin, and I have conveyed it to our esteemed Prime Minister. Apparently, he sees it your way," said Oakwood, "he's conservative in both senses."

"It would be simple to ground all Chinooks for a while," Burnley persisted. "There's been talk of a bug in the engine management software."

"Well I'm afraid the Government will not be intervening Paul. After my recent conversation with the PM and the Cabinet Secretary, they have decided to employ the utmost caution with Temporal Adjustments. We can continue preventing terrorist and criminal activity, and so forth, but incidents of national and international importance are off limits for the moment."

" 'For the moment,' what does that mean?" asked Riley.

"Dr Riley, you cannot be so naïve as to believe that the Government will not eventually make full use of this new technology, technology they have expensively funded over the years? Surely you realize that we will inevitably use it to advance British interests in many different directions?"

"But it's so dangerous," said Riley.

"So are nuclear weapons, Dr Riley. I'm afraid that you should have considered the consequences of Temporal Messaging before you developed it. As we speak, a committee is being formed to supervise Government use of TM technology. We have recruited some of the finest minds in the Civil Service to it."

"That's a relief," muttered Riley.

Oakwood continued without pausing. "You can rest assured that our future will be safe in their hands, with all future adjustments or interferences with the, er, Timestream, planned and implemented under its auspices."

Burnley looked up. "With all due respect, Dr Riley shouldn't be attending this meeting. The science team shouldn't have access to the content of the hard drives, it's bad security. They don't need to know what information we receive from the future. Their job is to keep the equipment running and find ways of improving it."

Riley bridled, this was what he had been expecting, although he was surprised that Burnley had brought the matter up in open session.

"If I get taken out of the loop, I'll resign and so will most of my team," he said.

All three of them knew that if this happened, despite the Official Secrets Act, TM would become public knowledge. Riley would make sure of it. He imagined the headlines, "The Father of Time Travel," and the smiling pictures of himself on the front pages of the newspapers, maybe even on the cover of Time magazine. The comparisons with Newton and Einstein, the total eclipse of that has-been Stephen Hawking with his fame and his books and his honors.

There was an awkward silence. Riley imagined that Burnley was planning a horrifying accident that would wipe out the TM team, enabling him to replace them with Government stooges. Oakwood, on the other hand, would be working out how to finesse the situation in his own interests.

"We'll leave it there gentlemen. I've told you what the PM's decision is, and other matters can be dealt with later when we have more time to thrash them out." The screen went blank.

Burnley picked up his papers and left without a word. Riley stayed where he was for a few minutes, trying to work out his next move.

It was ten days later; Friday night was curry night, and Riley and Estella were sitting in a booth in the Jaipur Restaurant. Riley was still fretting about his meeting with Oakwood and Burnley.

"Stop worrying, there's nothing you can do about it. Have a poppadum," said Estella as she broke one of hers and spread mango chutney on it.

"Anyway," she said, "the PM saw it your way, so everything's okay. Eat your poppadum."

"Yes, that was a surprise," he said, mollified. He reached across for the bowl of chopped onions and spooned some onto his plate. He leaned across and whispered, "I was surprised they didn't interfere with the helicopter accident, there were a lot of important people on board."

"Yes, but not as many as in the original reports," said Estella.

"What do you mean?"

"Well, there were thirty passengers and four crew, in the reports from two weeks downstream, but when they reported it today, they said there were twenty-four passengers."

"Probably an error in the first report," said Riley.

"God, Martin, you're not thinking. Today's report is the first report. They were both issued on the same day by the same newspaper, but the one from the future said thirty passengers and the one from the present said twenty-four. I expect the Government saved their most important people. A compromise, it's what us Brits are good at. Ah, here comes my Lamb Rogan Josh."

Riley toyed with his food and wondered whether the changes to the helicopter's manifest had been an official intervention, or had Burley's personal scruples overcome his sense of duty. He was sure that if friends of Burnley had received unofficial phone calls, warning them not to take the flight, the calls would not be traceable back to him. Covering his tracks would be second nature to Burnley, but he would still be punished, proof or no proof if the calls were not sanctioned.

Riley wondered if his own star might be rising after all.

Oakwood rang two days later. "Paul Burnley has been called to duties at Vauxhall Cross," he said. "He's still involved with the TM project but it's felt he has more to offer with the new supervisory committee. Positive vetting and all that I expect. You'll see him from time to time at Martlesham, but his major responsibility will be for the security aspects of the new committee."

Back to his old job snooping, thought Riley, as an image of a grey muzzled old Bloodhound came to mind. *He'll probably be more comfortable. Old dog, new tricks.*

"How do you feel about supervising his input and output teams, the, er, Gleaners and the Scrutineers I believe he calls them?"

Riley was pleasantly surprised, but cautious. "Security isn't my field, Dr Oakwood, perhaps you need somebody with more relevant experience."

"Not really, Martin. The new committee will make the decisions, we'll promote one each of the Gleaners and Scrutineers as group leaders, reporting to you for administrative purposes and to the new committee as far as operational matters are concerned. You'll still manage the science team of course, with an increase in your remuneration and promotion to grade five. This is rather a good opportunity for you, if you don't mind my saying so."

"Do I get a promotion too?" asked Estella playfully when he told her that evening.

"I'm not sure there's a grade for sex slaves," he said as he helped her out of her underwear and pushed her onto the bed.

"Oh, Martin, you are a naughty boy," she laughed as he struggled out of his shorts and joined her.

"They're trying to control the number of people inside the security bubble," he murmured as he nibbled one of her ear lobes. He moved his head down. "God, I do love a girl with brown nipples."

"Yes, I can see that," she giggled.

Chapter Six

England the 1990s

Oakwood had asked Riley to attend a meeting of the steering committee in London, and he was suited, booted and carrying his new leather briefcase, Estella's present for his thirty-second birthday. He enjoyed first class train travel and used the time to read a physics journal, even the coffee wasn't bad. He got off the train at Liverpool Street and took the Underground to the new SIS building at Vauxhall Cross, "Legoland" as its inhabitants had already dubbed it. The passes and paperwork that Oakwood had sent him, got him past the security desk and as far as the metal detectors. After the uniformed staff had searched his briefcase, they politely waved him through to the atrium. He made his way to the room on the third floor that Oakwood's letter had stipulated. The secretary in the outer office showed him straight through into a large conference room, it held an oval table with about two dozen people seated around it. They looked up as he entered. He noted the only empty chair, at what he assumed was the foot of the table, and sat down before anyone invited him to. It was only a small gesture, but he felt slightly more empowered by it.

Most of the occupants turned and continued their quiet conversations.

Oakwood was sitting at the opposite end of the table.

"Dr Riley, thank you for coming," he said, rising to his feet. The other delegates fell silent. "I've been briefing the newly formed, 'Temporal Adjustment Steering Committee,' or 'TASC' as we call ourselves." He paused and smiled, Riley thought he was probably pleased to be associated with such a muscular sounding acronym; it was almost as theatrical as the Government's 'COBRA' emergency committee.

"As one might expect, there is some understandable incredulity among the delegates, I'm hoping that you can show them evidence that will corroborate your theories."

Riley noticed that Oakwood had not introduced the individual Committee members, although he recognized several politicians from their appearances on television. Their uniforms advertised the representatives from the military. He assumed that the rest were either 'spooks' or senior civil servants. He had been expecting to deliver his presentation to a group of 'suits' but this was the first he had heard of a 'Temporal Adjustment Steering Committee' chaired by Oakwood, why wasn't he on it. They wanted him to feel he was just the hired help, the 'little man who does the science.' *The whole world is run by arts graduates,* he thought, *the scientists are pumping in the bilges while these bastards take all the credit.*

He noticed that Oakwood's introduction implied the theories 'belonged' to Riley at this point, but suspected that they'd also 'belong' to Oakwood if things went well. *Slimy bastard.*

Riley was nervous, Oakwood had warned him that funding of the project depended on the outcome of this meeting, he was sweating, always a bad sign. He liked to do presentations in shirtsleeves but his under-arm wet patches would be too much of a giveaway. He wondered what level of interference to expect from this band of bums and stiffs from now on. The Government would see TA as a huge political opportunity. The military would see it as a weapon and God alone knew what the security services would want to do with it. They'd see it as a threat because it made them largely redundant. Who needs spies if you can foretell the future?

He stood up, "Ladies, gentlemen, good morning, my name is Martin Riley and I am the inventor of time travel, I am here to tell you that the future is flexible, we can change it." Despite his nerves he chuckled inwardly at the group's startled reaction to his introduction. It was always best to begin a lecture with something to make the students sit up and pay attention, and he was pleased that his voice hadn't quavered.

Riley picked up the long pointer lying on the desk in front of him and felt his confidence return. He was in his element, he'd done this before.

"First image please," he called. A page from a newspaper appeared on the screen behind him. "Ladies and gentlemen this is the first scan we sent back to ourselves from twenty-four hours in our future." He turned and pointed to the date at the top of the page. "It may not look very impressive but I hope to convince you that it has tremendous implications. It is as historic an image as the photograph of Neil Armstrong's first boot print on the surface of the Moon."

As he talked, Riley saw Oakwood sit back, a small satisfied smile on his face. He watched, with a slight feeling of distaste as Oakwood chose a biscuit from the communal plate in front of him, and dunked it in his tea. He managed to transfer it to his mouth before it could collapse and form an unappetizing sludge at the bottom of his cup. Riley realized that Oakwood always supplied gingernut biscuits for meetings at his office because they were the best dunkers. He looked more relaxed than he had for months. Riley expected that Oakwood's next appointment would be to the House of Lords. Who'd have thought it; his parents had owned a fish and chip shop in Lowestoft.

He realized that he had paused momentarily and brought his attention back to the presentation.

"Next image," he called.

When Riley had finished, Oakwood led a discussion about possible types of Temporal Adjustment which could be made in the interests of the British Government.

"We have to be very conservative in our tamperings with the Timestream," said Riley. "We can't be sure what effect they'll have on the future."

"Yes, yes," said a white-haired Army officer whose red ringed, peaked cap lay on the desk in front of him. "But if there's a threat to the public or the sovereign, then we will need to act immediately. We've got a job to do, matter of duty."

Riley knew there was no point in trying to argue, but he was still not comfortable and spoke to Oakwood later when they took a comfort break.

"Yes, Martin, it's the old problem. Nobel invented dynamite and wanted people to use it exclusively for peaceful purposes. Einstein opposed nuclear weapons. No doubt the inventor of the bow and arrow wanted it to be used for hunting rather than warfare but unfortunately, that isn't the way the world works. It all comes down to the interests of the people who hold the purse strings. In this case, HMG."

Depression descended on Riley as he took the train back to Suffolk. Moodily he stared out of the window as the sky darkened and the fields streamed by. At least Einstein and Nobel had the satisfaction of recognition for their discoveries, even if they didn't like the uses people put them to. He, on the other hand, was just another commuter on the train home from London. He hadn't been invited to join TASC, they hadn't even bothered to make him an official adviser. It was bloody irritating, he would have to discuss his position with Oakwood.

As time passed it became clear to Riley that he would never be invited to join the Committee. He fretted about his status. It was a weekend in August and he and Estella had driven up to Aldeburgh for a walk by the sea and a visit to, their favorite fish and chip restaurant.

"Why is it that as far as the civil service is concerned, you can have the strongest Glaswegian accent, a Brummie or Geordie accent, a Welsh accent even a bloody awful Northern Irish accent, but just a hint of Cockney and you're a pariah, working class, only fit to sweep the roads."

"Oh, you're being too sensitive, Martin," said Estella as they walked along the footpath above the shingle beach.

"It's all right for you, you speak perfect BBC English."

"Yes, it always surprises me when I hear a recording of my voice. I sound much posher than I feel. Anyway," she said, changing the subject. "Just think about the work, and all the good we're doing. It makes me proud to be part of the team. I mean, that IRA bomb in Manchester in June. It would have devastated the whole city center if we hadn't been able to warn the Committee. Hundreds of people would have been killed or injured. Think of it."

Riley couldn't come up with an answer when she talked like that. He'd relaxed his guard while he was thinking, and a herring gull swooped down and snatched his ice cream.

"Bollocks!" he muttered as it flew away, mobbed by its companions.

"Never mind, Martin, you can have a lick of mine," giggled Estella.

That Autumn Dr Oakwood summoned Riley down to his offices in London.

Another interminable meeting, he thought as he gazed at the burned fields from the first-class compartment of his train, as it sped south from Ipswich towards London. The farmers seemed to begin ploughing earlier every year. The lack of an agenda or list of attendees to the meeting had puzzled him. Still, it was Friday; he might get back to Ipswich for an early start to the weekend.

Riley had a special interest in the racing at Ascot the next day.

He dozed for a while then stared at his paperwork, bloody holiday rosters, the bane of his life. Admin was the thing he hated most about the job; he just wanted to work on the science. An hour later, the train arrived at Liverpool Street Station. Stepping off, he joined the crowds shuffling towards the entrance to the Underground and took the Circle line to Victoria. The walk to the headquarters of the Office of Science and Technology in Victoria Street was a pleasant opportunity to stretch his legs. He made his way up to Oakwood's top floor office, and the secretary showed him into the inner sanctum. Oakwood and Burnley were there to greet him. They got up and shook hands.

"Ah, Martin, nice of you to come, sorry for the mystery, but I need a word in private. I am afraid that the matter is rather sensitive and, er, personal. Please take a seat."

Riley sat in the proffered chair, and noted the air of formality that pervaded the room. A silent alarm in his mind disturbed his composure. If Oakwood wanted a private word then what was Burnley doing there? Was he here as a witness?

"How can I help, Dr Oakwood?" he kept his voice flat as he stared at the other man.

"I'm afraid that it concerns your interest in 'the turf', Martin. The security people say you are continuing to place bets and win tidy amounts which you are presumably salting away for personal use. Technically, you are making a profit from a government project and this leaves you open to the risk of disciplinary action."

"I have only placed three bets since the project got official sanction two years ago," he said. "I've always assumed that the racing tips are my future self's way of validating Temporal Messaging. It's a simple and inexpensive proof that TM works."

"Be that as it may, it still looks rather dubious, almost fraudulent. After all, ministers are not allowed to make personal profits from their work in politics." Riley stifled a chuckle, while Burnley stayed impassive. "You know exactly what I mean, Martin," Oakwood snapped.

"Very well, Dr Oakwood," said Riley nodding his head. "You're right, I can see your point, and I will cease all involvement with betting at once. Next week I'll close all my bookmakers' accounts."

Riley enjoyed the look of surprise on Oakwood's face; presumably he hadn't been expecting such an easy capitulation.

Oakwood glanced across at Burnley. "Would you be prepared to sign a declaration to this effect, Martin?" he asked.

"Of course."

"Good, I have one ready here." Oakwood lifted a sheet of paper from his desk and passed it across to Riley, who signed and dated it after reading its brief contents. "I'll have a copy made for your records and forward it to you."

"I'll take a copy now if it's okay with you, Doctor," he said. "Is that all?"

"No, I have several other things I want to discuss while you're here; the proposed increase in the size of our intelligence gathering team is the first item on the agenda."

Riley's heart sank at the thought of even more admin. His life seemed to consist of nothing but budgets, holiday rosters and stationery indents. They'd be discussing the overuse of paperclips next.

Burnley stood up, shook hands with both of them and left. He had barely said a word. Riley assumed that he had only been there to witness the proceedings and report back to his masters. Bastards, wait until Monday and see who's feeling smug then.

At the end of the meeting Riley left the building and phoned Estella as he walked towards the entrance to the Underground. He had received a racing tip a week before by the usual method and, according to the email, it was to be the last. The Italian jockey, Frankie Detorri would win all seven races on Champions Day at Ascot next day and this opened the door to an accumulator bet of unprecedented proportions. People who made such bets were known to the bookmakers as "Mugs" or "Mug Punters." Riley had taken full advantage of the opportunity. He and Estella had broken up the bet and placed every penny they had with various turf accountants around London and Ipswich. His promise to Oakwood had been an irrelevance. He caught an early train home and took the rest of the afternoon off.

The next day, Saturday, Riley and Estella, with mounting excitement, watched all seven races on their TV, drinking champagne and cheering their horses on. By the time the winner of the seventh race, 'Fujiyama Crest,' crossed the finishing line, they were both shouting at the top of their voices, even though they already knew what the result would be. They hugged and jumped up and down laughing. Riley popped the cork from a second bottle. "I propose a toast to the Mug Punters revenge," he said, "and to the fact that, for the first time in our lives, we are financially independent of our employers, fuck the lot of them," they clinked glasses.

"Fuck the lot of them," shouted Estella.

Even though neither of them had any intention of resigning from the TM team, it was a nice feeling. "Let's finish this upstairs," he suggested. Estella smiled, picked up the bottle and led the way. They got drunk, screwed enthusiastically, and fell asleep in each other's arms.

A couple of hours later, he sat on the loo having a piss, Estella hated floor splashes. He thought about Oakwood's and Burley's reactions, when the security people reported the new balances in his and Estella's accounts. He guessed that Burnley would secretly find it funny. Oakwood wouldn't.

Riley knew he should feel good about the way things were going, so why did he still feel hollow and scared? He worried about everything, that Estella might leave him, that he might lose his job, that they were damaging the future; he worried about who was sending the racing tips. Was it his future self or was there another game in play, a game he wasn't aware of? His mind felt like a tangled plate of spaghetti, the worries winding and twining around each other, just as he pictured the wormholes they were manipulating. He got back into bed and looked across at Estella, blearily he noticed something wrong with her hair. Was she wearing a hairnet? He fell asleep before he could follow up on the thought.

Chapter Seven

England the 1990s

Estella walked into Riley's office clutching a sheaf of printouts. She stood in front of his desk, slow tears slid down her cheeks. He was a shocked; Estella was a toughie and seldom cried.

"What is it?" he asked half rising.

"It's Princess Diana. She and Dodi Fayed are going to die in a car accident in Paris in two weeks' time. These are the first reports." She placed them on the desk and sat down opposite him. He passed her his box of tissues. "I can't believe it; Princess Diana is such a force for good in the world. Look at her work with Aids victims and land mines. It's just not right." Her voice shook as she talked angrily, "The Royal Family has never forgiven her for that television interview." She paused for a moment, gathered herself, and spoke more calmly, "Remember, when she was going out with that heart surgeon Hasnat Khan. He had to hide from the press in the boot of her car when they drove to her apartment at Kensington Palace. I thought that was so funny and romantic, she was even going to convert to the Muslim faith to please his family, but I think they still made him break up with her. I liked him better than this Dodi

Fayed. Surely they won't let her die, Martin; surely the Government will intervene." She was speaking faster now, almost gabbling.

"I never know what they'll want adjusted and what they won't," Riley said. His mind was whirring with thoughts of the ramifications of Princess Diana's death, if TASC allowed it to happen. "I can't see the Royal Family wanting to intervene. Diana has been a thorn in their flesh for years, and they know that when Prince William takes the throne she'll come back into the Royal Family and become Queen Mother. She will have won." He chuckled mirthlessly. "A nightmare for the Establishment. The new occupant of Clarence House, married to a Muslim and possibly a Muslim herself, with Muslim children and grandchildren. They might find this accident providential. I don't think they'll want to change a thing."

Estella sat dabbing her eyes. He read several versions of the story before he picked up the phone to ring Dr Oakwood.

Oakwood arrived by helicopter an hour later, he'd already been briefed by Paul Burnley. Riley realized that this was a big issue when Government limousines carrying members of TASC started to arrive at Martlesham in quick succession. The group viewing the television footage that was being sent back grew to a dozen. They watched as the French police handled the situation, saw the mangled Mercedes, heard the pronouncement of the deaths of three of its occupants.

All other work came to a standstill in the TA laboratory as the story unfolded over the next few days. More of the Committee arrived; the admin staff booked local hotel rooms for them and equipped a conference room to show the TV footage in private. Riley watched the Prime Minister's televised speech made on the Sunday after Diana's death. When Tony Blair used the phrase "The People's Princess," he heard a politician mutter, "He owes Alastair Campbell big time for that one."

Two days later, a disheveled and jacketless Dr Oakwood sat in Riley's office drinking tea.

"The PM is seriously worried, Martin. Footage from two weeks ahead shows the newspapers are making much of the Queen's refusal to fly a flag at half-mast over Buckingham Palace, it's triggered an outcry. The crowds outside have grown bigger, there are acres of flowers, and Paul Burley's sources say there's a dangerous deadlock between the Prime Minister and the Queen. She's still refusing to speak publicly about Diana's death, the Committee are getting worried."

Riley was struck by the contrast between the mundane, present-day news reports he saw on TV at home, and the drama in those sent from just two weeks ahead. He and Oakwood rose and re-joined the members of TASC, who were filing back into the conference room after a lunch break.

"This is building up to be a perfect storm," said Robin Buckley, the Cabinet Secretary, sitting on Oakwood's right. He had arrived on the fourth day and stayed, cancelling his other business. "This could seriously damage the monarchy, we could have a revolution on our hands and be a republic before you know it."

Riley chuckled inwardly as he thought of the titles and privileges that would disappear if that happened.

They love their perquisites, he thought, *these accidents of birth, these inbreds.* He had become more embittered as time passed and the realization grew that the recognition he deserved would never be his. It was a constant simmering resentment, he was just another nameless scientist in the service of the British Government.

Over the next few days, the crowd outside Buckingham Palace continue to grow. Even Estella was surprised at the vast numbers of bouquets the public had laid at various palace gates, on pavements outside municipal buildings and even in supermarket car parks all over the country. Meanwhile, the Royal Family stayed remote and secluded on their Balmoral estate, five hundred miles away. Despite the efforts of the Prime Minister, the Queen remained intransigent, refusing to expose her grandsons' grief to the maudlin voyeurism of the press and public.

It was on the sixth day after Diana's death that the riot began. The Committee watched footage of the evening crowds massing outside Buckingham Palace, with its darkened windows and empty flagpole. They saw huge numbers of angry Diana supporters surge forward. The police were forced to unlocked the gates, at the front of the building, to prevent the crushing of the innocent. Over the screaming and shouting they heard explosions, as the police fired ineffectual baton rounds at the huge crowd funneling from the Mall into the forecourt of the Palace. They saw the front doors broken down and windows smashed as rioters, running amok, first sacked and then set the largely empty building ablaze.

The Committee and scientists sat in shocked silence as Buckingham Palace burned, and fire engines battled the flames that lit up the London night skyline.

Like the Red Army storming the Winter Palace, thought Riley as, with secret amusement and a carefully neutral expression, he surveyed the horrified looks of the 'Great and the Good,' sitting on their fat arses on either side of him. He remembered how easily Burnley had prevented the fire at Windsor Castle, five years earlier, after the warning from the TM team. He expected that most of the Committee were unaware of that early Temporal Adjustment; it had been before the formation of TASC. The clips of the original incident had been dramatic, but at least that had been an accident. This fire was purposeful, a metaphor, a lesson to the Establishment, the masses are a sleeping giant that will rise and roar if provoked.

One of the Generals stood up and remonstrated at the screen. Riley thought he might have a stroke, his face was red and blood vessels throbbed at his temples. "We'll shoot the bloody lot of them, leftie scum," he shouted, shaking his fist. "Flame throwers, that's what's needed, burn the bastards."

Oakwood took a deep breath, and held up his hands for silence. Reluctantly the general sat back down, still muttering.

"We need to decide now," said Oakwood to the rest of the Committee. "We can prevent the accident in the tunnel and save Diana if we choose to and none of this will happen; but we only have two more days. Those in favor please raise a hand and then sign the memo I am circulating." Oakwood would never risk-taking action on his own, thought Riley. The vote was unanimous and the Cabinet Secretary, who was murmuring into his cell phone nodded.

"The PM says to go ahead," he said.

Oakwood called Paul Burnley into the room. "We need to stop the accident. Can you arrange that?" he asked. More meddling, thought Riley, can't they see the danger?

"The early French police reports say that the driver of Diana and Dodi's car, was drunk. If we change the driver the accident won't happen."

"How can you change the driver?" asked Oakwood.

"We have an asset in their hotel in Paris, she's a waitress. She can give the driver a Mickey Finn an hour or so before he's due to drive Diana and Dodi. I'll get straight on to it." He left the room pulling his mobile phone out of his suit pocket. Riley was impressed, he and Estella always referred to Burnley as "Mr Bond" when they spoke of him at home.

Two days later, in the Ritz hotel Paris, Dodi Fayed's driver, Henri Paul, was kneeling, throwing up in the staff toilet. The bodyguard who was standing next to him phoned the head of security. "He isn't fit to drive the Boss," he said, his tone indifferent.

"Okay, get somebody else to drive. Make sure it's somebody careful. Send the car around the back now, they're ready to leave."

The Mercedes S280 drove up to the rear entrance of the hotel, security guards escorted Diana and Dodi to it. The driver was a well-trained, reliable member of Dodi's security team. He felt nervous and knew he needed to resist the urge to drive fast to get away from the paparazzi, waiting outside with their cameras and motorcycles. He didn't want to put his passengers at risk. As he let out the clutch, he looked into the rear-view mirror.

"Monsieur, Madam, please buckle your seat belts," he said. Surprised at the driver's presumption his passengers glanced at each other and then complied.

The next weekend, Estella, and Riley were spending a pleasant morning relaxing over coffee, croissants, and the Sunday papers, in their large modern kitchen. "How wonderful that we could save Diana's life," said Estella? "It makes me proud to be doing this job."

He took a deep breath. "Yes, but what about the ramifications? What effect have we had on the future?"

"You and your 'ramifications', we've made things better, that's all. Why beat yourself up?"

"Because Diana was supposed to die, and now we've changed history. We're living in a radically altered Timestream. For all I know, there might be two Timestreams, one with Diana dead, and one with her alive."

"How many Timestreams could there be?" asked Estella.

"There might be an infinite number of Timestreams, ask Stephen fucking Hawking." Riley was becoming agitated, he was jealous of Professor Hawking, and usually avoided mentioning him. "It worries me that our masters are manipulating history for their own ends. Power corrupts, and I have no idea where Temporal Adjustments of this significance will lead us."

"Yes, but if the government are working in the public interest, what's wrong with that. I may not be a royalist exactly, but I wouldn't have liked it if there had been a revolution or a coup or something. I think the Queen does a good job, it's the next incumbent that worries me."

Riley didn't reply. She popped another piece of pastry into her mouth and took a sip of coffee.

"Have some croissant with your jam why don't you," he said.

"Mind your own damn business Fatso; I'll have as much jam as I like." She smiled brightly at him. "Anyway, pregnant women often get an appetite for sweet things."

Riley had returned to his newspaper, he paused before looking up.

"Pregnant?" he asked.

Chapter Eight

England the 1990s

Riley sat next to Estella's bed with the baby cradled in his arms. Estella was still tired and sleepy from the labor, the birth and the anesthetics. The new baby was mewling quietly and making vague tentative movements with its arms. Riley felt more relaxed than he had for months. It was as if a huge emotional switch had operated in his brain. He pictured the one Dr Frankenstein pulled, in the movie, when he connected the lightning conductor to the monster. In Riley's case, the switch had a label over it that said 'Fatherhood.'

He had shown the baby to several of the other mothers in the recovery ward, but had become embarrassed because his baby was so obviously superior to theirs. He tried to be polite, but the other babies were such an ugly, puny bunch compared to his. Later he'd phoned his mother to tell her that the baby was safely delivered and that Estella was all right. She'd laughed when he told her how wonderful the baby was, and how he'd never seen one as beautiful.

"Why are you laughing?" he'd asked.

"I'm laughing at you," she said. "Don't you realize that everybody feels like that about their first baby."

He knew she'd agree with him when she saw Hank. They had decided to call him Hank, because Estella had a crush on the lead guitarist of Cliff Richard's backing band when she was a girl.

When mother and baby were sleeping, Riley drove home from the hospital for a shower and a shave. He needed to sleep, but first he sat in the garden, smoked a cigar and drank two fingers of whiskey. He decided that things had to change, for Hank's sake, they had to change. He decided that the TM technology should be put into the hands of the United Nations, so that it could be used for the benefit of all mankind. The fact that this would inevitably make him famous and very rich was immaterial. He owed it to humanity. He went into the house and lay on the bed, fully clothed. As he fell asleep, he pictured himself walking up the steps to shake hands with the King of Sweden, and accept his Nobel Prize for physics, or even the Nobel Peace Prize. His TM technology could help bring world peace under the right circumstances. What a wonderful gift to give to Hank's generation, world peace.

At work the next day, there were congratulations, backslapping and cake at the morning break. Paul Burnley rang to offer his congratulations as did Dr Oakwood. Riley started to tell him about his idea for making TM technology available to the world, but his boss cut across him.

"I think you're a little emotional at the moment, Martin, perhaps you should have a few days off, take your paternity leave, we can manage without you for a while. Actually, I insist, go home, Martin, we can discuss this later, and please don't mention your ideas to anybody else before we've discussed it."

Riley left the office and went to see Hank and Estella at the hospital. Estella was feeding Hank while he was there, and as he watched, Riley realized the changes that the baby would make to their lives. It wasn't about Estella and himself anymore, it was about Hank, and would be for the next twenty years.

"I've decided that we need to offer TM to the United Nations," he told Estella.

"You know we can't do that, Martin," she said, looking up from stroking Hank's cheek and suddenly serious. "Talking like that is dangerous, we have Hank to worry about now, so stop thinking about your legacy and start thinking about his future. I hope you haven't talked about this to anyone? You haven't, have you?"

"No, no," he said. He went home and tidied up the house to prepare for the mother and baby's arrival next day. After Estella and Hank came home, his emotions calmed as they adapted to his changed priorities. Estella had decided to stay off work for a year. It was going to be a different life, he thought. His mother told him he was a 'proper grownup' now, and she was right, as usual.

A week later, he was still on leave, the home phone rang, it was Oakwood.

"Hello, Martin, I'm in the café at Holywells Park, it's not far from your house, meet me here as soon as you can please. Walk, don't drive, and please check that you are not being followed," he rang off. Puzzled, Riley put a coat on and made his way to the Park. He looked around several times but had no way of knowing whether or not he was being followed, and anyway, by who? As he walked into the warm café, he smelled coffee and fried food. Several tables were occupied by older couples, out for an afternoon stroll. They all seemed to have small dogs on leads, looking out from under the tables.

Oakwood sat huddled at a corner table with his overcoat collar turned up, he was wearing a dark trilby, pulled low, and looked furtive and conspicuous. Martin drew out a chair and sat opposite. Oakwood was pale and nervous, his hand shook as he lifted his tea cup, his gaze flicked around the café as he spoke.

"This meeting never happened, Martin, nobody knows I'm here. Things are changing, Martin, it's the new Prime Minister. He has turned out to be a politician of a very different cut from Mr Major. Please do not mention handing TM technology over to the UN again. Not to me, not to anyone else, not at the office, not on the phone, not even in your home. You must assume that Paul Burnley or his minions are listening to every word you say."

"Has something happened, Dr Oakwood?" said Riley.

"I'm afraid I cannot discuss the matter, but if I tell you that when the Cabinet Secretary and I first told Mr Major about TM, some years ago, he was shocked. As you know, he wanted to use the technology cautiously.

When we briefed Mr Blair, soon after his election, he grinned, rubbed his hands together, and said, 'Control of the future, wait till I tell Alastair about this.' He calmed down after we explained the level of secrecy that we work under. In fact, he saw the ramifications and asked us about TASC. He looked at the list of members and immediately wanted to make changes. That was a year ago, I can't say any more. All I can say is that we need to watch our backs."

"Could I talk to him?" asked Riley. "Perhaps I could convince him that we should use the technology for the benefit of the whole human race."

Oakwood sighed, "Please don't do anything like that, Martin. Wait until you've regained your emotional balance. Finish your paternity leave, try not to think about TM, just concentrate on your new arrival." As he rose to leave, his knee caught the table and a jug of milk, a plate, and various cutlery fell noisily to the floor. Most of the people in the restaurant looked over as, clutching his coat around him, Oakwood left hurriedly. Riley noticed that one of the couples hadn't looked up at the noise but had continued looking at their menus. Their Spaniel had stayed supine under the table and cocked its ears as if it had seen it all before.

Riley wondered if the couple were deaf, but they were murmuring to each other without seeming to gesture or lip read. He decided to stay and have something to eat. The couple left the café, and he watched as they set off in different directions, the woman leading the dog, the man in the same direction as Oakwood.

Chapter Nine

England the 1990s

A dozen members of TASC sat in the committee room at Martlesham, Riley stood below a large overhead screen as he addressed them.

"My team have done a first-rate job of editing the video files to make this presentation," he said. "There are cameras all over the Sizewell B nuclear power station site and their output is continuously copied to the Électricité de France central office in Paris. The local files were destroyed during the incident you are about to see. Remember, this will happen in less than two weeks' time." He signaled for the room lights to be dimmed and pressed a button on the remote control he was holding.

The sleek, matt black, Zodiac rigid inflatable boat, with its three occupants, bounced at high speed across the low swells of the North Sea. It had probably been lowered from the deck of a freighter, a few miles off Felixstowe, on the Suffolk coast, while the ship continued its journey north.

The three men, masked and dressed in black, looked fit and thoroughly dangerous as their boat slowed and crunched ashore on the pebbly beach. They jumped out, dragged it a few yards further from the water and unloaded their back packs and light machine guns. Shouldering their equipment, they made their way up the beach, in single file, towards the huge white dome of Sizewell B. Nobody challenged them as they cut through the few strands of barbed wire and, using flash cord, cut through two of the eight-foot-high steel railings and stepped through onto the site.

The station was "guarded" by only half a dozen retired prison officers, plumbers, and traffic wardens, wearing the black "livery" of a local security firm.

The three masked men approached the airlocked entrance to the white domed concrete containment building. Reaching into his pack, the leader extracted a black box which he attached to the outer door. He twisted one switch and pressed another, they all took cover as, moments later, an explosion blew the lock to pieces and the door swung outwards on its hinges. Before the smoke had cleared the second man moved into the airlock, and came back out again almost at once. Moments later another explosion blew open the inner door. The first two men moved through the airlock and into the containment building while the third crouched and guarded the approach.

A door opened in a nearby office and, framed by the light inside, two guards came out carrying torches. Before they had moved more than a few steps, the watching mercenary gunned them down with four shots of silenced fire. He remained in position.

Inside the containment building, the two men made their way up steel stairways and along the walkways to the top of the reactor, where one of them placed a grenade. They took cover, as an explosion distorted the array of control rods which clustered there. The reactor was now out of control.

The soldiers calmly strapped two shaped charges to the heavy pipe work coming from one of the four heat exchangers. They made their way down the steel stairways and back out through the ruined airlock. Once in the open air they dumped their weapons and stripped off their outer clothing, revealing the blue overalls worn by all employees on the site. It was a short walk to the staff car park. There were two muffled explosions from the containment building as the mercenaries climbed into the side door of the van, which was waiting for them. They passed through the security barrier and drove away towards Yoxford and the A12.

Cameras in the containment building showed super-heated steam and boiling water gushing from the breached and ragged pipework. In the operations center, one of the technicians suddenly shouted, "We're losing primary and secondary cooling water, the core temperature's rising."

The shift supervisor could see the hopelessness of the situation on the flat screen displays. She picked up a microphone and her amplified voice could be heard above the noise of alarms and the flashing of emergency lights around the installation. "Attention. Emergency. All personnel must evacuate immediately. I repeat all personnel...."

Over the next hour, the core temperature rose unhindered until the fuel rods melted. The molten fuel burned through the bottom of the reactor flask and spilled through the pipework and open steel lattice floors of the containment building. There was a spectacular display of fire and sparks as the building filled with smoke and flames.

The fuel pooled under the reactor and melted through the concrete floor. It continued to burn deeper into the ground until, a few meters below, it reached the water table. Fire and water met and battled, there was a colossal and continuous steam explosion.

A jet of radioactive fuel particles, flames, gas, and water vapor roared horizontally out of the open containment airlock and over the sea, a volcano gone askew. The roar could be heard for miles across the quiet countryside. The concrete around the airlock began to melt and crumble. As the seaward side of the building disintegrated, the dome cracked, and large pieces of the roof fell crashing onto the ruined reactor.

A huge plume of radioactive smoke and steam rose above the small fishing village of Sizewell. The patrons of the Vulcan Arms public house stood speechlessly staring upwards from the outdoor smoking area. They inhaled fatal doses of radioactive dust as it drifted down onto them, their relatively harmless cigarettes held forgotten at their sides.

"This last clip was taken from a press helicopter flying upwind of the site next morning," said Riley, still seated. The screen showed a huge plume of radioactive steam and smoke slowly billowing from the hollow, jagged, concrete stump of the containment building. They could hear the emotional voice of a journalist reporting on the scene. Riley turned the volume down. "The plume is drifting towards Ipswich," he said. "If you look carefully, you can see that the reactor building has a double skin but both have been smashed to rubble." Nobody spoke, they were too stunned by the TV footage.

The presentation ended, and the lights came back on. Riley stood as the rest of the group sat in shocked silence for several seconds.

"What's the estimated death toll?" asked one of the committee.

"In the hundreds of thousands," said Riley.

"How can this have happened?" He turned to look at Oakwood. "You scientists have always assured us that nuclear power is safe."

"Nuclear power stations may be safe from accidents, but they have never been safe from informed targeted attack," Oakwood replied. "These men are professionals, mercenaries, possibly ex-French Foreign Legion. CCTV cameras show them boarding a scheduled flight at Norwich Airport, they were on their way home two hours after the reactor breached."

"This is a bloody shambles!" said another member of the group angrily. He was wearing civilian clothes but Riley suspected that he was military. "We need to protect installations like this. There should be soldiers or at least armed police patrolling. We're very vulnerable. Bacton Gas Terminal is only a few miles further up the coast, that could be next. I could easily list a dozen industrial sites as nationally important as this. It's really too bad."

"I don't imagine we need much discussion, ladies and gentlemen," said Oakwood. "Can I have a show of hands for an intervention? So, it's unanimous then, I'll speak to the Cabinet Secretary, I'm sure the PM will recommend that the military take measures to prevent the attack. Paul Burnley can initiate it. Although technically this comes under the auspices of MI5, as it's going to happen on home soil. We don't want to step on anybody's toes." He picked up the phone. "Send in Commander Burnley please Rachael."

Riley wanted to warn them again about making alterations but he worried that they were getting fed up with his prophecies of doom. They might dismiss him or demote him. Anyway, on this occasion he felt more comfortable, an intervention would save tens of thousands of lives.

After the meeting, he booked the day of the incident as part of a holiday. He decided he would take Hank and Estella to visit his mother in Liverpool. Their house was in Ipswich after all.

Two weeks later, as the Zodiac craft crunched onto the pebble beach at Sizewell, and its occupants gathered their weapons and equipment ready to disembark, a squadron of six paratroopers rose from the ground nearby. The light covering of pebbles that had hidden them fell from their uniforms as, without hesitation or challenge, they shot the mercenaries dead with brief bursts of automatic fire. They bundled the bodies back into the boat and dragged it up the beach to their lorry and trailer, parked behind a dune. They loaded it onto the trailer, covered it with a tarpaulin, roped it down, climbed aboard the lorry, and drove away. The operation was over in minutes.

Small waves broke on the shingle. The breeze blew through the coarse grasses and sea cabbage plants, as it had blown long before men arrived on this shore, and would continue to blow long after they had gone.

The soldiers sat in a row on the bench seat; they rocked companionably to the movement of the vehicle as it drove along the back lanes.

"Is it all right to smoke, Sarge?" asked one of the younger troopers. The whites of his eyes contrasted strangely with the green and black camouflage paint darkening his face. A fly moved unheeded across his forehead. He was trying to unscrew the silencer from his light machine gun, but in his excitement, he had forgotten that it had a left-hand thread.

"It certainly is, Son," said the sergeant as the lorry took them back towards their base in Colchester; he leaned forward and extracted a cigarette from the proffered pack, nodding his thanks. He reached into a tunic pocket for a light. "Left-hand thread, remember." The trooper reversed his action and continued to strip his weapon. He'd spent hours practicing this blindfolded.

"Sorry Sarge," he muttered.

The sergeant ignored the trooper's gaff. It's always nice when things go to plan, he thought, as he lit up and took a grateful pull. He still wondered how the two spooks that had accompanied them had known exactly where and when the mercenaries' boat would hit the beach. He and the spooks had used snow shovels to cover the troops lightly with shingle, half an hour before the boat arrived. The agents had moved back to the safety of their four by four, parked some distance away in the dunes. The sergeant had taken cover behind a beached fishing boat, ready to intervene if necessary. As soon as the action was over, and after handshakes all round, the spooks had left at speed, probably for London he thought.

The sergeant had liked to read the Greek myths when he was a boy. There was one about dragon's teeth being scattered on the ground and turning into armed warriors. He took another pull on his cigarette and looked affectionately at his troops and remembered them rising from the gravel, his dragon's teeth. He smiled contentedly to himself. They had all done well.

He knew there would be no press coverage, the incident hadn't happened. They would probably be decorated, but at a private ceremony. You never know, it might even be Prince Charles, the Colonel in Chief, who made the presentation. The Royals loved to associate themselves with successful operations, and he didn't seem to be a bad sort of bloke, he'd just married the wrong girl.

Chapter Ten

England the 1990s

Oakwood called at Martlesham a few weeks after the Sizewell B incident. He and Riley stood together in the laboratory watching, as Riley's team of technicians and scientists sat at their work stations, keeping the equipment focused on the wormholes leading into the past. Riley was proud of his facility. He looked across at the two, large, white painted Cyclotrons, the surrounding accessories had long been wired in professionally. The original carbonara of trailing leads and flexible pipes surrounding them was gone. Everything was neat, clean and professional.

Riley was still allowed to see the newspaper stories as they arrived from 'downstream' although he worried that Burnley would eventually cut him out of the loop. He was, after all, just the 'chief techie,' and still not a member of TASC. Now that the operation was running smoothly, and they didn't need him as much, he fretted that they might hire a more malleable replacement. Fortunately, there was no one on the team who fully understood the theory. Not yet.

A Rolling Stones number from his teenage years played in his head, "Who wants yesterday's paper?" wailed Mick.

Riley noticed that Oakwood had been unusually quiet, and seemed not to be interested in the new arrangements. Eventually they adjourned to his office.

"I have some news," Oakwood said suddenly. "I decided it best to tell you in person, Martin. I am afraid that the whole facility is moving to Langley. You're being taken over."

The news shocked Riley, he was momentarily speechless. "What do you mean, we're moving to Langley?" he had half risen from his seat and was staring at the other man, his expression bewildered. "Langley, Virginia? In America?"

"Now calm yourself, Martin," said the Government's senior scientist. "I'm afraid that it was pretty much inevitable that our American allies would get involved with Temporal Messaging in the end. We've been in no hurry to inform them of our activities, but somehow their National Security Agency has found out about us, and the US Government has put pressure on the Prime Minister. To all intents and purposes, they will be taking charge. As with so many things, it comes down to funding and they will be doing most of that. We will still have representation on their new Oversight Committee. You will, of course, still be the senior scientist, but the operations manager in day-to-day charge will be a US Army Colonel. Actually, I've managed to persuade the Americans to send him over, so that we can introduce him to the team, before you all move to Virginia. It might be less daunting for you if you've met your new boss before you go. He's in the reception area, I'll get him."

Oakwood left the office and returned a few moments later with a companion. "This is Colonel Wilson," he said. Wilson wore a grey suit, a white shirt and bootlace tie, with a turquoise and silver bolo clasp. He reminded Riley of Clint Eastwood, the same chiseled features and cold grey eyes. Slimmer than Riley, he was almost skinny, about the same height, just less than six feet, and tanned with greying hair. Riley's first impression was that he seemed slightly detached, as if he might not be an easy man to get to know. Riley hadn't liked Oakwood's use of the word 'boss.' Neither did he relish working under a military management style, where the officers keep their distance from the people under their command, in case they have to order them to do something unpleasant or, more likely, drop them in the shit to save themselves. He'd briefly joined the Army Cadets in his early teens but had only lasted two meetings. The experience had given him a jaundiced view of all things military.

They shook hands. "I'm looking forward to working with you, Dr Riley," said the Colonel, in a soft, east coast, American accent. His body language showed that nothing could be further from the truth. His handshake had been weak and dry; Riley noticed that he'd leaned backwards slightly as he gave it.

"Who will be funding us?" asked Riley, taking a direct approach. *Start as you mean to go on,* he thought.

"The Defense Advanced Research Projects Agency," said the Colonel. "But we'll report to an Oversight

Committee in Langley and through them, to the Executive Office of the President of the United States."

The Colonel stiffened as he said this, Riley imagined that he wanted to stand to attention or salute or pledge allegiance, possibly all three at the same time. Fucking flag waver, he thought.

"And of course, to TASC and the British Prime Minister," prompted Oakwood.

"Of course," said the Colonel hastily.

Riley wondered if the Yanks planned to replace him, in the long run. Oakwood's assurance to the contrary meant little, if they were providing the funding. He couldn't allow anybody to take over his project, it was too important to him.

"Dr Oakwood has briefed me on our mission, but I find the concept strange and difficult to believe," drawled the Colonel. "I'd just like to be sure I understand. So, we will receive reports about important events, two weeks before they happen." He looked at Riley for confirmation. He nodded, and the Colonel continued. "We'll pass the information on. Other agencies can then take measures to change these events if they do not suit our purposes. By which I mean the purposes of the United States Government," he paused cleared his throat and then continued "and their allies, the British Government." Oakwood nodded energetically. "What happens to the people two weeks in the future if we change their reality?" asked the Colonel.

"That's a good question," said Riley, impressed by the Colonel's quick grasp of the ramifications of Temporal Adjustments. "It depends on what our masters decide to do. Small changes will have little effect while others might be catastrophic for them."

97

"It is always our intention to change things for the better though," said Oakwood, smiling encouragingly.

Yes, thought Riley, *the road to Hell is paved with good intentions*, and for the first time, he fully understood the adage.

"Well working behind the lines always brings added risks," said the Colonel.

Chapter Eleven

USA the 2000s

Riley was surprised at how quickly the move to Langley was accomplished, and how lavish the new facilities were, it must have taken the Americans months to prepare them. As he stood in his new laboratory, looking at the six Cyclotrons, the rows of computer terminals and equipment benches, he wondered how long that slippery bastard Oakwood had known about the impending move. The same Oakwood who, after his new appointment would now be sliming all over a red leather bench in the House of Lords, Riley could only wish him a painful death. At least he was one irritation gone, but how bad was the replacement going to be?

Soon after their arrival in the USA, as new personnel were coming on board and the project began to bed into its new surroundings, Riley's attention was diverted by the birth of Cliff, he and Estella's second child. He didn't find the experience as much of an emotional jolt as Hank's birth, but he was still off balance when the Colonel walked into his office, without knocking, a few days later.

"Martin, I've decided that we should put on a demonstration for the powers that be. I want to show our new Oversight Committee the potential of Temporal Messaging. They report to the National Security Advisor among others and we should convince them we are an important resource, not just another irrelevant science project. Have a look at this." Riley bridled as the Colonel passed him a folder.

He opened the file and read a newspaper story, about a bank robbery that would take place in New York in ten days" time. A well-organized gang would steal an impressive amount of money and kill several security guards, before making their escape.

"What about it?" he asked, attempting to hand the folder back.

The Colonel ignored the folder. "We can prevent this robbery, catch the gang of criminals and show our potential in one hit. Everybody wins except the bad guys." He looked across at Riley to gauge his reaction.

"We can't just intervene willy-nilly," he said. "Interfering with the Timestream is a serious business"

"We need to do this. We need to prove ourselves. Anyway, I've already told the Oversight Committee that we will prevent this robbery."

"I hope the Oversight Committee isn't 'leaky'. If the rest of the world gets to hear about our tamperings, there'll be Hell to pay."

"Our security protocols over here are second to none, Martin. Don't worry, I'll be discreet when I warn the NYPD about the raid, I'll use an informer as a cut-out."

The Colonel had taken the decision out of his hands; once again he realized that he was only the hired help.

Later he sat with Estella in the cafeteria. "These people have no idea; they want to play cops and robbers now," he whispered. "They see TM as another resource they can squander, and never mind the consequences. If somebody blabs and their famously free press gets hold of this, we'll all be in the shit. We could find ourselves in court, or worse."

Estella smiled and patted his hand.

"Don't worry, Martin, I'll visit you, and bring you a cake with a file in it."

He leaned forward, "You'll probably be in the next cell," he hissed as he stood and walked towards the exit. Once again, he wondered why he was the only one aware of the dangers. He paused as he pushed through the doors. Looking back, he saw the Colonel standing talking to Estella, with a cup in his hand. Estella smiled and gestured at his empty chair. The Colonel sat down. As Riley stood watching them from a distance, he saw Estella touch her hair several times and smile with her head on one side, as they talked. He walked back to his office. Why could nobody see that every time they made a change it must have a knock-on effect on the Timestream? They were bending it, splitting it into alternatives, or distorting it, he had no way of knowing which, but he knew they were always changing the future. They should be careful, gather more data, only intervene if it was necessary. The Colonel was perverting the project to further his career and in the meantime Riley was getting no credit, again.

He sat at his desk and felt a furious urge to smash something, but instead he sat smoldering and had his usual fantasies about going to the press and blowing the whole project wide open. He imagined the fame, the honors, the interviews, the committees he would be invited to sit on. He sighed and pulled up a spreadsheet of the latest calibration results and began to go through them.

Ten days later Riley was at home with Estella, watching the news while they ate dinner. A tanned and toothy newsreader appeared on screen.

"And finally, ladies and gentlemen, just in from the security cameras of the First National Bank in New York. Exciting footage of a gang of thieves, who got a surprise they will have plenty of time to contemplate, from their prison cells."

The screen showed the quiet, Art Déco interior of a large bank. Customers were writing at desks in the public area, while others stood at the counters conferring with the tellers. The calm was disturbed by the noisy entrance of a group of men pushing a green plastic dumpster through the main doors. Dressed as refuse collectors, they wore overalls, hats, and dust masks. As they entered the foyer, a member of the gang hiding inside the dumpster threw back the lid, and began handing out machine pistols and sawn-off shotguns, before climbing out himself. The leader stepped into the main hall and fired a short and shocking burst of automatic fire into the ceiling.

"Get down on the floor, get down on the floor and nobody gets hurt," he shouted.

One of the gang moved up to the grill, and gestured at the staff on the other side with his weapon, "Nobody fuckin' touch nothin'. Get on the floor," he shouted and began to climb up onto the counter.

The rest of the gang pushed customers down and menaced them with their weapons.

"Where's the manager?" shouted the leader. He was holding a frightened young black woman by the shoulder, a gun against her temple. "Where's the manager?" he shouted even louder. "Get him out here now."

"Drop your weapons," said a loud, calm voice, over the bank's public-address system.

Behind the main counter a SWAT team of a dozen officers in black helmets, overalls, body armor and gas masks appeared. They crouched threateningly, with automatic weapons jutting through the grillwork. One of them reached through and grabbed the ankles of the masked criminal who was standing on the counter and jerked them from under him. Screaming, he crashed backwards to the marble floor, and lay still. Everything stopped. Nobody spoke. The intruders were exposed. They were the only ones standing, and they had no cover. Their masks hid the looks of surprise on their faces.

"Take hostages," the leader shouted, but the hoped-for hostages were not willing to cooperate. The "customers," who had dropped to the floor pulled out handguns and pointed them up at their assailants.

There was a moment of stillness as the newly reversed situation coalesced in the minds of the criminals. They realized that they were out gunned and their position was hopeless. The leader's "hostage" slowly stood up, stepped back, looked at the leader and, unsmiling, extended her hand. There was another pause, before he gave up his weapon, raised his hands above his head and knelt on the floor.

The other members of the gang hesitated, then knelt, laid down their weapons, and raised their hands. A group of uniformed police crashed through the bank's main doors and began handcuffing the prisoners and leading them away.

The "customers" stood and began to congratulate each other.

The scene shifted back to the TV studio, the newsreader smiled into the camera and shuffled his script.

"Well," he said, "and once again folks, we see that crime doesn't pay. And here's Mike with the weather. Mike."

Riley stood, switched off the television and topped up his wine glass.

"Now we're really cookin with gas," he said in a fake American accent. He walked out onto the deck and stared moodily up at the sky. Estella came out and stood beside him.

"Cheers," she said clinking glasses, "is this a private depression, or can anybody join in?"

Riley didn't reply. Baby Cliff began to cry in the nursery and Estella left to feed him.

Chapter Twelve

USA the 2000s

For Riley, the day had started normally, with the usual accumulation of irrelevant emails demanding attention and time he wanted to spend on research.

Doug, one of the newly recruited American technicians, rushed into Riley's office white faced.

"They're gonna blow up the World Trade Centre," he said. "The Twin Towers will be completely destroyed, two weeks from now." He rushed out and back to the main laboratory. Riley followed and stood behind his chair as he called up the video recording. Several others joined them, the evidence was on the computer screen; Riley ran to the Colonel's office.

"Come right away, you need to see this," he said.

They hurried back, and together they watched footage they would never forget. The Twin Towers, viewed from a distance, the North Tower smoking. Then, the unexpected impact of a second plane, into the South Tower, and the explosion as its full load of fuel ignited.

"Oh no," exclaimed the Colonel, unable to contain his emotions. The viewpoint pulled back to show both Towers smoking and burning. "Lock the doors," he shouted and the leader of the new team of Scrutineers complied.

The crowd around the screen grew. As more information arrived on the hard drives, the whole team began viewing footage from different TV stations on their screens. The Colonel was talking quietly into his cell phone, his hand shielding the mouthpiece when, about an hour later, the South Tower collapsed. He banged the desk hard with his bunched fist.

"No, no, no," he shouted.

"Did you see how it concertinaed? Like a demolition exercise," said Riley in an awed voice. Half an hour later the topmost floors of the North Tower dropped bodily into the dust cloud below. The scientists and technicians stood speechless. Riley felt as if he was watching the special effects of a Hollywood disaster movie. He was horrified to realize that, after the first collapse, the people in the second Tower knew their fate. What would they do, use their cell phones to say goodbye to loved ones? What else could they do? TV footage showed people in burning rooms making their decision and taking the big leap. Riley was cold, his skin crawled, he didn't speak. Other members of the team reacted in different ways, many of the men were angry, and many of the women tearful.

The Colonel was appalled. "Terrorists reducing our most important financial center to a pile of rubble, it would be an unbelievable coup for our enemies; we'd be a laughingstock in the eyes of the world. It's intolerable." He hurried back to his office and slammed the door. Riley knew the Committee would never allow this catastrophe to take place.

A week later, Wilson had invited Riley into his office to share a coffee break, an unusual occurrence. The Colonel seemed at peace, almost affable. Riley looked around, bemused by the regimental pictures, buddy photos, flags, pennants and other military paraphernalia.

"Saudi student pilots were going to fly the planes," said the Colonel. "Their instructors at the flying school told the CIA that they weren't interested in learning how to land a Jumbo jet, just how to take off in one. They should have been more suspicious. We deported the bastards back into the gentle hands of the Mabahith."

Riley looked puzzled.

"The Saudi secret police," said the Colonel. "Our towel head friends will be enjoying the fine hospitality of Al-Ha'ir Prison, and the best of luck to them."

He laughed loudly, another unusual event, his relief showing through, thought Riley

"They've promoted me to full bird colonel," he said.

Riley offered his congratulations. *He gets another badge, while I get fuck-all, and no mention of me to the Oversight Committee*, he thought.

"This has been our greatest success so far," said the Colonel. "The powers that be realize that destroying the 'Great Satan's' financial center would have had incalculable consequences. An enormous victory for the terrorists it would have made us look vulnerable, incompetent, humiliated. What a shame the public will never know what we accomplished here at Langley, Martin. From now on we can write our own ticket, we're flavor of the month with George W."

"Well, there's no turning back now," said Riley. "We've made a radical change this time."

"It's for the best, Martin," said the Colonel. "Think of the damage this would have done to America's standing, in the eyes of the world."

"Yes, and think of the children that won't be fatherless, the husbands that won't come home to a tearful, final message, on their answer phone," said Riley.

We saved thousands of lives, he thought as he remembered the people waiting in the North Tower, knowing they'd soon be plunging to their deaths. He couldn't forget the 'jumpers.' *Surely it was for the best? Surely it was justified?*

Two weeks after they had saved the Twin Towers, the Colonel invited Riley into his office for coffee again. Riley was suspicious of this new familiarity and wondered what the Colonel would reveal.

"It seems the Committee have seen things my way," said the Colonel. "Saving the World Trade Centre has finally put some fire in their bellies. Now they understand the awesome power we have at our fingertips. They want to be discerning though, play the long game in the national interest. They want us to collect and analyses more data, so we're gonna move the Gleaners to another site and hire more of them. We'll recruit more Scrutineers here, in their place. The Gleaners don't need to know who they're working for, it's the Scrutineers that should be inside the security bubble. The Committee want you to improve our reach beyond the two-week limit, so none of us is out of a job, quite the opposite," he chuckled. "We need to be vigilant, Martin. We're the keepers of the keys. We can unlock the future."

Or screw it up, thought Riley, wondering when he would meet this mysterious Committee.

He was disconsolate as he left the Colonel's office. When he got back to his desk, he found a letter lying on top of the budget report he had been working on. It was from HM Government and enquired whether he would be willing to accept a knighthood if one was offered to him

"But you've always despised the honors system," said Estella, when he told her the news that evening.

"Yes, but when you're offered one it's hard to refuse," he said, "don't piss on my bonfire. You never seem to be on my side, these days."

"Stephen Hawking refused a knighthood."

"Yes," he snapped, raising his voice, but still trying not to wake the baby, "but Professor Hawking has many other awards, so he can afford to refuse one if he wants to. I have nothing. I have invented one of the most important technologies in human history, possibly the most important, yet because of the Government's disclosure restrictions, nobody has even heard of me. Thanks to me we control the future." He was shouting by the end of his tirade. He went into his home office and slammed the door. In the nursery, Cliff began to cry.

That evening, after a late dinner, he sat at the table swirling a second glass of brandy. The boys were asleep.

"So, how are you feeling about the way things are going?" asked Estella.

Riley recognized an open-ended question when he heard one. "What do you mean?" he countered. He wondered whether she was talking about their marriage, or something more mundane.

"About the 'Dire Effects of our Interventions,' " she said in a deep, comic male voice. She took a drink from what he noticed was her fourth glass of wine. She seemed a little fuddled.

"Do you see any 'Appalling Ramifications' coming over the horizon?" She leaned back in her chair and looked at him, her brow furrowed. " 'The Destruction of the Timestream,' perhaps." He heard the sarcasm in her voice as she quoted his own phrases back at him. Their relationship was going through a low phase. He had answered several phone calls to the house where the caller had hung up without speaking.

"I'm okay about it," he said evenly, he didn't want a row, it wouldn't help. She was just a little drunk, she did this occasionally. "It's too late to do much about it, we've made our bed and now we have to lie on it." He stood. "I have emails to go through, I'll see you later," he walked into his home office and closed the door.

That night, in bed, Riley spooned up to Estella, kissed her shoulder and began to slide the strap of her nightdress over it.

"I'm sorry, Martin, I'm tired," she said, as she pushed the strap back into place. A faint wailing came from the baby alarm, building in volume. Riley sighed, got up and reached for his dressing gown, it was his turn.

"Best of luck," said Estella, as she pulled the quilt up and settled her pillow.

Riley walked around the nursery, rocking Cliff in his arms. He sang quietly, to help settle him. "The Twelve

Days of Christmas" was a useful song because, with all the repeats, there were seventy-eight verses. He'd pinned an old Christmas card up on the wall with pictures of "Geese a laying" and "Ladies dancing," as a prompt. He alternated with "Green Grow the Rushes, Oh" for the same reason.

He tried to remember the last time he and Estella had made love, it was months ago. They occupied the same house but it was as if they had forgotten what they liked about each other. He decided to give it some thought and resolved to try to be more attentive, buy her flowers perhaps? They were so tired most of the time, and living in a foreign land meant there were no mothers or mothers-in -law to look after the boys, while they spent a night out together. Estella wouldn't trust local teenage girls to baby sit the boys.

Chapter Thirteen

USA the 2000s

The Christmas break was two weeks away, when Doug walked into Riley's office. Doug the technician had quickly made himself indispensable. He was the guy who could unblock the photocopier, reload the water cooler, fix routine computer problems. Short and overweight he kept a low profile. On this occasion he had a half-eaten sandwich in one hand and the rest of it in his mouth.

"What's the good news Doug?" Riley asked.

Doug gulped down his mouthful.

"It's a Tsunami, caused by an earthquake in the Indian Ocean. It'll kill a quarter of a million people on the 26th of December." He placed a copy of a newspaper report on Riley's desk and went back to sit at his work station. He put in a pair of earbuds and returned to the virtual world that most of his generation seemed to prefer. Riley had noticed that many of the clever math types could be indifferent to other people's problems, the technicians were usually more grounded, but not Doug.

Doug's news made Riley feel optimistic. It would be easy to warn the population in the danger zone and save tens of thousands of lives, at no cost to the US taxpayer. He walked over to the Colonel's office and, on principle, entered without knocking. He laid the news print out on his desk.

"Where does the Tsunami strike?" asked the Colonel, after he had read the headline.

"Well, around the Indian Ocean, but the worst hit countries are Indonesia, Sri Lanka, India and Thailand. A quarter of a million people will die," Riley reiterated. "We could reduce the death toll if we warned them to move away from the coast and camp on higher ground. It should be easy to issue fake results from the seismic monitoring systems."

"Okay, I'll inform the Oversight Committee when they meet tomorrow."

The Tsunami slipped from his mind, it was the Festive Season, everybody had preparations to make, presents to buy, cards to send. When Christmas Day came, and there had been no warning, he became uneasy. On Boxing Day, Riley and his two young sons, Cliff and Hank, were sitting in front of a log fire in the lounge of their Scandinavian styled house. He was watching the TV news, while the boys played with their new toys. On screen, an assistant handed a piece of paper to the newsreader.

"Reports are just coming in of a Tsunami in the Indian Ocean. No reliable details are available, but our correspondent in Indonesia reports they have lost communication with the northern parts of the country."

Riley sat still. Estella came into the room holding a Christmas cake on a stand.

"Can I interest anybody in this?" she asked. The boys were very interested. "How about you, fatso?" She held a knife poised ready to make a cut, "Just a small slice for you?"

Riley couldn't speak. The whole scenario unfolded as he mentally ran the footage he had watched two weeks before at the laboratory. A quarter of a million-people dead, a quarter of a million. He stood up, walked into the hallway, put on a coat and left the house. He walked in the snow for hours, his mind churning.

By the time he got back, the boys had gone to bed. He sat by the fire in the lounge, with a blanket that Estella had wrapped around him, and sipped at a glass of single malt.

"I told the Colonel about the Tsunami," he said.

She looked shocked, "I remember. Didn't they give a warning? I haven't been keeping up with the news. Everybody at the lab knew about the Tsunami."

"No," he said, "they didn't give a warning. A quarter of a million-people dead, and we could have alerted them. We could have saved hundreds of thousands of men, women and children. Why didn't the Government warn them? The Colonel said he would tell the Committee. What sort of people are we working for?"

Estella stared at him, her hand in front of her mouth. There was nothing to say.

After the holiday Riley tried to tackle the Colonel.

"Sorry, Martin, I'm too busy to talk," he said over the phone. "I'm working on next year's budgets I can't be disturbed."

After several similar calls, Riley walked past Wilson's protesting secretary and into his inner office. He shut the door and stared at the Colonel who was standing at his ergonomic desk, reading a report. Wilson sighed and pushed his glasses up onto his forehead.

"Look, Martin," he said, "now, I know what you're thinking. The problem is that you and I don't see the big picture. What might appear significant in the short term, might look real unimportant in the long-term and vice versa. They see the big picture at Liberty Crossing." He was referring to the National Counterterrorism Centre, based nearby. "The Government ignored the warning for their own good reasons, I'm sure."

"Explain that to the victims and their families," said Riley more loudly than he meant.

"Well I share your concerns, but we have to trust our democratically elected leaders to work in our mutual national interests," said the Colonel, staring hard at Riley.

Probably for the recording that the FBI was making of conversations in this office, thought Riley. The mealy-mouthed bastard. The Colonel continued to stare at him intently as if he would like to say more. Riley noticed that he had stopped blinking.

"We should be working in the international interest," said Riley through gritted teeth. "If the victims had been Europeans or Americans, we'd have warned them," he shouted.

Riley worried about how he would explain himself to a jury if the TM team's activities ever became public knowledge. He didn't know whether he could justify his position. An image of the defendants in the Nuremberg war trials, seated in the dock under guard, haunted him. Their defense, "We were only following orders," seemed laughable now.

The Colonel abruptly changed his attitude, he approached Riley and placed a hand on his arm.

"You're overwrought, Martin. Why not take a few days rest?"

Riley went home and slept on the sofa until Estella arrived home with the boys.

"I don't know whether the Colonel will report our conversation to his superiors," said Riley, later that evening. "If he doesn't, they might accuse him of complicity, so he hasn't got much choice. Anyway, they're spying on us all the time, we're such a big security risk. To the Yanks all Europeans are commies and my outburst will have reinforced their prejudices."

"Yes," agreed Estella. "They seem to translate 'Liberal' into 'Communist' over here."

Riley stayed at home for a few days, he painted the lounge and read a few physics journals. Eventually he went back to work, made a sizeable donation to the Tsunami relief fund, and tried not to think about it.

The dark months passed and finally it was Spring. The delightful smell of newly mown grass was usually overlaid by the meaty fumes from his neighbors" barbeques. Riley and Estella were getting ready to go to a concert with their new friends, Alan and Diana. Estella had met Diana through the boys" nursery.

"They're probably FBI agents, tasked with watching us," Riley said. "Be careful what you say if they fish for information about work."

"Your trouble is that you think everybody has a hidden agenda, Martin. You think everybody wants something from you, or else they're out to get you," said Estella.

"You told me it was Diana who first approached you. We have to be careful."

Riley was having a third go at tying his bow tie.

"Why don't you wear an elasticated one like everybody else?" asked Estella as she leaned over and pulled the wrinkles out of her tights.

"Because I have standards," he replied.

"Oh yes, we know all about your standards."

Now there's a statement without content, he thought, as the tie unraveled again. He decided to follow her advice, but he wouldn't give her the satisfaction by admitting to it.

On the way home in the car they discussed the recent London bombings. "I don't understand why the British Government didn't intervene and prevent them," said Estella. "Perhaps George W didn't tell Tony about it. But I thought they were 'bestest' friends."

Riley had been paying more attention to the "big picture" as part of his long-term plan to get onto the Oversight Committee.

"If there's no terrorism at all, then why have an expensive security service? Better to have a limited amount of terrorist activity to keep the public worried, everybody in their jobs and the budgets healthy."

"Is our Government really that cynical?" she asked.

Riley turned to look at her for a moment.

"Nothing would surprise me," he said.

Next morning, before he stepped into the shower, he glimpsed himself as he walked past the long bathroom mirror. His stomach stuck out, he was developing a middle-aged spread. He quickly pulled it in and decided to start attending the gym. Perhaps he should buy a rowing machine or something, and put it in his home office, it was big enough. He went closer to the mirror and held his hair away from his forehead, his hairline was receding, and the greying of his temples was more pronounced. He reflected on his life as he brushed his teeth. The boys were wonderful, the job was interesting, he and Estella were solvent, but things were rocky between them. She'd started doing aerobics on Tuesday evenings and Spanish on Thursday evenings, they never seemed to spend time together. She'd rebuffed his advances in bed, several times, he found the experience humiliating, and left it to her to restart their love life, but she didn't seem to be in any hurry.

Barbara was a young woman he worked with. He remembered how they had kissed in a quiet corner of the laboratory, at the office party last Christmas. The kiss had lasted much longer than he expected and he was surprised by the feel of her tongue moving just inside his mouth, she was being more than polite. Who'd been holding the mistletoe? Surely not himself, he'd been a little drunk but he couldn't remember having mistletoe. Barbara was slimmer than Estella, and although she was no beauty, her strong features, direct manner, and good dress sense had caught his attention. She was about thirty, there was a twelve-year age difference between them, but he decided to ask her out for a drink, and see how things progressed. He noticed stirrings in regions he been trying to ignore, as he stepped into the shower.

At work, next day, he followed Barbara as she left the office to take her morning break in the staff restaurant. She sat by herself at a corner table.

He walked over, holding his coffee. "Mind if I join you?" he asked.

"Of course, not, Martin." She had a nicely modulated voice with just a hint of a Lancashire accent.

"How are things going?" he asked as he sat down.

"Things are going fine, Martin, thank you." She looked at him as if waiting to see what he'd say next. After a pause she asked, "How are things going with you?" She was half smiling.

"Er, Barbara, I wonder if you could help me with some calibration results?" She was one of Estella's mathematics team.

"Certainly, Martin, when would be a good time?"

"Actually, I'm rather busy all day, would you mind staying on for half an hour after close of play?"

"I'll see you at about five then." She finished her coffee and left.

Five o'clock came, and the laboratory and side offices emptied. He'd told Estella that he'd be an hour late coming home, she hadn't seemed bothered, they used separate cars.

"It's my aerobics evening, I need you back before seven, to put the boys to bed," she'd said.

Barbara arrived at his office a little after five.

"Ah, yes, Barbara, nice of you to stay on. I was wondering if ..."

She put her finger to her lips, took his arm, and led him to the cleaner's store. She shut the door behind them and leaned against it.

"I just wanted to ask you if ..." he began.

She pulled him to her, and kissed him firmly on his lips, then whispered in his ear, "You took your time, the office party was months ago. There are no cameras in here, Martin."

They kissed passionately, he'd forgotten how suddenly these things could happen. He lifted her onto the worktop and they made love, fully clothed, hurriedly, hungrily, violently. It was over very quickly.

"Jesus Barbara, that was a surprise," he panted, as they adjusted their clothing afterwards. "That wasn't the most elegant thing I've ever done."

"It was probably something we both needed, Martin."

"Can we go for a drink somewhere quiet? We need to talk about this."

They left the store and walked towards the laboratory exit.

"Night Doc, night Barbara," called Doug, hidden by the PC on his desk.

"Night Doug," they both called back, as they pushed through the double doors onto the main staircase.

"I thought the place was empty," said Riley.

"So did I. You know, that Doug gives me the creeps, there's something about him. Where I come from we'd say 'he's all about,' " said Barbara.

They went to a hotel bar and sat in a booth near the back.

"I wasn't expecting things to happen this fast," he said.

"It was a surprise for me as well. I didn't realize how much I fancied you until we kissed, again. It must be your pheromones." She stared into her drink, the ice rattled as she swirled it around her glass. "I know how this conversation's going to go, Martin, I've been here before, I had an affair with my tutor at Warwick and later, my prof at Cambridge. They were both married, I know the score, you needn't worry. I love my job, I love my apartment, I love my independence. I don't want a husband, kids, all that conventional stuff. I've seen how it holds women back, stunts their careers, limits their choices. I don't want to break up your marriage, ask you to leave your kids, endure the scandal at work, have to find another job. This is your lucky day, Martin, I'm offering sex without responsibility, every man's dream."

He remembered the adage, "If a deal looks too good to be true then it probably is." Did she habitually have affairs with men in a position to help her career or did she find powerful men sexy? Probably the former, which seemed quite reasonable, but he'd better be ready for the quid pro quo.

Riley arrived home. "Is that a new aftershave?" asked Estella.

"No, the same as usual," he said as he went upstairs, showered and changed. He'd have to be more careful about Barbara's perfume clinging to him.

"I want to start going to the gym on Wednesday evenings, if that's okay with you," he said.

"Fine," she called from the kitchen. "You can try to lose your love handles."

He wondered if Estella was playing the same game as himself. Her Spanish books were gathering dust in the lounge untouched, and aerobics was practically a euphemism. But he felt better than he had in months.

"I was thinking of changing my car," he said.

"What to," she called.

"Well, a Porsche Carrera actually, I've always wanted one." There was silence from the kitchen. Estella came through, drying her hands on a tea towel. She looked at him quizzically.

"You're not having an affair are you, Martin?" she asked.

Riley realized that he would have to be much more careful if he was going to deceive Estella. That night, in bed, she moved across to him in the darkness, and they made love. She turned her back to him, almost as if she wanted to keep the act anonymous, either that or she didn't want to see him enjoying himself. Still, it was better than nothing.

Chapter Eighteen

USA the 2000s

Riley gunned the engine as he joined the main road and headed for the Interstate. Even though he was driving too fast, his pulse rate fell, as he left the Langley complex further and further behind. He would never go back, he'd said too much. The members of the Committee would never trust him again, and he couldn't work with the Colonel. He called Estella, he wanted her to know where he would be sleeping, her cell phone went straight to voice mail. On second thoughts, he wouldn't be safe until he'd spoken to the press. He should disappear until he'd published his statement. He threw the cell phone out of the window. Track that, he thought, as he continued on towards the Potomac River and the Punter's mooring on the other side.

A few miles later, the Woodrow Wilson Bridge soared majestically on concrete stilts a dozen stories above the water. He drove onto it, but as he reached the central span, an explosion under his car flipped it upside-down and flung it over the low parapet.

Strapped in his seat, gripping the steering wheel he began the long screaming fall to oblivion, but the fall became slower, as if he was plunging into treacle. At first, he thought his brain was working faster than events, that any moment his life would flash before his eyes, an upload to the CosmicCloud. Still clutching the wheel in a white knuckled grip, he watched as airbags slowly inflated all around him, partly obscuring his vision and grazing his face. Surely airbags should inflate instantaneously. Time was truly running more and more slowly, and finally it stopped altogether. The car was suspended in space and time. Groggily he looked at the Potomac River twenty meters below him, there was no movement in the water, everything was still. He realized that he was weightless.

"Sorry to have to leave it until the last moment, Dr Riley," a female voice said from behind him. "Please unbuckle your seat belt and make your way back here to the portal."

Riley sat frozen in place, he could move, but this situation was so far from his normal experience that he had no idea how to respond to it. He wasn't frightened, he found that he was unexpectedly calm, but he felt unreal, disassociated from the situation. Was he dreaming, or in a hospital anaesthetized and hallucinating? Leaning forward he looked in the driving mirror of his inverted car and saw that a flexible, many colored membrane replaced the whole of its rear section. It was like a thick soap bubble, strange polychromatic patterns shifted over its surface. A woman sat on the other side in what appeared to be another vehicle. She wore a close-fitting suit of pastel colors which changed and sparkled in the dimly lit interior.

"Are you from the future?" he asked. He couldn't think of any other explanation.

"Yes, Martin? Just climb back here as fast as you can."

He sat rigidly, and tried to think what to do. How could he regain control of the situation? He wanted more time to think.

"Was the explosion an assassination attempt?" he asked.

"Yes, Martin. Please unbuckle your seat belt, now."

He saw the membrane fluctuate and a burst of new colors splashed across it.

"We can't hold this configuration indefinitely, Martin, let's get moving." Her voice had become harder.

"Won't this have repercussions, ripples in the Timestream?" he asked.

She sighed, "No, your involvement here was about to end a few seconds from now. We can extract you with no temporal reverberations. Come on, Dr Riley, no more questions, we're on the clock here."

"Why are you saving me?" Riley was still uncertain what to do, he was playing for time, the situation was out of his control. He still hoped for a way out, a way back to normality.

"The Commonwealth has a job for you."

Riley still hadn't moved. "The Commonwealth, what Commonwealth?"

The woman became exasperated, "If you don't come right now, I will have to disengage and leave you falling. You will die about three seconds later."

Realizing that he had no choice, he unbuckled his seat belt, grabbed his briefcase, and pulled himself towards the rear. Mixed with his feelings of confusion was an intense disappointment that the Colonel and his masters would think they'd won.

Fuck them all anyway, he thought, as he slid through the membrane and into the future.

Chapter Fourteen

USA the 2000s

Riley had always wanted a boat. The Chesapeake Bay was only an hour away from Langley so, on a whim, he bought a converted Skipjack fishing boat, without discussing it with Estella. He renamed her the "Punter's Revenge" which seemed appropriate as that one last big bet had been the source of the wherewithal. The previous owner had equipped her for fair weather sailors, by fitting a toilet, shower, and galley kitchen; it had all the modern conveniences that Estella would like. He visualized the family sailing the sounds and inlets of the offshore barrier islands, fishing and swimming in the warm, blue waters.

Cliff and Hank, now six and eight years old, were delirious with excitement when he took them all to see the Punter. Estella seemed less enthusiastic as she stood on the shore and watched the boys explore above and below decks. Their shrieks and shouts as they discovered the bridge and best of all their sleeping quarters made her smile.

"Can we sleep in the bunks Dad?" Hank called from below.

"Of course," he called back, "that's what they're for." They were just the right age for this sort of adventure, and began arguing about who would have the top one.

"Take it in turns," he shouted.

"You should have discussed this with me before you went ahead, Martin," Estella said, as she stood, arms folded, staring at the boat. "You know I get motion sickness. I'm afraid that you and the boys will have to do this by yourselves."

"How convenient, you can stay home alone at weekends with the three of us out of the way. You can spend more time with your fancy man." He was angry at her obstructive behavior and couldn't help saying more than he had intended.

Estella turned and stalked back to the car. She got into the passenger seat, slammed the door, and took out her cell phone. Riley ignored her.

"Who's ready for a trip around the Bay?"

Cliff and Hank couldn't have been readier. I'll soon have them crewing he thought, as the boys climbed aboard. He loosed the moorings, jumped aboard himself, took the wheel, and keyed the engine into life.

Riley wished he hadn't alerted Estella to his suspicions. All marriages go through low spots; if she was having an affair, it would be best to ignore it and hope it burned itself out. He just couldn't bear the idea of losing his family, his boys. He was furious at the thought of another man screwing his wife, but the possibility of the same miserable bastard bringing up his children made Riley murderously angry. He wanted to sink an axe into his head, whoever he was. His knuckles were white on the wheel as he steered the boat away from the shore, the boys standing on either side of him holding on to the grab rails.

Riley imagined Estella and this stranger coupling in their marital bed, he wanted to throw up. Surely, she wouldn't stoop that low. Surely, she'd insist they use hotel rooms. The thought of him on top of Estella, thrusting into her as she cried out with pleasure, or worse, having her.... He pushed away the shockingly detailed pictures that were forming, uncalled for, in his mind. He tried to concentrate his thoughts on the boat, the boys, and the Chesapeake Bay, but he was shaking with anger. He looked over at his wife, still sitting in the car. The boys waved and shouted as they motored past but she stared straight ahead and wouldn't look at them. He took off across the Bay for half an hour, then returned to their mooring. As they drove home, he and the boys chatted excitedly about the boat, and the trips they would make in her. Estella stared silently out of the side window.

The Punter was a big success; the three of them spent happy times together that summer. Riley was sorry that Estella would never join them, though the boys, especially Cliff, the younger one, pleaded with her. She cited motion sickness, even when the forecast promised a flat calm. In the meantime, the marriage continued to tread water and Riley made a point of not asking questions. He hoped that she would come back to him, eventually.

He risked discussing his feelings with Barbara on the next Wednesday evening at her apartment. They lay side by side, their empty wine glasses on the floor beside her bed.

"Honestly, Martin, you men, always applying the double standard. If you can have an affair which isn't rocking your marital boat, why can't she? The French do it all the time, it's just part of life to them. The aristocracy have been the same over the generations."

"Because it feels different, that's why. If I have an affair, I won't get pregnant. If Estella has an affair, I could end up bringing up another man's kids."

"But we have birth control now, Martin, this is the twenty-first century."

"It's all right for you," he said. "You don't have a long emotional involvement, kids, a whole history together." He had got out of bed and dressed as he talked. He was shaking as he sat on the bed and tried to knot his shoe laces.

"It's probably best if we take a little break, Martin," she said, leaning across to pick a cigarette out of an antique silver cigarette box, she liked to smoke after sex. "I really don't want this to get messy, remember that Estella is my boss. Let's leave it for a few weeks, see how you feel about things. Go to the gym next Wednesday, it's good cover, anyway."

"I'll see you at work tomorrow," he said as he left.

Chapter Fifteen

USA the 2000s

Riley was sitting in his office, staring absently out into the laboratory area. It was nearing the end of the day, and he was grappling with the staff holiday roster, a job he hated. It was an almost insoluble problem, even for a man with a doctorate in particle physics. Everybody with kids requested the school holidays off, and it left him with little or no cover. He'd always wanted to be a leader, but never a manager. Surely this admin was the Colonel's job, but he insisted that Riley was responsible for his 'Limeys,' and that was that.

He noticed Barbara stand up and go over to the main printer, she picked up a sheet of paper from the output tray. Workplace romances were dangerous, and this one wasn't going smoothly. He sighed, he should get on with the holiday roster, but instead he watched as Barbara folded the paper. She logged out of her workstation, picked up her handbag and jacket, and walked over to his office. His door was open, and she knocked on it once as she walked in and took a seat. Neither of them spoke for a moment. Riley could sense something unusual in her manner.

"Hello Barbara," he said, "how can I help?"

She paused, and stared at him for a moment.

"Well, Martin, it's a Policy Four matter." She sat clutching the paper in her lap and staring intently at him.

Policy Four was one of the Colonel's bureaucratic novelties. It stipulated that, if any of the team found a news item of direct concern to another team member, a road accident for instance, they were to report it to a superior. They were not to discuss it with the interested party.

"I see. You wish to report something which will affect another member of the team?"

She nodded.

"So, what's the problem?"

"The problem, Martin, is that it's a news item that affects you, so I should report it to the Colonel, but judging by the date on it he's already aware."

He smiled and tried to appear relaxed, but a cold feeling had come over him. He paused, "I assume it's important or you wouldn't be here, would you?"

"You're right, Martin, it's very important." Barbara sighed as she appeared to come to a decision. She placied the folded sheet of paper on his desk, stood up and walked out of his office. He watched as she continued to the main exit and left the lab. Riley would never see her again.

He went to the rest room and unfolded the paper in the privacy of a locked cubicle. It was a copy of a newspaper story. He read of the death of his older son Hank, in five days' time.

Chesapeake Examiner July 14 2008
Tragic death as boy drowns in boating accident.

The body of ten-year-old Hank Riley was found this morning, floating by the side of the family's converted Skipjack, "The Punter's Revenge." The boy's father, Dr Martin Riley (48,) discovered the body but was not available for interview. A spokeswoman for the family said they were understandably distraught, and hoped that they will be allowed to grieve privately. The cause of death has not been announced, but local police do not suspect foul play. Hank's mother, Mrs Estella Riley (44,) was away visiting a friend for the weekend, while Dr Riley, who is a Government employee, and his sons, Hank and Cliff, were fishing and sailing in the Bay. On Saturday night they moored up and enjoyed a barbeque before retiring. It appears that Mr Riley's son, Hank, fell from the boat during the small hours and drowned. He was not wearing a life jacket.

This publication has every sympathy with the feelings of the Riley family, but it is our editorial duty to once again remind readers that preventable accidents, such as this, occur every year. We cannot emphasize too strongly the responsibility of parents to make sure that their children wear proper safety equipment, when they are on or near the water.

The Medical Examiner's office has stated that there will be an investigation to establish the cause of death. The date of the inquest has yet to be announced.

He tore the paper to shreds and flushed it away. Leaning his head against the door of the cubicle he stood trembling, thinking of his poor boy, his life barely begun, lost to him and Estella. He cried quietly for several minutes. By force of will he regained his composure. This didn't have to happen; he would not let it happen. What was the point of having the power and not using it? If the Government could save the Twin

Towers, then he could save Hank. He realized that he would expose Barbara if he approached the Colonel, she had broken the rules. He had to think what to do.

Riley left the cubicle, washed his face, and returned to his desk. He was trembling and couldn't concentrate on administrative trivia. He told his secretary that he had a headache, he drove home and sat in the empty house. Information arrived two weeks in advance, yet according to the date in the newspaper, Hank's accident was only five days away. The Colonel must have seen the report more than a week ago and he hadn't mentioned it. Riley was furious to think the Committee must have discussed it and decided not to warn him. He poured himself a whiskey, gulped it and sat staring at the fireplace. His emotions were fluctuating between anger and distress. Those bastards, what sort of people was he working for? Where was their loyalty? They expected his, but where was theirs? Riley threw his empty glass at the wood burner, it smashed to pieces. He sat back on the sofa, head in his hands and thought about his life, his wife, his job, his boys. Those faceless fuckers on the Oversight Committee, he would never trust them again, nor that jumped up wanker Wilson. The whiskey warmed his stomach and, as the alcohol entered his blood stream, he calmed down. His breathing steadied, and he felt better, he cleared up the broken glass. He hoped that Estella wouldn't notice the missing tumbler, it was one of the expensive ones.

Estella arrived home, she had already heard something was wrong.

"Sonia told me you have a headache and seemed upset," she said, but he shrugged it off. When the boys came home from school, he spent a long time on the floor with them, playing with their train set.

That night, as he lay in bed with his back turned to Estella, she leaned over his shoulder.

"You were very good with the boys this evening, it was lovely to see you getting so involved with them." He grunted and said nothing. Riley had to deal with this himself; he didn't want to implicate her in whatever action he took. She kissed his ear. He turned to face her, and they made love, gently, for the first time in weeks, probably months. He wondered if things would get better between them, he hoped so.

The next day the Colonel came into Riley's office.

"Barbara's been called home on urgent family business," he said. "Her mother has had a stroke or something; she'll be away for a while." He turned, and flipping his glasses down off his forehead, walked back towards his office, reading the document he was carrying.

When the weekend came, Riley considered cancelling the sailing trip, but decided to change events in the Timestream as little as possible. He wanted to minimize the "ripples", so he went ahead as planned. Estella had left early for a weekend with "friends," although Riley suspected that the "friends" were one male "friend."

On the Saturday night, after the boys were asleep, he locked the cabin door, pocketed the only key and sat reading and drinking coffee. At about two o'clock in the morning Hank woke up, he climbed out of his bunk and, still half asleep, fumbled at the cabin door. Riley unlocked it for him and followed him up the steps. Hank stood on the deck and pissed over the side of the boat, as his father had taught him. There was no point in filling up a boat's septic tank with unnecessary toilet flushes.

As Hank finished, he overbalanced forward. Riley grabbed the back of his tee shirt and hauled him upright. Hank regained his balance and stumbled below, rubbing his eyes; he probably wouldn't remember the incident next morning. Riley followed him, and after he had settled Hank in his bunk, he poured himself a celebratory drink. It was a huge relief, he'd saved his boy; he'd been scared that he might fall asleep. If he had, and Hank had drowned, what then? He would have to send himself a TM, send it back two weeks, and make a retrospective Temporal Adjustment to save Hank, something expressly forbidden.

Had saving Hank generated a new Timestream, or a new branch? He didn't know, although he cared deeply. What mattered most was that he'd saved Hank. He had overcome the cold-hearted indifference of the Colonel and the Committee, they were welcome to do whatever they liked when they found out; his boy was worth more than all of them put together. With trembling hands, he re-locked the cabin door and pocketed the key. He put some cushions in front of it and lay down to sleep on them. He wasn't taking any chances.

Riley was at his desk early on Monday morning, as usual. The Colonel came into his office, he didn't speak. Riley looked up at him over the top of his screen.

"Good morning, Colonel."

"Good weekend, Martin?"

"Yes," he said "I took the boys sailing, lovely weather." They stared at each other for a long moment.

"Great," said the Colonel and turned to leave.

"You know what your problem is Wilson?" asked Riley, he felt a cold, white anger.

The Colonel turned back and stared but didn't answer.

"You're a cunt, Colonel, that's what your problem is." Riley wanted to knock him to the floor, kneel on his arms and choke the life out of him. He imagined his thumbs crossed over Wilson's scrawny windpipe. He could see it happening in his mind, but knew he was too inhibited to do it.

The Colonel left the office, closing the door quietly behind him.

You conniving bastard, thought Riley, if I ever get the chance, I'll fuck you up.

A week later, after Riley had got over his initial anger, a memo arrived from the Human Resources section. Attached to it was a copy of Barbara's neatly typed and signed letter of resignation. It said her mother, who lived back in the UK, had suffered a stroke and needed care for the foreseeable future. As her only daughter, it fell to Barbara to return home and look after her. She apologized for any inconvenience to the team, and said she was very disappointed to be leaving etc., etc. Riley compared the signature to the one on last year's holiday request form, it looked genuine. The Colonel came in to discuss a replacement.

"It's very inconvenient for you, Martin I know, but I suggest we follow the usual procedure and recruit somebody from one of the core technical positions, outside the TM team security bubble. It'll have to be a Brit, of course. We don't want to fill the place up with Yanks, do we?" He was referring to the agreed ratio of

US and UK personnel. Riley realized he was making an effort to lighten the atmosphere between them. They hadn't spoken about Riley's unofficial TA.

"Yes, but it's always such a pain, briefing new recruits," said Riley. "They need days to get their heads around the time-slip thing. People find it so hard to take in, I'm sick of explaining it, to be honest."

While they were talking Riley was wondering what had really happened to Barbara.

When he got home that evening, he hand wrote a letter to his brother Phillip, who was a sergeant in the Flying Squad back in London. He asked him to investigate Barbara's supposed return to England, and to be circumspect in his reply. He placed the letter in the pocket of his jacket, and left the house. There was a posting box just inside the entrance to the local mall. After passing through the automatic doors, he slid the letter into it as he walked past, without breaking step. He hoped to fool the FBI agent, or anybody else, who might be following him; he was getting more paranoid every day.

Two weeks later, Phillip phoned from England. "Hello, Martin, long time no chat, how's things?"

"Fine Phil, fine, how's the job going, caught any dangerous villains lately?"

"Not really, the only thing I've caught lately is a cold." They both laughed then chatted about family matters, the weather back home and the Beijing Olympics. After ten minutes, Phillip brought the conversation around to more personal interests. "Talking of my divorce, which we weren't, I decided it was time to start dating again. It's been six months since Eileen left. The decree nisi isn't through yet, but I realize she won't be coming back. Just for a start, I wanted to see if any of my old girlfriends are free and single. You never know your luck, and it's easier than trying to meet new women, especially in this job, working shifts. I tried to get in touch with that girl Maggie, the one I was engaged to fifteen years ago. She used to live next door, when we lived on Whitehouse Avenue, you remember?"

"Oh yes," said Riley, "I haven't seen her in years. How did you get on?" There had never been a girl called Maggie living next door to them. Their friend Dave had lived next door, Phillip obviously meant Barbara.

"I had her Mum's phone number, but when I rang somebody else answered. They said they'd bought the house after the old lady died of a heart attack, two years ago."

"So, did you find Maggie?"

"No," said Phillip. "There was no trace of her; she left the country four years ago, and hasn't been back since, except for her Mum's funeral. Anyway, plenty more fish in the sea." They moved on to other things, and after a few more minutes, agreed that they'd talk again soon. Riley replaced the receiver. He was grateful that Phillip was used to keeping his cards close to his chest.

He hoped that Barbara hadn't suffered.

Riley had to talk to somebody, the only person with a common interest was Estella. He took her for a walk in the park near their home, he was becoming ever more worried about "bugs." She was shocked when he told her of Hank's accident and his intervention. She stood and stared at him with her hand over her mouth.

"You mean he drowned, but then you stopped it from happening? I can't believe it."

"Well, I'm surprised that you have difficulty with the idea, after all, Temporal Adjustment is what we do."

"I suppose I've never seen it used so close to home before," she said. "How did you find out it was going to happen? Did the Colonel warn you?"

"No, it was Barbara."

"The one who resigned to go back and look after her mother?"

"She didn't resign; the US Government has assassinated her."

"You can't believe that, Martin, you're getting more suspicious every month. You should talk to somebody."

"I asked my brother Phillip to investigate; he told me that Barbara's mother died two years ago. Barbara hasn't re-entered the UK, she's disappeared. Into a convenient US Government incinerator somewhere if you ask me. Keep moving."

Estella rubbed her forehead as they walked. "What does it all mean?" she asked staring sideways at him.

"It means that we're very vulnerable. The idea that the press might get wind of our activities must petrify the present Government. They might decide to exterminate the whole team and airbrush Temporal Messaging from history; it wouldn't be difficult, very few people are aware of us. Or the incoming administration might expose us as a Republican conspiracy, when the CIA briefs them about TM. They could have us arrested, but if they do, they'll make sure the story is never reported, otherwise we'd have read it two weeks earlier, and made a run for it. We have to stay alert, what else can we do?" He was trembling by now. Estella took his arm.

"I often wonder how the Timestream reacts to our interference," said Estella. "Did it branch when you saved Hank? Are there two Timestreams now, one where he's dead and you and I are inconsolable, and one where he's alive? Or is there still only one, this one, which we've altered?"

"That's the sixty-four-thousand-dollar question," said Riley. "If there are multiple time branches then every molecule in the universe could give rise to a new branch an infinite number of times a second. There could be an infinite number of copies of us, playing out every possible storyline. It might be a limitation of my imagination, but I just don't see how that could be true. Perhaps all the possible realities are ghosts, and only one is real. Perhaps our actions change which one that is, crystallizes it so to speak. At least we know Hank is alive and kicking in this one, that's the important thing." Estella took hold of his arm with both hands and they walked on in silence.

Chapter Sixteen

USA the 2000s

Riley had always liked Peter Abrahams. He'd joined the team several years earlier, another eager young thing with a PhD in high energy physics from Cambridge. His CV was impressive, Riley had been part of the board that interviewed him. They'd worked closely together and Riley had mentored him through a brief but difficult period when he had lost confidence.

"The thing is," Abrahams had explained, "everybody around me is so intelligent. They all know more than me. I don't deserve to be here."

"You're suffering from 'Impostor Syndrome,' " said Riley. "It's quite common; I've been there myself occasionally, although my insecurities tend to concern personal relationships, rather than scientific competence. Your confidence will grow when you have a project you can immerse yourself in, something you know more about than anybody else. I'm sure you'll begin to feel useful after a few months. In the meantime, don't beat yourself up, enjoy the food, find yourself a girlfriend."

Abrahams had been grateful for the support. At the time, Riley wondered if his lack of confidence might stem partly from his slight build and shortness of stature. Yet here he was, two years later, eating a working lunch with Riley, in a quiet corner of the staff restaurant, and very much the confident research team leader.

"The thing is, Martin," he said, "I've found a way around the two-week barrier. I think we can move information a lot further back upstream, further into the past. I realize that we never make retrospective changes, but I thought I should let you know my direction of travel, so to speak." He looked down, picking at his food, and Riley noticed the hair grip that held his black kippah in place on the back of his head. Momentarily it took his attention, he'd never noticed it before. Abrahams was staring at him, expecting an answer.

"Er, how are you proposing to get past the two-week limit? What's your methodology?" he asked.

"Leapfrogging, Martin, we'll be sending data through a series of linked wormholes that reach back, theoretically as far as we want. We'll break the data into chunks, duplicate it, send it through different routes, and then join it up at the target date. The error checking is the biggest problem. I'm sure there'll be limitations that become apparent as we run the tests."

"Yes, I'm sure there will," said Riley. "Nothing's ever as simple as it seems in basic research, something always jumps out of the bushes and bites you on the backside. My problem with this is that it's so dangerous." Riley leaned forward and spoke quietly. "If you get it up and running the Yanks might want to save Jesus from the cross, or warn President Lincoln not to go to the theatre, or something equally bloody stupid. Can we keep this between ourselves for the moment,

Peter? We need to think up a title to baffle the Colonel. Could you call it something obscure and I'll sign the checks so to speak?" Abrahams looked doubtful, and was about to answer, but Riley stood up, patting his mouth with a paper napkin. "Must dash, another meeting, let me know how it goes. I want a weekly report for my eyes only, nothing too detailed, but come and find me if you make any breakthroughs." Abrahams seemed crestfallen; he probably wants recognition for his efforts thought Riley, as he walked away, and if it's kept secret, he won't get it. Well join the club mate.

Over the months, Abraham's research progressed well. Riley was careful to keep himself up to date with the software and procedures, almost looking over Abraham's shoulder at times.

They hadn't been able to keep the project secret for long, the Colonel was too efficient an administrator for that, but at least the Oversight Committee didn't ask Abrahams to send messages deep into the past, or do anything Riley found questionable. Bland messages sent back by Peter Abrahams, appeared on the hard drives from four weeks ahead, eight weeks ahead, sixteen weeks ahead and so on. The technique was seen as a powerful tool without a current use.

Hank's near accident had been a pivotal moment for Riley. He no longer felt any loyalty towards his masters and didn't trust them to do the right thing anymore. He constantly worried that a nutty politician might influence the Committee to make use of his inventions for a partisan end and bring reality crashing down around their ears. He worried that somebody else might invent the technique independently, the North Koreans for instance.

Tonight, he was alone in the lab, it was late. He'd had to wait for everybody to go home. Doug the technician had been the last, he'd hung around the kitchen drinking coffee while Riley sat in his office shuffling paperwork. Eventually he'd gone home, and now Riley had logged on to Abraham's application, in the main laboratory. He was entering data, copied from his notebook, that would arrive on a hard disc at Cambridge University on various dates about twenty years in the past. He was sending the racing tips that had started the whole TM process. Even though it was a retrospective TM, it had to be done, if not, his earlier self would never invent Temporal Messaging, and history would take a different course. He didn't want to risk a refusal by explaining his actions to the Colonel, and through him the Oversight Committee. He'd just pressed the return key on the final email and the progress bar was slowly filling from left to right.

"Working late Doc?" said Doug from behind him. Riley hadn't heard his approach and jumped part way out of his chair.

"Bloody hell Doug, don't creep up on me like that," he snapped.

"Sorry Doc, it's these brothel creepers, I shoulda coughed or somethin." He peered at the flat screen and screwed his eyes up as he read aloud.

"Frankie Detorri. Who's this Frankie Detorri guy and where's Ascot?"

The progress bar was full, and the text disappeared. Inwardly Riley was furious that Doug was reading his private emails over his shoulder, but he didn't want to draw attention to what he was doing.

"It's a Brit thing Doug," he said swiveling around to face the other man. "A famous horse race meeting, a big celebration, dressing up, men in suits, women in fancy hats, all that sort of thing. Foreigners love it, it's a tourist draw, like a rodeo." He knew that he was gabbling and making himself look guilty.

"Uh-huh," said Doug. Riley could tell that he wasn't convinced. He was still curious about the email.

Riley shut the computer down, stood and picked up his briefcase.

"Are you going or staying?" he asked.

"I'm goin Doc, I'll walk out with ya. So, this Detorri guy, he's a jockey, right?"

"Yes, probably the best jockey in the world." They were standing waiting for the elevator by this time. Riley was pretty sure that Doug hadn't realized that he'd been sending information back upstream.

"Look Doug, I probably shouldn't be using US Government equipment to email my bookmaker in England, but it was only a small bet, and it's a tradition. Everybody back home has a small bet on British Champions Day at Ascot. I'd be grateful if we could keep this between ourselves." Riley hated to grovel, particularly to an underling, but he needed to put Doug off the scent. He didn't want him reporting his observations to the Colonel.

"That's okay Doc, we're both men of the world," said Doug. "Who knows, I might need a favor off a you, one day."

They got out of the elevator, walked across the atrium and swiped out of the building.

"Thanks Doug, I appreciate it." They shook hands and set off in different directions across the near empty car park.

"Let me know if ya make a killing Doc," Doug shouted across to him. "Those bookies deserve a shaftin'."

Chapter Seventeen

USA the 2000s

It was a Monday, and Riley had arrived at the laboratory at eight o'clock that morning. Doug had been on weekend call staying in the staff quarters. He came into Riley's office looking, disheveled and unshaven, he placed his handover sheet on the desk, another of the Colonel's bureaucratic novelties.

"Did ya hear about the earthquake yet?" he asked. He was chewing gum as usual.

"No, what earthquake?"

"The one that's gonna happen in Haiti in two weeks. It's gonna kill a lotta people, about a quarter of a mill." Doug left, as emotionally unaffected as ever.

Riley read the report, carried it through to the Colonel's office, and placed it on top of his keyboard. The Colonel looked at Riley over his reading glasses then, after a pause and a small sigh, he picked it up and began reading it.

"Okay, Martin, this looks serious, I'll pass it on to the Committee," he said when he'd finished.

Teo weeks passed with no warning given. On the day after the quake, the Colonel invited Riley into his office.

He wants to get the inevitable confrontation over as soon as possible, thought Riley. The Colonel was standing behind his desk as Martin entered.

"I don't make policy, Martin, I'm sorry that we didn't warn those poor people in Haiti," he said, "but we have to keep this technology secret. The same way you Limeys protected your code breaking in World War Two. Alan Turing, Bletchley Park, the Enigma code, all that good stuff. The Government has to take painful decisions for the greater good. Sacrifices have to be made."

Riley was furious. He placed his hands on the desk and, leaned forward into the Colonel's face.

"They've counted 170,000 bodies so far, and they estimate there'll be a quarter of a million." He spoke through gritted teeth. "Do you know what 250,000 casualties means? Men, women, children, mothers, fathers, babies. Even now hundreds of people are lying trapped and dying with broken limbs in the darkness of cellars under collapsed buildings, calling out for water, calling for their God. You could have warned them, it wouldn't have cost you anything, you and your precious Committee, you could have easily warned them?" He was shouting, his hands were shaking, he stepped back.

"I refuse to work with you people any longer, you are mass murderers, I quit." He heard the slight break in his voice. "Oh, and by the way, I know about you and Estella. You, are a man without honor," he said slowly and carefully, before he turned and left the office. He would always regret that his inhibitions stopped him from punching the Colonel in his stupid face and then kicking the shit out of him while he lay curled up on the floor. He wanted to stamp on his head.

Riley walked into the main laboratory looking for Estella, he felt the embers of a dangerous, violent anger being fanned into flame. She was sitting at one of the work stations; he leaned down close to her ear.

"Come with me," he hissed. She looked up in surprise, and then followed him into the conference room. He shut the door and tried to drop the blind on the laboratory side.

"What's the matter, Martin?" she asked, as he pulled ineffectually at the draw strings. He threw them down, leaving the blind high on one side.

He turned and looked at her. "I know about you and him," he said.

"Me and who? What do you mean?"

He noticed that her blink rate didn't increase; it was normally a sure sign of tension with her, one of those useful indicators that a spouse notices but never discloses. A separate, logical part of him, found her personal control interesting, almost admirable. She was going to try to deny this thing.

"You and the Colonel."

"You're imagining things, Martin."

"He's been leaving his car parked at the back of the house, on the nights he stayed with you, nights when the boys and I have been away."

"How would you know if you were out on the Bay sailing your fucking boat?" she asked, hands on hips.

"Our home security cameras, I cut into their data loop, they store the last week's images. He parked near one at the back of the house, careless, probably overeager to see you. I watched him come to the back door with his wine and his flowers."

Estella stood staring at him, her mouth clamped shut, her face reddening with anger or embarrassment, he didn't know which.

"It makes sense to me now. He knew even better than you what my movements were, when I had to go away for meetings, when I was taking the late or weekend shift. The sneaky bastard, the two of you must have been running rings around me for months, years. How long has it been going on? How many others have there been? Who fathered the children for Christ's sake?" he was shouting by this time.

He took several deep calming breaths and spoke more quietly. "You've put so much at risk. Our jobs, our family, everything, just for a bit of excitement."

"What did you expect? Always worrying about 'ripples in the Timestream' or out on the Bay with the boys, you never had any time for me. He loves me, Martin, he's going to leave Pauline and make a life with me, Hank and Cliff."

Riley laughed derisively. "The only way he'll leave Pauline is with her boot up his arse when she finds out what he's been up to with you. He wants an affair, he wants sexual variety, and married women are safest, you're just his bit on the side. Wait until the chips are down, do you think he'll swap his daughter for our boys, not unless he's pushed? Even if you both try to make a go of it, how can you ever trust him? If he'll do this to his own family, he'll do it to you when he meets somebody else. You'll never be sure he isn't cheating, and he'll feel the same about you, because he knows you cheated on me, the father of your children. What a pair you'll make, watching each other's every move, checking each other's cell phones, hiring detectives." He laughed mirthlessly.

He moved towards the door. "I can't work here anymore, not with you, not with him, not with the Committee, I've quit. I need to get away. I'm going home now, to prepare a statement to the press. Bollocks to the disclosure restrictions. The world should know about our achievements here."

Estella stood rigidly, her arms by her sides, hands clenched, face red as he walked out of the room. The pneumatic closer denied him the satisfaction of slamming the door so he punched the water cooler hard as he passed it in the corridor. It fell over, the plastic bottle detached and rolled across the floor spilling water. Riley was aware of surprised looks from the staff sitting at nearby work stations.

"It's only a fucking water cooler," he shouted at them. "It's water, not blood."

He turned and shouted back at Estella, "He loves Pauline, they were childhood sweethearts and even if she kicks him out, he'll always love her more than he loves you. You'll always be second best."

He went back to his office, picked up his briefcase, and walked out of the building. He was upset, but the anger was mixed with relief, he had lanced the boil, it had hurt, but it was done, what would happen next was anybody's guess. As he walked to the car park, Riley decided he would spend the night on the boat. He needed time alone, time to get his thoughts in order. He wanted to feel the Punter's gentle rocking beneath his feet, to hear the slap of water on her hull, take melancholy comfort in the sun setting over the Bay. He needed a drink, he wanted peace. He drove the Jaguar out of the complex for the last time.

The Colonel watched from his office window as Riley drove through the main gate. He picked up his phone and tapped a number, it was answered at the first ring.

He sighed, "Colonel Wilson here, we have a problem, the one we discussed two weeks ago."

Chapter Nineteen

In transit

Riley looked around, he was inside a spherical space several meters across. The extremities of the sphere were insubstantial, misty and it was dimly lit. He turned to look back through the portal which covered part of the wall behind him. He watched as his now empty car finished its fall and smashed, upside-down, onto the water. Fragments of glass burst out all around it as the roof collapsed. The beams from its headlights slowly dimmed as it slid into the murky depths.

The portal shrank to a point and disappeared, the light level increased and he could see the interior more clearly. There were two seats set facing one another and no sign of any controls. The interior was grey and almost featureless. His skin was tight, it felt sunburned nearly to the point of pain. He wondered if it was something to do with passing through the membrane. Might it be radioactive? He rubbed his forearms trying to take away the burning sensation. His rescuer sat looking at him, hands placed on her thighs. Her suit no longer sparkled, she appeared relaxed, he guessed that she was about thirty and attractive in an understated way. Somehow, she reminded him of a librarian, well groomed, bobbed hair, minimal makeup, slim, almost athletic looking.

"Take a seat, Martin," she smiled and gestured towards the one opposite her. "The decontamination process has caused the strange sensation in your skin; the discomfort will fade shortly. I'm going to turn off the neuro-suppression field now. It has been damping your emotional responses, like a tranquillizer. You might feel panicky at first, as your defensive responses kick back in, but it will pass after a few minutes."

Suddenly Riley's heart began to race, he started to tremble and sweat, his legs felt hollow, he was terrified. He collapsed into the seat and the woman reached across with a beaker.

"Drink this, it will help calm you."

He could hardly hold the beaker, he was shaking so much. Gradually, he gained control of himself as he sipped the drink. Thank God, he hadn't thrown up, that would have been even more difficult to cope with. The woman sat quietly, allowing him time to calm down.

His emotional control began to return, he looked up. "I think you'd better tell me who you are and what just happened," he said.

"My name is Farina, I am a time traveler."

"Well who just tried to kill me?"

"Think about it, Martin. The Committee received a message about your outburst two weeks ago, through the secure feed. They decided to stage an accident. The charges were aligned to blow your car off the Bridge rather than into bits. They've been in place, hidden under the wheel arches, for over a week."

"But I didn't see anything about my accident in the press reports from the future."

"No, the Colonel made sure of that, Martin."

"Bastards, how will they explain what happened?"

"They'll say you were overwrought, driving erratically, your car clipped the parapet and somersaulted over into the River. Your friends will be shocked and sorry. The car is recovered later, they assume your body has been washed out into the Bay."

"So, the Government shuts me up, you capture me, Estella is free to break up the Colonel's marriage. Everybody wins a prize except me," he was shouting again. He felt the suppression field come on and dampen his emotions.

"We have saved you from certain death, Martin, remember that. I can show you your funeral if you like, but you might find it a macabre experience." Riley was too numb to speak, he wondered how Estella would feel about his apparent death, he regretted that their last words had been so hostile.

His mind seethed with questions, but one was uppermost.

"What about Cliff and Hank?" he asked. "I can't protect them anymore."

"They'll miss you, but the Colonel treats them well; Estella sees to that, a mother's loyalty is to her children first and to her partner second."

"I hope she remembers that he was willing to let one of them drown," he said bitterly.

"Let's go slowly, Martin, and try not to get overwhelmed. This is a lot for you to cope with. I'm sorry, I should have removed the field gradually, I've re-established it at low level."

"So, you're a time traveler, what do you do as you travel through time?"

"I am a historian, I specialize in your era, your customs, languages and politics. I discovered your progress in time manipulation by accident, it was a great surprise, but we'll talk of that later."

"Okay," he said, "why don't you tell me where we're going and why you need me." He lay back in the seat with his eyes closed. He felt drained.

"We are travelling up to what I call the present, but you think of as the future.

"But why are you taking me there?"

"I work for the 'Commonwealth,' the world government. Their representatives want to speak with you about Temporal Messaging."

Riley sat up and looked around him. "Why haven't we already arrived? I'm surprised the transition isn't instantaneous."

"It is a matter of manipulating the wormhole we're going through now." She sat back looking at him, her head tilted.

"Why do I feel like a specimen on a microscope slide?" he asked.

"Sorry, Doctor, may I call you Martin or would you prefer Dr Riley?"

"Martin will do. There are so many questions I want to ask."

"Start with whatever is uppermost in your mind."

"I've been worrying about reverberations affecting the future since I discovered Temporal Messaging. Surely you're concerned as well, your whole civilization could disappear like a burst soap bubble, if a shortsighted politician made a sufficiently radical alteration to your past."

"Very good, Martin, substitute the word 'scientist' for 'politician' and you're getting close to the purpose of our journey. I can see why they want a copy of you."

"A copy of me?" he was puzzled.

Farina changed the subject. "What sort of outlook would you like as we travel downstream?" she asked. "How about, 'Martian desert?'" The surface of the globe transformed, and they appeared to be travelling over the sands of the Red planet. "Or there's, 'Underwater exploration.' " The scene became clear water with many types of colorful marine life disporting around them. "Or, 'Centre of the Galaxy,' as a physicist, this one might appeal to you."

"Bollocks to your screen savers, what do you mean by 'a copy' of me?" He'd half risen from his seat but he felt the field increase and he sat back down.

"We're getting ahead of ourselves, Tolland will explain the details, but we need to make a copy of your brain state, and store it."

"That's a weird idea," he said, and thought about it for a few seconds. "Will it be conscious?"

"Only if we activate it."

"Can you communicate with these things, I mean, how detailed are they?"

"They're very detailed, if you want to put it that way, but it would be better if you wait and let Tolland explain more. I was only tasked to extract you. Your indoctrination will be a lengthy process; you must be patient."

"Who's this Tolland?"

"He is your Advocate, your representative with the Council. Like me, he has studied your language and culture, although unlike me he has no practical experience of your era, so he may sometimes appear gauche to you."

"So, how do you manipulate wormholes and send matter through them? We could only send information?"

"I cannot answer your questions about the technicalities, Martin. Please try to relax, we will arrive shortly."

Riley sat back; their vehicle appeared to be moving through the cosmos at a leisurely pace. He watched the swirls of gaseous nebulas, stars, galaxies and dust clouds which surrounded them.

"Okay," he said, breathing deeply and lowering his shoulders, as Estella had taught him to. "Have you contacted any extra-terrestrials yet?" he joked.

"We've made contact, yes, but they are light years away and communications take decades to exchange, so we won't be meeting up in a hurry."

"What have you said to each other?"

"Not much more than 'Hello,' we're not sure of their intentions, so we keep our cards close to our chests."

"How far into the future are we going?"

"To about two thousand years PC."

"PC?"

"Post Collision."

"Okay, so what collision?"

"Well, about two hundred years after your 'accident,' a large asteroid hit the Earth, it was big, not just a 'city killer.' Fortunately, it was a glancing blow. It pulverized several thousand square kilometers of North America, and continued on its journey into the deeps, with a cloud of debris trailing behind it. Some of the debris fell into orbit, Earth has rings now, just like Saturn. The impact triggered a series of volcanic events that nearly ended life on Earth. Ah, we've arrived."

Riley had more questions, but the star fields vanished, as did the insubstantial boundary of the sphere. They were in the center of a large cylindrical space. The circular ceiling was twenty meters above them, the walls were about fifty meters away. Farina stood up, took his hand and led him several paces. He was unsteady on his feet, it was like coming ashore after a long boat trip. Their seats melted into the floor and disappeared, like chocolate in a warm saucepan. He looked up, and saw what he assumed were ducts and cabling snaking across the ceiling and down the walls. They appeared more organic than industrial. There was a bluish actinic light, with no obvious source.

"The whole place looks as if it's been grown rather than built, so many curves, so few straight lines."

"Yes, Martin, parts of the Tower are organic."

"Are the surfaces bioluminescent?"

"Yes, gene splicing, Martin, it was used in your time on a small scale."

The floor was spongy under his feet and they were moving across it at walking pace. He looked down but could see no mechanism.

"Is this surface a liquid, or are we floating just above it?" he asked.

"It's what you might call a traction gel. I am controlling it with my implants." Farina tapped the side of her head. They moved across the hangar and stopped near the wall, Farina pointed and, looking up he saw a hole about five meters across in the ceiling. He could see similar holes in the floors above, their alignment shifting slightly at each level.

"Let me guess, no elevator?" he said.

"Antigravity, Martin, didn't you read Dan Dare or Jeff Hawke when you were a child?"

They lifted into the air, and moved upwards several levels. Looking downwards Riley panicked and grabbed hold of a branch of ducting. He was sweating, his legs began to feel hollow again. He couldn't let go. Suddenly he was calm and relaxed, he released his hold, leaned backwards and turned a slow somersault.

"You've switched the field on again, haven't you?" he recognized the slight feeling of disassociation again.

"This is a lot for you to cope with unaided, Martin."

"Yes, it's not easy being a Neanderthal among Cro-Magnons," he laughed.

They rose rapidly through several hundreds of meters and dozens of floors, following a curve around the inner wall of the cylinder.

"I'm taking you to your quarters; you can rest and freshen up before you meet Tolland."

They stepped out onto the next level and walked along a corridor. The floor was still spongy, cables and ducting "grew" over the walls and ceiling, he felt as if he was on a film set. Farina stopped in front of a door, it slid into the wall, she took him into what appeared to be an ordinary twenty-first century apartment, carpeted and equipped with standard appliances from his time.

"We arranged this specially for you, Martin," she said as she showed him around. "There is food in the refrigerator, the microwave oven works." She put a dish of food in it and shut the door. "Eat something, try to relax. I've set the bed to Deepsleep you for two hours, I advise you to use it. Please make yourself at home. If you need anything, call my name, I can be back here in a few moments." She left him.

Riley walked around the apartment and noted the sofa, the armchairs, the large flat screen TV. There were bookshelves with paperbacks, DVDs, vases of real flowers in the lounge. He went into the kitchen; the cupboards and worktops wouldn't have been out of place in the homes of any of his friends. There was an indefinable mismatching of colors, light fittings, and fabric patterns. He couldn't put his finger on it, but there was an element of foreignness in the design.

In the lounge he looked out of the window at the cityscape below, and wondered if it was real.

"Underwater exploration," he said loudly, and instantly the submarine view appeared. The apartment's entrance door was featureless and didn't respond to his voice. He wasn't surprised. The food was hot and savory, but he couldn't tell what it was, probably pasta. The Talisker whisky tasted authentic, he felt he deserved to be generous with himself. Eventually, he lay on the bed and fell asleep at once.

While he slept, Farina returned, she walked through to the bedroom and stood looking down at him. In her hand was a silvery flexible mesh which she carefully arranged over his head. She went back to the lounge, sat in an armchair and closed her eyes. After ten minutes, she stood up, went back to the bedroom, and removed the mesh. The entrance door opened at her approach, and she left the apartment.

Outside in the corridor, she sub-vocalized to an unseen observer.

"The copy is intact and verified, but dormant. I have transferred it to Tower Memory."

There was a pause.

"I agree, it only becomes illegal if we activate it. We can gain his permission at a later date, when he will be better able to make an informed decision. I have my orders; his mind is unique, we cannot risk losing it."

After two hours, Riley was woken by a quiet, genderless voice which he didn't recognize.

"Please wake up, Dr Riley, Farina requests entry."

"Come in," he called as he sat up rubbing his face, aware of the covering of stubble. He felt more relaxed than he had in months.

Farina came into the apartment. She was wearing clothing that continually morphed in style, color and pattern. One moment she appeared to be in flames, the next she was monk-like in black, briefly she was naked, the sequence never repeated. He found it disconcerting but very interesting, he was looking forward to seeing her naked again, perhaps that was the point. Was this how all the women of the future dressed. He hoped so.

"Love the frock," he said.

She ignored the comment, but the "frock" stabilized as a simple dark trouser suit.

"Time to meet Tolland," she said.

Chapter Twenty

Kenya the 4400s

Farina led Riley out of the apartment and they walked together along the corridor. They entered an impressively large room, with floor to ceiling curved windows making up one wall. She guided him over towards them and, looking out, he saw that they were hundreds of meters above the ground. The landscape was agricultural, with large irregular fields laid out below them. Riley couldn't guess at the scale. A man was standing gazing out of the windows, his hands clasped behind his back. He turned, smiling, and approached. He was tall and well built, with swept back red hair, wearing a conservative business suit; he appeared to be in his early fifties. He shook hands with Riley, who noticed that he wasn't very good at it, the shake up and down was too emphatic, and he didn't seem to know when to let go.

"Welcome, Doctor Martin Riley, my name is Tolland; I have waited a long time to meet you. You are our honored guest."

"Thank you for saving my life, Mr Tolland. I am indebted to you."

The three sat in armchairs around a low circular table.

"May I offer you refreshments? Whisky, tea, milk, biscuits, all are available. Perhaps you would prefer cake, or French fries."

"No thanks, I'm quite comfortable, and please call me, Martin."

"And you should call me Tolland, we have no titles here."

Riley sat back and looked around, "Well, Tolland, you have the advantage of me."

"I must tell you that this meeting is being watched by many interested parties, we have chosen this simple format to avoid intimidating you. I assume that you have questions you would like to ask?"

"Yes, rather a lot. First, where are we?"

"We are in Metrotower 3, sited in an area that was once called Kenya." A three-dimensional image of the Earth, complete with clouds and oceans, appeared in the air above the table. Riley could see that several towers projected from different parts of the equator, the one sited in Africa had a marker which pulsed red. There were other towers on other land masses. Above the towers, in near Earth orbit and still in the equatorial plane, a train of incomplete, white, ragged spherical constructions formed a broken necklace encircling the planet. They appeared to be a work in progress. Further out were a series of flat rings, like those around Saturn. Both the necklace and the rings of debris were rotating relative to the Earth.

"The model is not to scale. If it was, you wouldn't be able to see the Towers or the String units, the white spheres," said Tolland, "they'd be too small." He pointed to the hologram, "We are sweeping up ring fragments to use as raw material for the new String structure. Eventually it will encircle our blue planet, like a string of pearls around the neck of a beautiful woman." He smiled.

"What will you use it for, accommodation?" asked Riley peering closely at the display.

"We are expanding Tower Memory and moving it up to the String, where it will have almost infinite capacity. The 'Corporeals,' that is normal physical people will continue to inhabit the Towers, while the 'Incorporeals,' the brain state copies, will inhabit the String units, as digital entities."

" 'Digital entities,' you mean they're dead?" asked Riley.

"They are usually no longer active in the physical world, although there are exceptions, but we need not concern ourselves with the fine details," said Tolland. He pointed, "The three equatorial Towers incorporate space elevators, the other Towers were built in centers of population as the Fightback from the Collision progressed."

Riley watched as the model continued to rotate. The world, the String of white spheres and the rings were all rotating at different speeds, suddenly the hologram disappeared, he returned his attention to Tolland.

"I have so many questions, Tolland, I'm not sure where to start. It will take me a long time to catch up on the history and scientific advances you've made since my century, but my first question has to be, why am I here?"

Tolland smiled, "Does the phrase 'a fly in the ointment' mean anything to you, Martin? I believe the saying is cotemporaneous with your period." He continued without waiting for an answer. "We discovered you and your assistant Peter Abrahams by accident; you appear to be anomalies in the Timestream. The results of your actions, your, er, Temporal Adjustments, were initially detected by Farina. She found a section of history that did not match our expectations, although the religious beliefs of a particular tribal leader, on a small island, in the twenty-first century, would generally be of little interest to us."

Riley was puzzled by the reference but let it pass.

"Mankind should not discover how to manipulate Time until far into your future. Your achievements impress us, believe me, but your activities have pushed the Timestream away from its original path."

"Yes, I've worried about that since I first started the TM project."

"The Timestream has a certain temporal inertia," said Tolland. "Like a river, it isn't easy to change its course, but if an event does, then the results can be catastrophic for people downstream as it finds another route. Most of your alterations came to nothing because of the Collision. It has been our greatest protection from you, because it brought human history to a full stop and then it had to restart. Even so, we are well aware that we need to protect our history. As you said to Farina, even a small change to the past could cause our civilization to disappear, like a burst soap bubble. The reason you are here is to make sure that events proceed as we expect them to, as our history predicts. You could think of the Timestream as a guitar string being pulled to one side, as your Temporal Adjustments distort it. It will stretch so far, and then either break or spring back. In our

Timeline, it sprang back, we call this the 'Realignment.' It realigned when your team made a Retrospective Temporal Adjustment in 2051, to reverse your first significant intervention in 1997. It is most important that this happens, and we need you to make it so.

"Surely the fact that we're here proves that it has already happened?" said Riley.

"I wish it was that simple, Martin, your grasp of the theory does not include the loops, twists, spurs and discontinuities that we know are possible in the Timestream. We guard our past most carefully."

"Farina said that you wanted a copy of me."

"Your abduction was also motivated by curiosity on our part, Martin. We were amazed to find that you and Peter Abrahams had made such progress with the tools and techniques that were available to you. Almost as surprising as if the Ancient Greeks had somehow placed a man on the Moon. Your approach to the problem of time travel was different from ours, so you may have discovered things we have not, things we need to understand. When the Timestream corrects itself, that knowledge will disappear. In the new reality Abrahams will die in a motorcycle accident when he is nineteen. You will fail to gain government funding for your project, and so will not invent Temporal Messaging. If we are to save all your knowledge, we must extract a copy of Abrahams before the moment of correction. We need to send you back to do this."

"Why not just abduct him, as you have me?"

"We could abduct you without causing temporal ripples because you were about to die, Martin. We cannot abduct Dr Abrahams because that would be a Retroactive Temporal Adjustment for us, and, as you well know, the effect on our present would be completely unpredictable. We could make a copy of Doctor Abrahams now, but we wish to make the copy as close to his disappearance as possible. Just before the Realignment of the Timestream, and your inevitable disappearances in fact."

Riley didn't like the sound of this but decided to stick to the main issue.

"If we let the Timestream correct itself, then all the terrible events we have prevented through our Temporal Adjustments will happen. The destruction of the Twin Towers in New York, for instance, and the meltdown of the Sizewell B nuclear reactor. I couldn't be involved in allowing such atrocities. I quit Langley because of the Government's callous attitude to human life, and now I find the same attitude here."

"There is no hurry, Doctor, we will give you time to understand the issues. We prefer that you help us from a sense of conviction. Farina will be your guide while you are here."

Riley looked at Farina, she returned his stare, without expression.

"Tell me more about the copies."

"We have copies of the brain states of various people who might one day be useful to us. They inhabit Tower Memory. Most of them are scientists and intellectuals but we also have politicians and artists."

"What do they do in there? Are they frozen?"

"No, no, not frozen, they are software entities who live in virtual worlds of their own invention. Many of them interact; I believe Sir Isaac Newton is an accomplished player of a game of tokens called 'Bridge.' His partnership with Professor Hawking has so far proved unbeatable. Apparently, Professor Einstein and Alan Turing are catching up. An ancient game called 'Go' is popular with the Incorporeals. Some are also active in the Corporeal world, involving themselves as committee members within government, or pursuing academic specializations. The Mathematicians are particularly prolific." He chuckled, "there is a rumor that we have a dormant copy of Genghis Khan for emergency use if we are ever invaded, but I'm not sure of the truth of this."

Riley stood, and walked over to the curved window, there was no glass, but he felt increasing resistance when he tried to push his hand through it. He stared out over a land that was once called Kenya, now farmed, presumably by automatic machinery. He was completely eclipsed by these people and their civilization. If he returned to 2051, as they suggested he would, it would be forty years after his extraction. Estella would be nearly ninety, if she was still alive. Hank and Cliff would both be over fifty. The whole situation was mind boggling. Early morning or not, he decided to have the whiskey that Tolland had offered him. He returned to the table, from where the other two were silently observing him, and sat down.

Chapter Twenty-One

Kenya the 2300s

Seated in the time capsule again, Riley and Farina floated over a frozen, broken landscape. At Riley's request, they had travelled back to see the Earth a hundred years after the Collision. Farina had made the upper half of the sphere transparent and the lower half partly so. He had felt uncomfortable floating hundreds of meters above the ground, sitting in an armchair with no visible vehicle around him. They were invisible to the world they were over flying.

"I can't believe it," he said. "The clouds, the ice, the snow, it's like Antarctica, there's no life, no plants, no animals, just rocks and snow."

"We will soon reach the equatorial strip where life clings on," said Farina.

The landscape began to show patches of green, through the white, Riley spotted herds of reindeer, and what looked like fur clad nomads herding them.

"Animal skin tepees, has mankind been reduced to this?"

"Life on Earth was almost extinguished, Martin, there were various off-world colonies: Armstrong on the Moon, Olympus Mons on Mars, and Arks on their way to the nearer stars, they all offered help. The Arks turned back, and eventually went into Earth orbit. Humanity re-established itself in the equatorial regions where the temperatures were highest, and then began the Fightback as the ice receded."

"What caused the ice age, after the asteroid hit the Earth?"

They were floating over pine forests now. Smoke rose from occasional cabins built in clearings. Riley could just hear dogs barking as they passed over.

"The Collision killed millions instantly in North America, and it was energetic enough to disturb the subduction zone on the western coast of the United States. A string of volcanoes along there suddenly came to life, but it was the ash from the super volcanos at Yellowstone and Long Valley that did the most harm. Dust clouds covered the globe, blocking out the sun for decades. Temperatures dropped, crops failed year after year. The ice advanced from both poles. In fact, we're still rebuilding and reintroducing species now, two thousand years later. Billions of people died, mainly of starvation, but there were plagues, and roaming gangs. It's best not to dwell on the suffering. The first five years after the Collision were the worst that humanity has ever experienced. Look down there, Martin, that is the beginning of the Fightback, the new city of Kisumu, you can see the small spaceport."

He watched a squat, box-like vehicle, landing almost silently, on four jets of blue flame.

"Probably one of the Ark shuttles bringing medical supplies," she said. "This was where the British Government made half-hearted, and then eventually panic-stricken preparations for the Collision. But that's another story. This would be a good time to return to the Tower."

"I'd like to see the rings," said Riley. "They're edge on from the equator, so they'll be almost invisible from the Tower."

"I can take you further north if you like."

The walls of the sphere misted over and then cleared a few moments later.

Riley gasped; Earth's rings arched over the darkening sky from east to west. They were brightly lit with striations separating them into different colored bands.

"My God, they're huge, they're wonderful."

"They are at their best in the evening, illuminated by the Sun when it has moved below the horizon," said Farina, who was also looking upwards. "I have chosen a latitude that displays them at their most impressive. Their aspect changes with the season."

"Beautiful," said Riley. "I wish I had a telescope."

"There is not much to see. They are rock fragments varying in size from dust to boulders. They often collide; large pieces sometimes fall to Earth near the equator. We have to keep a constant watch for them."

Riley gazed at the face of the full Moon. "La Bella Luna, she doesn't change."

"We should return to the Tower now. We can view the rings again, on another occasion." The sphere misted over and cleared, they were back in the arrivals area. They stepped out of the capsule, the seats melted away again. Like an old hand, he allowed the floor to take him across to the elevation shaft.

"Let me try this without the suppression field," he said, and managed his fear of the vertical journey by not looking down. "Would you like to eat with me?" he asked when they reached the door of his apartment. "I do a pretty good ragu sauce."

"Thank you, Martin, I would enjoy that."

Riley prepared the meal, the food in the fridge and freezer was vegetarian, although the protein came in various flavors and textures, some looked like meat. They sat down at the table and he opened a bottle of red wine.

"Thank God you guys still approve of alcohol," he said as they clinked glasses. Suddenly he was overcome by a powerful pang of sadness; the meal reminded him of Estella and the boys. His throat constricted, he couldn't speak and his eyes filled. Farina stared for a moment then stood, took his hand and led him to a couch. They sat for a few moments, still holding hands. She leaned forward and kissed him. The kiss felt natural to him, they lingered and she began to help him out of his clothes. Farina released her body stocking at the shoulder and it fell away in one piece.

"Have you switched the field on, Farina?" he asked as his heart rate fell and his breathing slowed.

"Yes, Martin, but only lightly, I hate to see you suffering."

"Switch it off, I don't need it."

She lay with her hands behind her head, one leg bent at the knee, he lay next to her.

"How do you wish me to respond to your lovemaking?" she asked.

"That's a rather clinical question. Lovemaking is supposed to be spontaneous." He was puzzled.

"I believe you have not yet realized, Martin, I am a Synthetic Person."

Riley rolled over and stared at her for a moment.

"A Synthetic, you're an android?" He ran his fingers over her skin, pushed gently into her ribs and breasts and stomach. She felt warm, soft, normal. He sat up, "You're a robot? I was going to screw a robot?"

"Not a robot, Martin, I am a Synthetic Person. I have normal human ratings for emotional and cognitive awareness. I have legal rights and responsibilities. I have citizenship."

"I was just about to screw a robot," he said more loudly. He sat shaking his head, laughing despite his perplexity. "After everything that's happened in the last forty-eight hours this takes the biscuit."

"I am not a robot, Martin, I am both sentient and organic." Her voice had risen and Riley noticed a slight flush in her cheeks.

"That's very good," he said, leaning forward and brushing his finger over her blushing cheek. "Very convincing, very convincing in all respects. Tell me, do you enjoy lovemaking or are you programmed to pretend?"

She sat up. "I have pleasure centers much like your own. I am a person, not a prehistoric sex toy, with limited responses and a few pre-recorded erotic phrases."

Riley looked at her smooth nakedness and had to admit that, synthetic or not, he found her appealing, and things had not been going well between Estella and himself. It had been a long time since he'd had the comfort of human contact.

Farina laid her hand on his thigh. "Come, Martin," she whispered, "I have switched off the field." She lay down again and tilted her head back on the pillow. Staring up at him she ran the tip of her tongue around her lips.

God, he thought, the male sexual reflex is so easy to manipulate. He lay next to her; his excitement grew as she reached across to stroke him gently. He would never know whether she was telling the truth about her enjoyment, but so what? In that respect Synth sex wouldn't be very different from human sex.

"How would you like me?" she whispered as she gripped his shoulder with her other hand to pull him down. She dug her nails lightly into his skin.

"Pleasant enthusiasm will do for starters," he said. "We'll see how it goes from there."

Afterwards they lay side by side.

"How was it for you?" he asked, laughing quietly.

"Very pleasant, thank you, Martin. You reached a satisfactory orgasm? I assume that you found our love making gratifying."

"No, I was faking it." Farina's brow furrowed. "Sorry, just joking."

"I can arrange for various enhancements if you wish." A rotating ring of embarrassingly explicit holographic images appeared in the air above them.

"Let's talk about that another time, I'm tired now. Will you be staying the night?"

"If that is your wish, Martin."

"Yes," he said getting up, "that is my wish. Show me how to set the 'Deepsleep' thing on the bed. Then you can tell me the plan for tomorrow."

Chapter Twenty-Two

Kenya the 4400s

"Seven o'clock, time to get up, I hope you had a restful sleep, Dr Riley," the bed's gender-neutral voice murmured in his ear. He half expected to see Farina leaning over him as he opened his eyes, there was a shared quality to their voices, but he could hear her rattling crockery in the kitchen. She came into the bedroom with a cup and saucer, sat on the bed, and handed it to him. He smelled the coffee and took a sip. It was weak and thin but at least it was hot. He sipped it.

"I hope it is to your taste, Martin."

Jesus, he thought, am I really honeymooning with a piece of software?

"To be honest, it's bloody awful, Farina, how much coffee did you use?"

"Five grams per cup."

"Well, use ten next time, the temperature is right though."

"The temperature was eighty-three degrees Centigrade as I handed it to you, Martin. I will remember."

"What are we doing today?" He hadn't been listening the night before, the bed had taken him, as he lay with Farina spooning into his back, her arms around him.

"We are to meet with Tolland again. He wishes to discuss your indoctrination plan."

"Okay, tell me, do you need to sleep, have downtime, or whatever you call it? Or were you lying beside me all night, staring at the ceiling?"

"I need little 'downtime' as you call it, but I used your 'sleep time' usefully."

"Doing what?"

"I connected to Tower Memory and communicated with some of my friends, Incorporeals and Synthetics, based in other Metrotowers. Then I performed a routine backup, and after that I reviewed and deleted some redundant files."

Well, that's told me, he thought.

"I hope my snoring didn't disturb you."

"You did not snore much, Martin, but you had a lot of rapid eye movement, you were dreaming for about forty percent of your sleep time. This is an unusually high figure, but not surprising given your recent experiences. I expect you were deleting redundant files of your own."

He wondered what she meant by that.

An hour later they had retraced their steps to Tolland's office.

"You seem in good spirits, Martin. I believe Farina has shown you the effects of the Collision, and I hope your sexual interlude was enjoyable."

"Actually, Tolland, in my culture we don't discuss our sex lives much. We consider it to be a private matter between the individuals involved."

Tolland seemed surprised, "Oh, I had the impression that your society was obsessed with the subject. I will not mention it again." Riley realized that his every move was being scrutinized. He'd talk to Farina about it, he wanted some guaranteed privacy.

"I've thought about our discussion yesterday," he said, "and I see a flaw in your explanation."

"And that is?"

"If you have copies of these various scientists and politicians in Tower Memory, then you could have taken copies of Peter Abrahams and myself any time you wanted, while we were asleep or even drugged. Your explanation doesn't make sense. You don't need me here, that is to say my Corporeal self, you must have other reasons."

"Yes, you are right, Martin, I was trying not to overload you with information, your indoctrination is just beginning. Like your government in the 21st Century, we never make retrospective Temporal Adjustments. It is too dangerous; the results would be unpredictable. The Collision would probably protect us if we did make a TA back in your time, but the Council has no appetite to risk our reality. We prefer not to even enter your era, we only observe it.

In your year 2051, you help to make the adjustment which realigns the Timestream, and we do not wish to interfere with that. We also know that you make various appearances in the Timestream, after your accident in 2020. It is our intention to facilitate the inevitable. To help you achieve the Realignment. To smooth the path."

"What about the Tsunami in 2004, and the 2010 Earthquake? I'll only cooperate if we give warnings. We could save hundreds of thousands of lives."

"But no warnings were given, Martin, our hands are tied. It would change our past if we intervened, and frankly those events pale into insignificance when you consider the billions that died soon after the Collision. We have to 'follow the script,' Martin. We cannot go back through history making alteration after alteration; you of all people must see that."

Riley sighed, Tolland's logic was indisputable.

"Yes, I understand, but those catastrophes were so personal to me. I feel responsible for not giving warnings and guilty about the loss of life."

"Martin, what you do over the next few months will be in the long-term interests of the whole human race."

Riley and Farina returned to the time capsule.

"This will be your first reappearance," said Farina, smiling, as the walls clouded and a few moments later cleared again.

Riley looked out through the membrane at a suburban garden, it was evening; he could hear voices on the other side of a hedge. One was protesting loudly; the other was placatory; he couldn't make out the words. Suddenly there was a cry, and the sound of a scuffle, followed by several car doors slamming. Riley stepped through the membrane, and into the front garden of the house he'd shared with Estella, before they were married, before Cliff and Hank were born. The air was cool, with a damp organic smell; he heard traffic noise from a main road some distance away. Orange sodium street lights lit the scene. He walked across the lawn to the front gate, and stepped out into the street. The red tail lights of a black Range Rover were receding from him; he couldn't make out any of the occupants. A bicycle leaned against the hedge. He remembered buying it at the cycle shop on Great Northern Road twenty years before; it was an expensive racing model. He stroked the handlebar, resisting the urge to ring the bell, wheeled it through the gate and down the side of the house. He leaned it against the shed in the back garden. There were no lights visible, Estella wasn't home yet, so there was no point peering through the windows, hoping to catch a glimpse of her. After a final look around, he stepped back through the membrane, ignoring the discomfort of the decontamination field, and sat in the empty chair.

"Why did you move the bicycle, Martin?" asked Farina gently.

"Because someone might have stolen it. Do you think I've caused a ripple in the Timestream? I wasn't thinking, it just seemed the right thing to do."

"It was the right thing to do, Martin. Where did you find it when you got back from the safe house?"

He thought for a moment. "I remember thinking it might have been stolen and being relieved when I found it leaning against the shed."

"You're right, it was leaning against the shed, and you were supposed to move it. The question is, did you have any choice?"

"Of course, I had a choice. Nobody made me move the bike."

"No, nobody made you, you just did it, you followed the script, and that is what we want."

"The script?"

"Like most humans of your time, you think your conscious self is making your decisions, but you are mistaken. Most of your actions are automatic and unconscious. When you play a physical game, such as tennis, there is no time to consider all the variables involved. The approaching ball's velocity and spin, the angle of the racket in your hand, the path of your swing, the strength of the impact, are all dealt with too quickly for conscious analysis. But when you get a slow shot, and have time to think and plan it, you are more likely to make a mistake. Most of the time it is your unconscious that is playing the game, while your conscious self is observing.

The unconscious part of your brain is an operating system that runs your infrastructure, while your consciousness rides on top, thinking it's in charge. Like a child with a toy steering wheel, sitting next to its parent, thinking it is driving the car. Determinism is very similar, you think you're in control but free will is just an illusion."

"So, I'm not the 'Master of my fate, the Captain of my soul,' I'm an automaton, clock-working my way through life, with no choice or responsibility for my actions?"

"Some cultures call it predestination, some call it destiny, others call it the will of God, you can call it what you like."

Riley shrugged, "Thanks for that, you've just inverted my whole perspective on life. Where are we going next? I feel like the ghost of Christmas past."

Farina paused, and then said, "Charles Dickens, A Christmas Carol, published 1843."

"How did you do that?" he asked.

"Implants, Martin, I am in constant touch with Tower Memory. All Corporeals have them, both humans and Synthetics."

"Is that how you control the capsule?" he asked.

"Yes, Martin. Shall we return to your quarters?"

"Your turn to cook."

"I am accessing 21st Century recipe files as we speak."

Later, they lay in each other's arms. Riley was convinced that she enjoyed their couplings, but now he was back in worry mode, nibbling at his finger nails.

"Something's been puzzling me," he was leaning up on one elbow.

"Really, Martin? Tell me, I will explain anything I am able to."

"Well, Tolland mentioned 'the religion of a particular tribal chief on a small island in the 21st Century,' what did he mean by that?"

"The tribal chief was a prospective King of England, Prince George, the son of William V. He secretly converted to Islam, and married an Arabian princess, a princess of the House of Saud. It was a love match, although there was a certain amount of encouragement and manipulation by the boy's grandparents, Diana and Dodi Fayed. There was public turmoil in England as Prince George's coronation approached. The divisions were both religious and racial, both potent stimuli at the time. As the political unrest gathered momentum, the situation was resolved by the realignment of the Timestream. It became irrelevant, you need not concern yourself with it."

"An interesting story though."

"Yes, but hardly original. You need to rest, shall I set the Deepsleep?"

"I'll tell you when I need to rest, Farina. You're not my mother, try to stick to one role at a time. I want to avoid the Deepsleep and for you to stop using the suppression field, I don't like being taken over, and all this talk of determinism makes it even worse."

Chapter Twenty-Three

Kenya 2331

The capsule had clouded and cleared again. Through the membrane Riley could see a dystopian scene, winter near Kisumu Spaceport. There were people dressed in smart military uniforms, while others wore coarse, homespun fabric and animal skins. Everybody carried a firearm. The military hand guns were sleek and modern, while the civilians carried heavy muzzle loaders that looked homemade. Vehicles showed a similar polarization: dog sleds and snow mobiles, hover cars and horse drawn wagons. In the distance, a shuttle was taking off on a pillar of blue light, the engines almost silent. Riley didn't recognize the technology. A horse and buggy rattled past.

"Are we visible?" he asked.

"No, Martin, you will become visible as you step through the membrane. I will position us behind a building so that you can leave the capsule unobserved."

He pushed a hand through his hair. "What are we doing here?" he asked.

"Tolland wants you to witness the fragility of the Fightback, Martin. You need to see how easily it could fail, and the human race be starved into extinction. It would be a Chronoclasm for the Commonwealth, our civilization would disappear, like a burst soap bubble, as you have said."

"So many choices, so many turnings," said Riley.

"Not really, Martin, not if you believe in determinism and that our path is laid out before us."

"Bugger me, this is a bucket of spiders," he said. "What do you want me to do?"

"This is the lowest point in the Fightback, the time of smallest human population. Tolland wants you to experience it at first hand, to see it, smell it, touch it. He wants you to immerse yourself in it for a few hours, keeping a low profile, and then come back to the capsule. I'll be drifting above you, just in case of problems."

Riley stepped through the membrane and walked around the building and onto the icy street. Farina had provided him with a fur coat, homespun clothing and boots. He carried the requisite blunderbuss and had a pack of furs on his back. He walked towards the trading post that Farina had pointed out. The town was a mix of single-story log buildings and larger ones made from sawn weatherboard. There was little use of brick or stone. He smelled wood-smoke, sewage and rotting meat. Scrawny cats and dogs eyed each other over piles of stinking refuse. It wasn't easy to love humanity when it smelt like this, he thought.

The furs were not for sale, they were part of his cover. Farina had told him she'd bought the clothes and other props from a native, and had been evasive about the medium of exchange. He wondered if it had involved a sexual favor.

He noted wooden signs hanging outside the buildings as he walked past. There was a leather worker, a wood yard, an undertaker, a chandler, a general store. Feeling reasonably confident of his disguise, he entered a tavern, its sign showed a Bear and Penguin and it advertised itself as a 'Freehouse.' The bartender looked up and smiled as he pushed open the door and walked across the bare wooded boards to the bar.

"What's your pleasure sir?" he asked as he dried his hands on a dirty grey rag.

Riley looked at the price list chalked on a board behind him. "A Boilermaker please."

The barman nodded, reached down a tankard, and pulling on the turned wooden handle of a beer engine, filled it with a cloudy brew of flat looking beer. He placed it on the bar, sat a shot glass next to it and filled that from a bottle of clear spirit.

"Both made on the premises sir, using only the finest Kenyan beet sugar and malted barley."

Riley sipped the beer, it was passable. He tried the spirit, it had almost no flavor, just a sense of burning as he swallowed. He hoped the burning in his throat wasn't mirrored in his brain cells.

"Four times through the still sir," said the barman smiling. "The boss is proud of his 'flash'. Can I pour you another?"

"Yes, yes please," said Riley feeling that things were going well, he took another swig of beer and downed the spirit. The barman looked expectant, Riley realized that he had no idea how he would pay. The furs he thought, surely, they'll accept one or two skins in exchange for a couple of drinks. He broached the matter with the barman.

"You mean you ain't got no Ark tokens?" The barman's friendliness had disappeared. He looked Riley up and down, then leaned back through an open doorway behind him and called, "Hey boss, another penniless trapper who can't pay for his drinks."

A few moments later a figure emerged, bearded, unkempt, hostile and, Riley thought, probably drunk on his own merchandise. He stared through red-rimmed eyes as the barman muttered something in his ear and jerked his head in Riley's direction.

The landlord lifted the bar hatch and strode up to Riley who was hurriedly extracting one of the furs from his pack. He snatched the fur and examined it closely, he sniffed it, pulled a tuft of hair from the skin and rubbed it between his finger and thumb. He thrust his face close to Riley's.

"Old," he said, "old and musty and stiff and worthless, like you," his voice rose to a shout, as his spittle flecked Riley's face. His eyes bulged, his breath stank. "You miserable sniveling bastard, you come in here, smelling like a whore's parlor, drinking my flash and wanting to pay me with a few skanky beaver skins. Well, you can piss off, you scrounging freeloader."

He drew his fist back, and punched Riley full in the face, knocking him backwards onto the floor. He followed up by trying to kick and stamp on any part of Riley he could get to. He stepped back and took a flying kick at Riley's head but missed and fell over. Riley dragged himself under a table and struggled to release the canister of pepper spray that Farina had given him. An arm reached in and the landlord grabbed his shoulder and pulled him out. Riley sprayed his assailant's face liberally, he gave an ear-splitting scream as the aerosol took effect then sank to his knees, covering his face with his hands.

"Where the fuck have you been? I recognize you now," he wailed. "Five years, five years you bastards. Five years I've been stuck here in this stinking pit."

Riley scrambled to his feet on the other side of the table as the barman approached holding an ancient battered cricket bat. He crashed through the door and into the street, turned and ran back the way he'd come. Rounding the building, he saw the faint ripple of the capsule's membrane and dived through it. He looked back and glimpsed the barman standing holding his weapon and peering around as the membrane shrank to a point and disappeared.

"Can we go home now?" he said as he lay on the floor coughing and bleeding. "I've had enough fun for one day."

They arrived back at the Tower and Farina helped him to his quarters.

"Well, thanks for that," he said as he stood naked in his bathroom. He had showered and Farina was kneeling, treating his bruises with a combination of sprays, quiet sympathy and a mysterious device that tingled as she moved it over his bruises. "The furs were worthless, the clothes stank, the gun was rusty and jammed, I hope you didn't give too much for them," he said nastily. Farina didn't answer as she glanced at the heap of clothing in the corner. "I'd burn them if I was you. And what was that 'five years' he was shouting? I'm sure I recognized him from somewhere. There was something familiar about his face behind that beard."

"I'm sorry, Martin, I cannot tell you that, Tolland has not given his permission. I expect he will make it clear, eventually. The Council wished to show you that the survival of the small group of humans in the equatorial zone after the Collision is critical to the continuity of the race. Their hold on life was tenuous, fragile, it was difficult to grow enough food, and if there had been even a slight change in the weather pattern, the crops might fail and starvation could have wiped them out. The planet would warm up over the millennia, plants and animals would repopulate territory north and south, but there would be no humans, no cities, no Metrotowers. The Arks in Earth space could not wait for the temperature to rise, they would have left, to try their luck on distant, more hospitable worlds."

"Yes, and Synthetics would never be developed either," he said. "This is just as much your problem as it is ours."

She sighed, sat back on her heels and looked up at him. "I have finished, there is no lasting physical damage."

"Oh, so you're a fucking doctor now are you?" he asked angrily. He felt no urge to let her off the hook, the whole incident had been her fault, she'd dropped him into the situation ill prepared.

"I have extensive files on human anatomy, Martin, and Tower Memory agrees with my diagnosis."

"You can tell Tower Memory to go and fuck itself," he shouted. He grabbed her collar with his left hand and drew his right hand back, ready to punch her in the face.

"Please do not damage me, Martin," she stammered, leaning back and holding her hands in front of her face.

"I'm sorry that our expedition went wrong, I'm sorry if I have made you angry."

He felt himself relaxing and realized that she had switched on the neuro-suppression field again. He let go of her and sat on the edge of the bath with his head in his hands.

"It's okay, Farina, you can switch it off now."

She stood, and began to put away her medical kit, not meeting his eye. "I could not stop you without using the field, Martin, Synthetics are not equipped to fight humans. If a human attacks us we can run away or try to block blows, but we are not aggressive, it is intrinsic to our design. You were between me and the door, I could not escape." She left him, and after a few moments, he stepped back under the shower and stayed there for a long time. In the bedroom, as he dressed in clean clothes, he could feel that his injuries were already less painful. He limped into the living room, apparently Farina had gone.

Riley was ashamed of his behavior. He felt wretched, homesick and lonely. He sat staring into space for some minutes. Activity was the only available remedy he decided, so he retrieved his journal from his briefcase and, after he'd written a summary of recent events, he wrote a list of questions and subjects he wanted to discuss with Farina in the morning.

The prepacked meal he reheated tasted okay but he couldn't eat it. In the lounge, he poured himself a large whiskey and chose a book from the shelf next to the television. It was a Cold War spy novel by an author he'd never heard of, he replaced it after a few minutes, finished his whiskey and went to bed. He set the Deepsleep, he didn't want to become dependent on it, but it was better than lying awake worrying. Did Farina feel, fear or embarrassment, she'd said she had normal human emotional responses but.....He slept.

Next morning, the bed woke him as before, the door announced Farina's arrival while he was eating his breakfast. She came into the kitchen, he couldn't bring himself to apologies, not yet.

"I've been thinking about the 'Bear and Penguin,' " he said, hoping to lighten the atmosphere.

Farina looked at him but said nothing. She seemed apprehensive, but it was difficult to tell.

"Polar bears live at the North Pole, and penguins live at the South Pole. Penguins should never be in the company of polar bears."

Farina smiled, she seemed relieved, had he missed something?

"Well, Martin, after the Collision, the Northern and Southern ice fields advanced so far towards the Equator that for a short time they touched in places. At the time you visited Kisumu, both species had crossed over, extending both the range of the penguins and the diet of the polar bears, who apparently find penguins very appetizing."

Riley changed the subject. "So, what happened to the TM unit at Langley after my accident?" he asked as he took a sip of orange juice.

"Peter Abrahams took over as lead scientist. He was the obvious choice, the only one who fully understood the science, and his colleagues respected him for that."

"How did he get on with the Colonel?"

"They got on well, Colonel Wilson was avuncular towards Dr Abrahams, there was little rivalry between them, probably because of their age difference. Eventually Wilson developed medical problems and wanted to retire."

"And his relationship with Estella?"

"They stayed married, until the Colonel died."

"Died, how?"

"He was flying across the Atlantic for a meeting with MI6 in London when his aircraft disappeared from the radar screens."

"Sabotage?"

"Yes, Martin, apparently he knew far too much to be allowed to retire. His political masters must have decided it was the expedient thing to do."

"Don't tell me, they hid the press reports, so he didn't get two weeks advanced warning, just like me." Riley chuckled. "How ironic, his 'Policy Four' certainly worked that time. I wonder how Estella took it. What year was this?"

"2021, eleven years after your 'accident.' She lived for another nineteen years but didn't remarry."

"God, that's a strange thing to hear. I wonder what happened to the boys, what did they do for a living, what did they look like, did they have kids?"

"We can arrange for you to have sight of them until 2051, or we can provide a report, but are you sure you want to do this to yourself? Perhaps you should concentrate on the program we have arranged for you."

"I don't know what I want; this is too difficult to take in all at once. Let's stick to the program for now. What's next? Whose turn is it to give me a good kicking?"

"No more kicking, Martin. Let's go to the Capsule and I'll explain on the way?"

They walked along the corridor and stepped into the elevation shaft. Riley would never be comfortable with the experience of floating down the many stories to the 'underground car park,' as he thought of it, but he felt less panicked. If Farina had switched the field on, he couldn't feel it. The chairs coalesced upwards from the floor and they sat down. The sphere of mist formed and cleared. Riley saw that they were drifting, invisible, over Trafalgar Square in London.

"It is 2050, Martin. What do you notice?"

Riley looked at the throngs of tourists as they walked across the Square. Children and teenagers climbed on the bronze lions at the foot of Nelson's Column, and dodgy looking vendors stood behind hover stalls selling highly colored food and drink.

"No pigeons," he said.

"They eliminated the rock doves for public health reasons, but what about the clothes?"

"Well there appear to be a lot of Muslim tourists, judging by the hijabs and prayer hats. What of it? Perhaps they've taken over from the Americans and Japanese."

The scene greyed out to be replaced by a different view.

"The market place at Bungay, a small town in Suffolk," said Farina. "No tourists here, and notice the ethnicities of the people wearing the hijabs."

Riley peered through the membrane. "Well, most of them appear to be European."

"Today is Sunday, look over at the church."

Riley could see people entering the church. Most of the women wore hijabs and long colorful dresses, the younger men wore prayer hats. "Okay, so what are you trying to tell me?" he asked. "That the Muslims bought the church in Bungay and are using it as a Mosque?"

"No, Martin, this is a Sunday, not a Friday, they are all Christians, but Islamic dress has become popular. This was one of the signs that led me to discover your activities. The original Collision survivors in Kenya, the ones funded by the British Government, left good records, we know that they wore European clothes. When I travelled back upstream and found a period where British people wore Islamic fashions it puzzled me. I travelled further back, and discovered that the accident that killed Princess Diana and Dodi Fayed had never happened. It was Princess Diana who had started the fashion, after she married Dodi Fayed and converted to Islam. I realized that this was a branching of the Timestream, or some sort of distortion. Our knowledge of pre-Collision history was rather sketchy, many records having been lost, but I found that in this continuum the Twin Towers had not been destroyed. I investigated further, and found other discrepancies. My researches upstream revealed you and your Temporal Messaging technology, and downstream from there I discovered Peter Abrahams and his improvements. Then, in 2051, you and he cause the realignment of the Timestream. The Council see this as a very significant event, and have tasked Tolland and myself to help you accomplish it."

"So, just to be clear, saving Princess Diana in 1997 put a kink in the Timestream, and to straighten it out, we have to go back and allow her to die? And that's what you mean by the Realignment?"

"Yes, Martin, like quantum mechanics, Time can seem counter-intuitive. The best way I can explain it is to say that the view back into the past from before 2051, looked different from the view back after 2051.

Anyway, now we want you to observe Mary Lee, she is a drone pilot, with an important involvement in the Realignment."

Part Two

Mary Lee – The Drone Pilot

CHRONOSCAPE

Chapter Twenty-Four

UK the 2040s

Mary Lee walked across the parade ground at RAF Waddington. Although she moved purposefully and wore her smart Air Force blues, she had a hangover from her weekend activities in the officers' mess. Being young and single, indulging in the three D's – Drinking, Dancing and Dating – was pretty much mandatory. She noted the activities around her. Vehicles carried personnel and supplies from one part of the station to another. There was a shrieking from the engine test bays and the smell of jet fuel. Looking up, she watched a pair of fighters execute an impossibly sharp and noisy turn. There could be no humans on board, they'd be unconscious from the g-force. Artificial intelligences have taken over all the best jobs. She sighed and tried to put the thought out of her head as she entered the operations building to start her shift. In the changing rooms her ear lobe tingled, her software sprite spoke quietly in her ear.

"*The boss wants you in his office, ma'am.*" Its familiarity level was set to 'respectful'; there was no point in being friendly with software that wasn't even self-aware.

"Okay, tell him I'm on my way," she sub-vocalized. After buttoning her jacket, she ran a hand through her bobbed black hair and walked back to the admin area. The Group Captain's door was ajar, he was standing talking to a civilian, she knocked and waited in the doorway. Her boss beckoned her in.

"This is Flying Officer Lee, Dr Abrahams," he said. "Dr Abrahams is over from Langley, Mary." She shook hands with the newcomer. He was the same height as her, short for a man, about sixty, and lightly built. Mary thought he looked like a jockey. "Dr Abrahams is a scientist with a 'special interest.' I'd like you to show him the drone control room, answer any of his questions and bring him back in an hour, we have to attend a meeting later."

Mary knew better than to ask about Abraham's 'special interest,' he was obviously a spook if he worked at Langley. His English accent suggested he wasn't CIA, perhaps he was SIS, the UK's Secret Intelligence Service.

"I understand you're a drone pilot," said Abrahams, making conversation as they walked along the corridor. They entered the control room with its dozen black upholstered couches and racks of related equipment. "What type of drones do you fly?"

"Small ones," she said, and took him over to a mahogany display case. It contained an array of dead, but carefully mounted flies, of various types and sizes, from the humble house fly, to a large horse fly. They were labelled with both their Latin and their common names. "If you look closely, you can see that their thoraxes are enlarged." Abrahams looked blankly at the display, Mary pointed to the squadron emblem on the wall. It depicted a member of the same genus 'diptera,' with the motto 'Non muscae super me.' "No flies on me," she joked.

"Oh, those are the drones. Well, I'm impressed by the miniaturization." He peered at the specimens with more interest. "Are they real insects or fabrications?" he asked.

"They're modified insects. No point in re-inventing the wheel when the natural version is so efficient." Thinking she might have sounded sarcastic, she continued in a more careful tone. "They insert a small pack of quantum electronics at the pupal stage, while the maggot's anatomy has melted into an organic soup. As the adult insect forms, the pack makes millions of connections into its central nervous system, and 'bish bash bosh,' you have your drone. It's more complicated than that, but I only have to know enough to fly the little buggers. They don't need any maintenance, they die after a few weeks, and we get issued with replacements as necessary. The wranglers look after them, feed them, transport them around. They have insectaries all over the country. The electronics are easy to produce so the drones are cheap to manufacture." Mary picked up a virtual reality visor and put it on. She turned its mirrored surface towards him, hoping to surprise him with the distorted reflection of his own face.

"What does it feel like when you're flying them?"

She sat on the couch. "As pilots, we have total sensory integration and control. When I lie back like this, put on my visor and place my hands in these sensor depressions, I am the fly." The visor muffled her voice.

"But how can you handle six legs and two wings?"

"The software handles many of the functions, we point our host in the direction we want to go and the computer does the rest. It's not that different from riding a horse. Probably more like being a centaur because you're so well integrated with your host's nervous system."

Abrahams was about to ask something else when the next shift arrived, wearing their black sensuits. The pilots began to get into position on the couches, their orderlies checking their straps and connections before fitting visors over their faces.

"While we inhabit our hosts, we're not exactly high dependency patients, but we need to be monitored. That's why we have orderlies. The restraints are necessary too, you wouldn't want to act out the movements of your host while you're piloting. It can happen if the feedback filters are tuned out of resonance, like sleep walking." She vacated the couch as its scheduled occupant arrived, smiling, followed by her orderly, a corporal burdened with her visor and other equipment. They left the control room and walked down the corridor to the canteen. Abrahams ordered coffee as they sat at a table. Mary drank hers gratefully, her headache diminished, either from the caffeine or the hydration, she didn't care which.

"How secret is the fly drone program? I wasn't aware of it, I expected something bigger and more mechanical."

"Very secret," she said. "We get all sorts of requests from SIS and MI5. Sometimes we leave flies in odd corners and on lampshades, curled up and apparently dead, but their electronics can still function as surveillance devices for weeks. I heard of a pilot who flew a drone into an enemy's code room and landed on an operator's shoulder. He recorded the clear data as the operator typed it into the encryption program. The enemy assumed we'd broken their code and had to change all their security protocols, very disruptive and expensive for them."

"What about assassination," he asked hesitantly, "are they ever used for that?"

Ah, thought Mary, *one of them*. A pity, he'd seemed alright until now.

"There have been stories of horse flies being adapted to deliver poisons: they have a strong bite so you could prime their jaws. I suppose you could use wasps with a modified poison in their sting. There could be another team doing that sort of thing but I'm not aware of it. I'm currently on 'Royalty Protection' keeping an eye on Prince George and his family."

"How did you get involved in the first place?" asked Abrahams.

"I trained as a fighter pilot, but as they use AIs to fly most military aircraft now, it isn't easy to get a seat flying anything. They offered me this; it was a big change from flying jets to flying insects though."

"Now, every time I see a spider or a fly, I'll wonder if it's spying on me and reporting back," laughed Abrahams. "I'll be adding fly spray to my office supplies list. In future I want it to be a no-fly zone. Are you all right, you've gone quite pale?"

"Not spiders," she said with a shudder. "Arachnids don't go through a pupal stage, so we can't insert the little box of tricks into them. No, not spiders, you're safe from being spied on by them."

He laughed, " 'Spiders, spied on,' very good."

Holding her emotions in close control she took him back to the Group Captain's office for his meeting.

Mary went to the changing room, she needed a few moments alone. Sitting on a bench with her head in her hands, she remembered the horrifying incident two years before, when the spider had caught her. She was on 'Royalty Protection' at Clarence House, spying on Diana the Queen Mother. The Establishment hated her and watched her every move. Mary had been following her from a reception room to her bedroom, flying just below the high ceiling, when she found herself entangled in the sticky cables of a web. Puzzled at first, as she bounced back and forth, it was a few moments before she activated the disengagement procedure. The software was slow, and she lived through the horror of the first few seconds, helpless, as the enormous, hairy, grey beast approached, its strange array of shiny black eyes unblinking, its palps quivering. It grabbed her and stuck its foot-long fangs into her poor body, turning her insides to liquid pain as its venom and digestive juices did their work. Then she was spinning round and round as her attacker wrapped her in a gossamer shroud. Helpless and disorientated, she screamed silently.

The system bumped her out, but her heart rate and other vital signs had gone into the red. It had only taken a few seconds, but it had seemed much longer. Groggily she returned to consciousness, an alarm was sounding nearby. She could move her head but the wrist and ankle straps still held her.

"Doctor, doctor, over here quickly, she's having a fit," her orderly was shouting. *Maureen's panicking,* she thought, *that's not a good sign.*

Dr Tom came and sat on the orderly's seat. "Don't worry Mary, you're back now," his voice was calm, and she heard the hiss of the aerosol on her arm. "You'll feel much better in a few seconds." He held her hand while the drug took effect, and she felt herself floating away, Maureen removed her visor and undid her restraints.

Several hours later, she woke up in the psychological evaluation unit. She lay entranced by the shadows cast by the gentle light shining through the venetian blinds as they moved slowly across the wall opposite her bed. An hour passed before the medics noticed that she was fully conscious. They brought her a cup of tea, how glorious it tasted. She sighed contentedly and leaned forward as a nurse plumped her pillows.

They kept her sedated for two days before they started the therapy. She never got the pictures out of her head but the treatment helped her to live with them, most of the time.

A week later, Mary was sitting in the hospital day room when the unit's civilian software engineer came to see her. Patrick worked for General Electronics, the drone control system's manufacturer. He was a quiet, dark haired, good-looking, young man. She had spoken to him before from time to time and he often led the update training on the squadron. He asked after her health, looked suitably sympathetic and then explained his visit.

"They want me to find a way of avoiding all this trauma," he said. "We can't exterminate spiders, but we can make the system bump the pilots out quicker, before they experience the spider attack. Currently the decoupling routines are too slow, and disengaging abruptly is also unpleasant and dangerous, like ejecting out of a cockpit. I want to make it fast and safe."

"What will you use as the trigger?" she asked.

"It'll be the moment that the fangs touch the fly's epidermis, and then it's probably just a matter of putting in a software buffer. That's what I'll try first."

An hour later, when he had all the information he needed, he said goodbye, and left. The next afternoon he returned.

"How are you today?" he asked as he sat opposite her in the dayroom. Mary put down her magazine.

"I thought you'd finished interviewing me," she said, pretending not to see the flowers that lay across his lap (he might have just called in to clarify something on the way to visit his mother.)

"Well, I'm not here on official business," he said as he handed them to her.

"How nice," she held them to her face and inhaled. "I love the smell of freesias. It reminds me of my childhood. My grandmother used to grow them on her balcony, back in Singapore. Mum and I used to visit her every year, and there was always the scent of freesias hanging in the air." Mary realized that warm tears were running down her cheeks. She put a hand to her forehead and wept quietly for a moment, Patrick passed the box of tissues from the side table.

"I'm sorry, they've taken me off the tranks and my emotions haven't settled yet, they warned me this might happen."

Patrick moved over to her sofa, took the flowers and put his arm around her shoulders.

"This isn't very military of me," she said.

"It's alright, you've been through a terrible experience, like something out of a horror movie. Hardly anybody else has experienced anything as alien and awful as being attacked by a giant spider. The only other person I can think of is Frodo Baggins."

"He doesn't count, he's a fictional character," she said. They both laughed.

Patrick visited her every day, and when she returned to work a few weeks later they started to see each other socially. After a couple of months Mary moved in with him - sharing a bed helped a lot in the small hours, when the nightmares came.

Tied up, lying helpless in total darkness, unable to move, she sensed a nameless silent horror slowly approaching. She screamed and struggled with her bonds, but they were too strong. There were delicate, feathery probings at her throat and collar bone. The next thing would be the fangs, rapiers pushing relentlessly through the base of her neck and down behind her ribcage, into her heart and lungs, before the filthy, burning poisons were injected. Mary thrashed wildly and tried to scream.

Suddenly she was aware of the sheet wrapped tightly around her, the mattress supporting her, and the warmth of Patrick's body next to her. After disentangling herself, she rolled onto her back and lay panting, waiting for her pulse to stop hammering. She wiped her forehead, her sprite told her that it was four in the morning, Patrick was still asleep, she moved across the bed and spooned into his back. He smelled of sweat and aftershave. She felt such comfort with him beside her. He was a gentle soul on the surface, but strong and dependable underneath. As she calmed down, her thoughts returned to a conversation she'd had with her shrink, a few weeks earlier.

***

"I've never been phobic about spiders," she'd said. "In the tropics, I've seen really big ones, as big as your hand. I was brought up to respect spiders of all sizes, because even the small ones might be poisonous, but I'm not afraid of them on a day-to-day basis." Mary walked over to a corner of the room where a long-legged house spider hung in a web near the ceiling. She made a cage of her hands, caught it gently, carried it over and dropped it onto his desk. He flinched and moved his chair back as the spider ran to the edge and abseiled to the floor. *Physician, heal thyself*, she thought as she sat down again.

"It's when I'm working, always expecting one to creep up on me, the thought of having to go through all that horror again, I hate it, I can't concentrate on the job, I'm always looking over my shoulder, or would be, if a fly had a shoulder."

"But you've told me that your drone has been caught by a bird. You said it's a fairly common occurrence in the summer." He was peering around at the floor and had pulled his feet under his chair.

"Yes, but if you're caught by a swallow or a swift, your host dies instantaneously. You find yourself "back in the room," lying on your couch, almost at once. It's physically unpleasant for a few seconds, but spiders are a different matter, they make you suffer." A soft chime sounded.

"Right, well, we can continue this on Tuesday," he said, nodding encouragingly as his keyboard appeared in front of him. Mary stood up and walked towards the door, she spotted the spider running madly across the floor, seeking the safety of the skirting board. She stepped on it, ground it into the carpet and glanced back: the shrink was watching, he looked down, began tapping at his keyboard, and moved his feet back in front of him.

***

She lay in the dark next to Patrick, worrying about the next day: they'd be testing the beta copy of his new software, she wasn't looking forward to it.

Now she was in the shower, they were crawling out of the shower head and the drain, crawling all over her. She was screaming and stamping on them, but more and more came, no matter how many she killed, bigger and bigger, climbing up her legs, over her body, onto her face. She couldn't kill them fast enough. They were in her hair, biting her scalp as she tried to tear them off. She closed her eyes and mouth but they forced their way in. Small ones were creeping into her ears, her nostrils.

She woke with a jerk and sat up gasping.

"I'll get you a glass of water," said Patrick. He went into the bathroom as she lay panting, then came back, sat on her side of the bed and handed her the glass. "It'll go away eventually," he said. "It'll just take time but you'll be alright in the end." She drank, then put the glass on the bedside table, he got in next to her and put his arms around her. "I'll look after you, Mary," he whispered. "It's my job. Go to sleep, it'll be better in the morning." He pulled the covers over them both and she drifted off again.

The next day, Mary lay trembling slightly on her couch as her orderly checked everything for the third time. *Now I know how Anne Boleyn felt on her last morning*, she thought. *I do not want to do this, but I have to show Patrick that I have faith in him.*

"I'm sure everything's okay, Corporal, stop fussing around," Mary snapped, then said more gently, "Sorry, Maureen, I'm very grateful for your help."

The orderly shrugged and smiled, "That's alright ma'am, I'd be feelin' edgy meself."

This is as bad as root canal work, Mary thought, and tried to control her shaking. If the software worked, it would give her confidence for the future, and she had every reason to believe it would work. It had worked when Patrick stuck a tiny pin into her captive drone yesterday. Mary had found herself 'back in the room' as soon as he touched her host's dermis.

Today's test was the real thing though. Her host was in one part of a plastic box in the next room, she felt sorry for it: the box was divided into two sections by a thin separator, in the other half sat a big, grey, garden spider. Patrick had caught it a week earlier and had shown her its impressive markings; he hadn't fed it since its capture.

"Okay, ma'am?" asked her orderly as she presented Mary's visor. Mary nodded and lifted her head.

She lay back and spoke to her sprite. "Let's get this over with."

"I'm sorry, ma'am, I don't under....."

"Initiate insertion," she interrupted.

A few moments later, Mary was standing on a smooth vertical surface, stable on her six sticky feet. She moved around until she could see the separator.

"Patrick wants to know if he can start?" said her sprite.

"Okay, go," she said, and watched as, a moment later, the separator flipped up out of the way. The spider was enormous, it horrified her. She felt her host's agitation, but held it in check as its wings buzzed and it tried to flee. The spider jerked as it saw her, and then paused. It raised its front legs and slowly began to approach, its movements unbearably menacing. She saw lights reflected in its cluster of polished jet eyes, the spiky hairs that covered it, its jaws working. Mary couldn't face it and turned off her vision channel. She waited in the darkness as her unseen assailant crept up on her and struck.

And she was back in the room, jerking on her restraints and shouting, 'FUCK,' as she tried desperately to shake off her visor. Her orderly whisked it away and Dr Tom was already sitting on the jump seat holding her arm, ready with his aerosol. Patrick was hovering anxiously nearby.

"I'm okay," said Mary breathlessly, "I'm okay, I didn't feel a thing. It worked just fine, but I couldn't handle the sight of the spider as it closed in on me." She was shallow panting. Dr Tom stood back and looked at her vital signs, on the screen above the couch, the aerosol wand held at his side. Maureen stepped in and undid the Velcro straps, with some difficulty because the stitching had been partly ripped.

"They'll need repairing," she pointed them out to the Doctor. "I've never seen anything like it, it can't be good for her." She sponged sweat from Mary's face, and helped her up. Patrick supported her, as she walked slowly towards the changing rooms.

"It wasn't my idea," said the Doctor, as Maureen busied herself wiping the couch and tidying up. He sighed and walked back to his office, shaking his head.

The membrane shrank and disappeared. Riley and Farina's seats rotated to face one another.

"Peter Abrahams looked a lot older," said Riley.

"Well, over thirty subjective years have passed; he's an old man by contemporary standards. What did you think of Mary Lee?"

"She's very attractive," he smiled mischievously and paused for a moment to watch Farina's reaction. He was disappointed when there wasn't one. "She has guts, but that's not surprising, she was a fast jet pilot and they're risk takers."

"You need to become more familiar with her and her world of your future, Martin. We will continue with your indoctrination tomorrow."

Back in the flat it was Farina's turn to cook.

"These aliens you mentioned when you first abducted me, don't they worry you?" asked Riley. "I mean, given the number of habitable planets in the galaxy, we should pick up comms chatter and entertainment transmissions from all directions and you've only found one distant transmission."

"Ah, the Fermi paradox," said Farina. "What do you think is the explanation, Martin?"

"Perhaps the noisy ones have already been subsumed or exterminated by a warlike space faring civilization, and the rest are keeping quiet hoping to avoid detection."

"Do you really believe that, Martin?" she asked seriously.

"Yes, I do, and if this alien civilization you've been talking to has been listening to your broadcasts for the last hundred years, it's had all that time to prepare and launch an invasion fleet. You might meet them sooner than you imagine, they could be edging into the solar system as we speak. This could be a good time to wake up Genghis Khan." Farina looked concerned, Riley burst out laughing. "Just kidding, I'm sure they're friendly. Tell me, do Synths have a sense of humor?"

"Not really, Martin," she said laughing along with him. "But we can simulate one, to help with human relations." She became instantly serious. "I need to communicate with Tolland about this. Sun Tzu might be a better choice as war leader."

It was Riley's turn to feel discomfited. "Do you think so?" he asked anxiously.

"No, Martin, I thought you realized that I was joking about the aliens, we haven't found any, Fermi's paradox is still holding." She chuckled as she spooned his rice and vegetables onto a plate. "Do Synths have a sense of humor?" she mimicked his voice. "No, but we can simulate one," she said in a squeaky, comic, robot voice and carried on laughing quietly to herself.

Riley realized he'd been bested.

Chapter Twenty-Five

USA the 2040s

Mary finished her Royalty Protection shift and walked to the changing rooms. Maureen helped her out of her sensuit and hung it in the maintenance locker, she heard the cleaning cycle start. In the shower her sprite spoke.

"The boss wants to speak to you ma'am."

"Tell him I'll be there in ten."

The Group Captain was standing talking to a secretary, in the admin area as she arrived. He turned to face her.

"Hello, Mary, can I offer you anything? I know you've just finished for the day."

"A cappuccino please, sir."

They walked into his office, sat down, and made small talk about her shift for a few minutes until the coffee arrived. As he added sugar to his cup, the Group Captain came straight to the point.

"How would you like a posting to America?" he asked. "It'd be a two-year tour, and you'd be promoted to Squadron Leader. What are your immediate thoughts?"

Mary's immediate thought was that it might mean a break up with Patrick, but she didn't say this.

"Promotion sounds good sir, what would the job be?"

"Do you recall that civilian you showed around a couple of weeks ago? Name of Abrahams, smallish chap, looked Middle Eastern, spook, doctor of something or other."

"Yes, I remember him, Peter Abrahams."

"Well apparently, he took a shine to you, in a professional way I mean. He's requested you as drone pilot on some sort of hush-hush, Anglo American surveillance project at Langley. It's with the CIA or Homeland Security, something like that, they haven't been specific. Anyway, he wants you on the team. What do you say? Need to sleep on it? I would. You might want to talk it over with Patrick."

"Actually sir, I'm sure that the answer will be yes but, you're right, I ought to discuss it with Patrick first."

She left his office, told her sprite to order a car and waited outside the building, enjoying the afternoon sunshine. Somewhere nearby, she heard a drill sergeant screaming. His voice got louder as a platoon of recruits marched around the corner of the building, swinging their arms in the approved manner. The sergeant did an 'eyes right' and saluted her. She saluted back smartly, and smiled to herself as they marched past. The sergeant continued shouting, it was all pleasantly familiar.

As the car drove her back to their house, she thought about life without Patrick. They could visit each other, maybe every month, even take the "Ballistic" to cut the journey time. It wouldn't be so bad, it was definitely doable. They planned to have a family when she retired from the Air Force, aged forty-four; she was only thirty now so there was plenty of time. The promotion would mean a bigger pension. The challenge of a new project lifted her spirits. She felt confident and ready for a change.

Patrick was less enthusiastic when she told him over dinner that evening.

"There's no way I'm stepping onto a suborbital airliner again, not even for you, Mary. I can't handle weightlessness, it's something to do with my middle ear. The only time I experienced it I threw up everywhere, missed the sick bag completely, the whole cabin had globules of vomit floating around, sticking to everyone and everything. It was very embarrassing; the smell was unbearable. The flight attendants were very nice about it, flying around with little fishing nets, collecting it all up and spraying deodorant, but no thanks, tried it once, didn't like it."

"It's a pain, I know," she carefully placed her wine glass on the table, "but look at the advantages, the salary, the pension, and it would only be for a couple of years. I could write my own ticket afterwards, maybe get a job at the Ministry of Defense in London. I'd really like to give it a go, Patrick."

The next morning, she reported to the Group Captain. He smiled, "I'm pleased for you, Mary; although I'll be sorry to see you go. Who knows, they might send you back here at the end of the posting. By the way, they want you there next week so you'd better get cracking."

Less than a week later, she stood outside the "New Building" at Langley. They still called it "new" even though it was built at the turn of the century. Her personal chip got her through security at the front doors and then as far as the tenth floor.

The holographic AI running reception smiled a greeting.

"Please take a seat Squadron Leader Lee. Dr Abrahams will be here in a few minutes. Can I offer you any refreshment?"

"No," she said and sat in an armchair, briefcase on her knees, her forage cap beside her. The AI would be analyzing her blink rate and other physiological signs, adding the information to her personal file. She didn't like the bloody things, they'd stolen her aeroplanes. Still, she was impressed that it knew her new rank, even though she hadn't had time to update the insignia on her uniform.

"You might like to try a more appropriate smile," she said helpfully. She knew AIs still had problems mimicking human facial anatomy. The AI went through its library of smiles, holding each for a couple of seconds, until Mary raised a finger at a particularly cheesy one.

"That's it," said Mary, spitefully pleased that it would take ages for it to adapt back to normal. She chuckled to herself.

Peter Abrahams bustled into the room.

"Well, well, Flight Lieutenant Lee, (he used the English pronunciation for her rank) how are you? Oh, sorry, it's Squadron Leader, now isn't it? I really enjoyed your briefing on insect drones at RAF Waddington. What a surprise they were, I haven't felt completely alone since then." They shook hands. "Come through into my parlor." He laughed at his little joke, Mary shuddered slightly but said nothing. They walked through the doorway and into an open plan area that reminded Mary of an air traffic control center. There were a dozen large screens with people sitting in front of them gesturing at menus and sub vocalizing commands. Other electronic equipment occupied benches around the periphery.

Her sprite whispered, *"They've just added a new security clearance to your personal chip ma'am, you can come and go as you please in most of this area."*

"This is our main laboratory," he gestured expansively. He led her off to one side, and through a door marked 'Drone Control, no admittance.' Inside there were two couches with their familiar ancillary equipment and a US Air Force sergeant, who had been making adjustments on one of the flat screens. She stood to attention.

"Never been used yet," said Abrahams gesturing at the couches. "This is Sergeant Harbaugh; she'll be your orderly and technician."

The sergeant was a woman of about thirty, dressed in fatigues; she was more heavily built than Mary, who had inherited her mother's slim, oriental figure. She saluted, Mary did the same. They shook hands. Mary hoped she would be as caring and reliable as Maureen back at RAF Waddington.

"I'm sure we can get by without too much formality," said Mary.

The sergeant smiled and appeared to relax.

"Whatever you say ma'am," she said. They exchanged pleasantries and began discussing the equipment.

"I'll arrange for you to spend time together and to do a few trial flights," said Abrahams, interrupting them. He seemed to want to press on.

"We call them 'circuits and bumps,' " said Mary and she and the sergeant smiled at the familiarity of the shared Air Force jargon.

Mary and Abrahams moved on through the control room to Abraham's private office, and sat at the conference table. A small arbeiter wheeled in with two mugs of coffee on its top surface.

"You're our only drone pilot, Mary. The Americans could have provided one, but we have an agreement to mix US and UK personnel on the Temporal Messaging programme and your experience with SIS amply qualifies you."

Mary was intrigued to know the name of the programme at last. Back in England her superiors had been evasive. "Special Project" was all they said. It sounded more interesting, now she was finally getting to the bottom of things.

"Temporal Messaging?" she looked at Abrahams. "It sounds as if you're involved with time travel."

"I suppose in a way we are." He leaned forward. "To put it simply, we have a team in another part of the States who send scans of newspaper reports and clips from TV news channels. They think they're gathering general intelligence for the FBI. Our technology allows us to see these files two weeks before they're sent. Effectively we can see two weeks into the future. We call it Temporal Messaging. If they don't like what they see, the Government can alter things before they happen. We call that 'Temporal Adjustment' or 'TA'."

Mary sat and considered this while Abrahams sipped his coffee and watched her over the rim of his cup.

"You mean to say you can change the future?" she asked.

"Not us, we just report our findings, it's up to the politicians to decide on the changes, and the spooks to implement them."

"Is that a good idea, it sounds dangerous?"

"They're very careful, an Oversight Committee scrutinizes every move. You'd be amazed at the atrocities we've prevented, the lives we've saved."

"Why only two weeks, why not longer?" asked Mary. She was more interested in the practicality than the ethics.

"There's a theoretical limitation, like the sound barrier, or the speed of light," he said.

"Who else has this technology, is anybody else tampering with our reality?" she asked. "I find the idea of Temporal Adjustment disturbing, alien."

"We are the only ones capable of Temporal Messaging. An English physicist called Martin Riley invented the technique back in the 1990's. The British Government financed the research and threw a security blanket over it, but it got to be too expensive. Eventually our American allies became the major underwriters, and here we are."

"I've never heard of this Martin Riley."

"No, I'm not surprised, but I knew him well, he was my mentor, the man was a genius."

"Was? He's dead then?"

"Yes, he died in a car accident over thirty years ago. Tragic, he wasn't even fifty; he could have achieved so much more."

"I find this time travel stuff difficult. Surely you could change all sorts of things. I mean, what if you assassinated Hitler in 1935, just think how that would change history?"

"We can only send information back, not people and we only ever make alterations in our present, which then alters our future, so time appears to flow normally to us. We never alter things in our past, too dangerous, there'd be unpredictable effects on our present."

"What type of changes have you made?"

"Most of them are secret. They'll tell you about some of them, as part of your indoctrination. I can tell you about one thing that the TA team did before the Americans got involved though. Martin Riley saved Princess Diana."

"Saved her from what?"

"Well, originally she died in a car accident in Paris, in 1997."

Mary thought for a moment. "He brought her back to life?"

"No, no, they altered the events leading up to the crash, so it didn't happen. SIS arranged for the driver to be changed. The original was drunk."

"They must have regretted saving her," said Mary. "She's been a thorn in the Royal flesh for years, what with converting to Islam and having kids with Dodi. She's always made the Establishment uncomfortable. The papers can't mention her without spluttering 'Islamification of the Royal Family.' "

Abrahams laughed, "Yes, and Prince George marrying a Princess of the House of Saud was an interesting development. Apparently, he won't say whether he's converted to Islam, which probably means he has. Anyway, enough royal gossip, you'd know much more about that than me, having been on 'Royalty Protection.' Do you have any questions?"

"This will take some getting used to," said Mary. "It changes my whole perception of reality." Bringing people back to life and giving them another chance? Could technology really cheat death like that, she wondered? What other changes had the politicians made?

Abrahams leaned forward and looked at her intently. "I hope you realize the political ramifications of this? The world would be a different place if it weren't for our interventions, but if the public knew about TA, there would be hell to pay. If anybody got wobbly and talked to the wrong people, our masters wouldn't hesitate." He continued staring.

"Wouldn't hesitate to what?"

Abrahams didn't reply. They sat in silence for a short while and Mary decided not to voice the question that had popped into her mind. This Martin Riley had died young, was his death an accident?

"Anyway," said Abrahams, with forced cheerfulness, "let's discuss your immediate duties. We want you to help us with a new technology we're developing. It's a spin-off from the science we use here. We want you to help us with targeting. Your job is to fly a drone to a specific point and wait until we tell you to, er, 'bump out.' Your drone will be emitting a signal that we can use as a target."

"Target for what? Guns, missiles, laser beams?" she asked.

"Well, yes, all of those things. Anything, fired from land, sea or air anywhere in the world. From a particle beam weapon on one of the orbital platforms, to a sniper's steerable bullet. It allows surgical strikes of any sort."

Mary wasn't convinced about the targeting job, it seemed insignificant in comparison with the TA project. She suspected that Abrahams hadn't told her everything.

"Lunch," said Abrahams standing up and smiling. "You'll love the food here, be prepared to put on a kilogram in the first fortnight. Our cousins have never heard the phrase 'portion control.' "

The weeks passed easily enough for Mary. Her job was simple; she flew her host to a given spot and sat there for a few minutes. Her sprite told her when she should bump out, and she would find herself back in the drone control room with Sergeant Harbaugh sitting on the jump seat at the side of her couch. The sergeant's name was Ruth. She and Mary were soon on first name terms, as long as there were no other military staff present. After about two weeks of this Abrahams collected her from the drone control room, and took her back to his office.

"Now you have your feet under the table so to speak," he said, "it's time to explain the real reason for your recruitment. Until now you've been helping us to calibrate our systems. Everything's gone well, and the powers that be are happy with your performance. They want me to put you more fully in the picture."

Mary said nothing; she waited for Abrahams to draw back the veil of secrecy. Surely nothing could be more astonishing than Temporal Messaging?

"The thing is, Mary, you don't mind if I call you Mary? The thing is, Mary that we've recently made a breakthrough. After years of research we've found a way to manipulate individual wormholes and increase their size. We can send, not just information, but also small amounts of matter, as far back upstream into the past as we like. It takes a lot of power, and the masses are tiny, only a few thousands of molecules, not enough to see with the naked eye. As soon as they arrive, an equal amount of anti-matter spontaneously condenses out of the quantum matrix; it's to do with the conservation of energy." He waved his hands and shook his head dismissively, to signal that the scientific details were not important to his explanation. "As the two masses meet, they annihilate one another, releasing a flash of electromagnetic radiation. We call the process 'Temporal Displacement' or 'TD.' If we were dealing with larger amounts of matter, there'd be an explosion. Who knows, a few years from now..." He was distracted for a moment, but then continued. "With the help of a targeting signal from, say, a fly drone, we can place the puff of energy to within a millimeter. The thing is, Mary," she was getting fed up with his 'thing is' habit, "we're ready for our first trial run."

"You said it was dangerous to interfere with the past," she said.

"Oh, we only send the packet back a microsecond. We could send them much further back, if we had a signal drone in place as a target. But that would be a retrospective TA and we're not allowed to do that."

"Then why send the packet back a microsecond, what's the point?"

"Because if we didn't give it a temporal displacement it would arrive and just sit there. There'd be no need for the quantum matrix to react, you see, so there'd be no anti-matter, and no energy release."

"Can you send the end of the wormhole into the future?"

"How could we do that? The future hasn't happened yet," he said.

Mary thought about this, but decided that she didn't want to pursue it. "What will you use Temporal Displacement for?"

"We'll use it to prevent some very nasty people from doing some very nasty things. We can target the release of energy accurately enough to make it happen inside a subject's head. The effect is similar to a cerebral hemorrhage, a stroke."

"Which are you talking about, Dr Abrahams, assassination or execution?" Mary was shocked but kept her emotions from showing.

"What's the difference?" he asked.

"A trial, lawyers, judges, juries, all that old-fashioned stuff, you know, democracy and the rule of law." Mary's voice was even and controlled.

"Look, you're a military pilot; your superiors might order you to kill an enemy in the line of duty, this is the same as firing a bullet or a missile. You don't go to court every time you press the button or pull the trigger." He seemed surprised at her disapproval.

Mary was disgusted, she understood the logic, but these sounded like the actions of a police state. She realized that she knew too much now, and had reached a point of no return. If she wasn't careful a puff of energy might manifest itself in her own head, targeted by her replacement. A bloody rite of passage for a new recruit, a sharing of the tribe's guilt.

Abrahams continued in a louder voice, "You don't have to kill anybody. You just have to do the targeting; we'll be pulling the trigger back here. The energies involved are far too great to be generated by a fly drone." He sounded agitated.

Mary wondered if Abraham's anger was a symptom of his own moral scruples and the helplessness of his own position.

"Who came up with the idea in the first place?" she asked.

"Well, actually, it was me," he said. "I wasn't planning on using it as an assassination weapon; I thought the applications would be medical or manufacturing. Unfortunately, our masters are currently only interested in funding its military use." They finished their meeting and went their separate ways for the weekend.

Mary did a session in the gym, and later, in the evening, HoloSkyped Patrick for a couple of hours. She didn't dare discuss developments at Langley, and he knew better than to ask. They had a few drinks, gossiped about friends in England and then spent some 'private time' together.

The next Monday morning the team was scheduled to begin targeting live pigs. The pigs lived in field about ten miles away. A drone wrangler released Mary's host from a car nearby and olfactory feedback made the herd easy to find. She reprogrammed her end of the interface to substitute the smell of cinnamon for that of pig shit, that way both she and her host were happy. It wasn't difficult for her to pick out the pig with the blue paint mark on its back. She landed between its ears and moved to the small black cross that was marked there. Gripping the pig's skin with the sticky pads on her feet, she used her claws lightly enough not to advertise her presence. A scratching session, on the part of the pig, wouldn't be helpful.

"They have acquisition," said her sprite after a few seconds and then, *"Packet arrival,"* a moment later.

She released her hold, flew to a nearby post, and watched as the pig slumped to the ground, its legs sticking out in different directions. Its eyes were closed, it jerked for several minutes before it went limp. Mary's view was being patched to the screens back at the TM lab.

"They say they'll try a larger packet next time, and they want you to pick out the one with the green marking."

Mary sighed and complied. Another day, another dollar. She decided that she'd try the vegetarian option in the mess that evening.

After the live pigs, came the human cadavers. The subjects were laid out in the pathology department at a hospital in Cincinnati; army doctors were there to perform autopsies after the TD strikes.

Mary found landing on the head of a corpse unnerving, particularly if its eyes were open. Each time she did, empathic feedback leaked from her host's nervous system into hers. The flies liked the corpses, they liked them a lot. On one occasion, she had submitted to the urgent need of her female host to lay half a dozen eggs before she returned it to its wrangler. The happy feedback made her more relaxed during the mission, but she spent longer in the shower afterwards.

After her third day with the corpses, Abrahams met her in the drone control room. She was sitting on the couch, still in her sensuit, feeling sweaty and unclean. Irrationally she worried that she might smell of decay. He appeared not to notice her discomfort and focused his conversation on the project, as always.

"The problem is, Mary, that although cadavers are good practice for target acquisition, they don't allow us to calibrate our packets for termination with minimum intrusion. We need to go live, if that isn't a contradiction. Ha, ha," he laughed nervously.

Mary scoffed, "Sounds like an acronym trying to get out there, Dr Abrahams, 'Termination With Minimum Intrusion,' TWMI? no it's just not coming to me. How about calling it 'Managed Unilateral Removal by Directed Energy Release,' it rolls off the tongue so easily."

Abrahams looked at her for a moment, then stood up and walked away, clenching and unclenching his fists as he passed through the doorway and turned down the corridor. She sat on the couch and, as Ruth unplugged leads and loosened the straps of her sensuit, Mary's emotions got the better of her.

"We'll be using live subjects next, and I don't think I can face it." Mary stood and wept quietly.

Ruth put her arms around her. She whispered in Mary's ear, "We don't have any choice ma'am, they're not going to let us go, we know too much."

Mary was grateful that the sergeant knew when they could relax protocol. She laid her head on Ruth's shoulder, and allowed herself a few moments weakness, before shaking herself and stepping back.

"Thanks Ruth," she said. "It's nice to have someone I can lean on, but then that's your job isn't it, part nurse, part technician?"

"And part friend," said Ruth as she helped her out of her suit. "Maybe on Sunday you'd like to come to the service at the Mormon Church I go to, it's not far. I could pick you up."

Mary thought fast. "Actually Ruth, I'm a Buddhist. Sorry."

Ruth shrugged, "Same God," she said, as she picked up the sensuit and carried it to the cleaning locker.

Mary didn't bother to correct her, she picked up a towel, wiped her eyes, and headed for the shower.

"Remind me what the date is here," said Riley.

"It is 2045, Martin."

"Now this is very interesting," he said. "Peter has found a way of manipulating individual wormholes. Even if he's only sending a handful of molecules through one, he must have increased its size by several magnitudes, and how is he anchoring the upstream end? This is a step change."

"The technical details do not concern us at the moment, Martin," said Farina. "What matters is that Abrahams accomplished this in the 21st century. It is far too early. It shows that his mind is as unique as your own, and the Commonwealth needs us to take a copy before the Realignment in six years. Any time from now would be acceptable."

"But if we know the date of the Realignment, it makes sense to make the copy as near to it as possible.

That way you capture all his research results before we all disappear."

Farina nodded. "Tolland wants me to show you the use that your governments made of Temporal Displacement."

Once again, the walls of the craft misted and then cleared.

Chapter Twenty-Six

USA, 2040s

They were volunteers, of a sort, prisoners from death row. The Government had promised to commute their sentences to life, in another prison, if they took part in a 'simple medical procedure.' All the inmates on the 'row' had signed up, they had nothing to lose. Three or four of them each day, they packed up their effects and sat on their bunks waiting for the call.

Two correctional officers led a shackled prisoner wearing orange overalls, into the white tiled room. They helped him into a chair and strapped him in. A small cross had been drawn on his newly shaved head.

"Sit still, it's important you don't move your head," said the older officer as he tightened the straps. The second officer said something unintelligible and laughed.

"Shut the fuck up George," said the other. They left the room and closed the door.

The prisoner warily looked around, keeping his head still. A pulse at his temple throbbed, sweat misted his forehead. Soft music began to play, and he relaxed as he got more used to his surroundings, his shoulders began to drop. His eyes turned upwards as he felt a fly land on his forehead. A few moments later the upper half of his head exploded, splattering the walls and ceiling with blood, bone fragments and brain matter. The body remained in place for a moment, its facial expression frozen in an expression of supplication, before it fell forward against its restraints.

The picture on the video link paused. "We need to calibrate the packet more accurately," said Abrahams, shaking his head, "that was at least ten times more powerful than it needed to be. We didn't have this problem with the cadavers."

"Maybe the problem's geographical Doc," said Doug the technician. "We're closer to the prison than we were to the morgue in Cincinnati where the deaders were."

"Well, we need to sort this out; we can't keep making a mess like this, the Governor at Greensville has called me twice now to complain about it."

Mary said nothing, she was horrified that the scientists could disassociate themselves from the effects of their activities. How could they sit and watch as they executed a man, without turning a hair? She wanted to run screaming from the room but instead she voiced her thoughts calmly.

"Should we be doing this, murdering people, lying to them first, and then executing them? How can this be legal?"

"I see it as collateral damage," said Abrahams. "The courts have found these people guilty of murder, or worse, and sentenced them to death. We have given them hope against all the odds, and their deaths are unexpected and instantaneous. It's mercy killing." The other men in the room nodded their heads in agreement.

Sycophantic bastards she thought. "I'm glad that your system of ethics is so flexible, Doctor."

Doug turned to her, "Look, Mary, as the saying goes 'The Lord said "Let there be light" and the Devil did the wiring.' We're just Satan's electricians." Everybody laughed except Mary.

"Well boys, perhaps you should get some funny lapel badges made," she walked towards the door but looked back before leaving. "The thing is, Peter, if they're Satan's electricians, what does that make you?"

The video restarted. a man of about thirty, wearing green scrubs, entered the room, pulling on blue vinyl gloves. He had a hand-rolled cigarette in his mouth. He wore a surgical mask but had pulled it down below his chin to facilitate his habit. He took a plastic bag from a back pocket and placed it over the ruined head of the corpse, sealed it in place with surgical tape around the neck and left, puffing smoke as he removed the gloves and threw them in a waste bin by the door.

Two prisoners, wearing orange overalls, pushed a battered metal gurney into the room. Two more followed carrying buckets and brushes. Between them they unstrapped the corpse, lay it on the floor, zipped it into a body bag and lifted it onto the gurney. The first two pushed it out of the room, while the other two hosed and brushed the walls and floor, ready for the next recruit, from the legion of the damned.

Abrahams closed the link, and the virtual screen disappeared. The small group of scientists and technicians drifted back to their stations. Mary left for the gym, she wanted to try to work the images out of her head.

Mary arrived home tired, but she still followed her routine, moving around the small apartment with a fly swat and torch, looking in light fittings and corners. Satisfied, she changed into shorts and tee shirt, ate her takeaway and sat down to watch the News. Two slow tequilas later, her eyelids began to droop, she crawled into bed and quickly fell asleep.

She woke, to find two men using the bedclothes to hold her down, a third pushed a pad over her mouth and nose. Mary smelled the chloroform, tried not to breathe and struggled against the sheets pinning her arms and legs. She lost consciousness and came to, strapped in a chair, in a white-tiled room, naked, and surrounded by her colleagues, who were smiling expectantly. Doug stepped forward and ceremonially drew a cross on her shaved head, bowed, and backed away laughing. She shouted at him to let her go. As she drew breath, she heard the buzzing of a fly and anxiously looked around for it. She fought to pull free from her bonds but the plastic cable ties cut into her flesh, blood ran down her hands, dripping off her fingers. Shaking her head, she shrieked and thrashed, but the buzzing kept getting louder. Her workmates laughed and pointed.

Mary screamed and screamed, and woke from her nightmare sweating and trembling. She reached across the bed for Patrick, but his side was empty, he was back at Waddington, thousands of miles away. She climbed out, shuffled to the bathroom and stared into her own bloodshot eyes for a moment, before opening the mirrored cabinet, and reaching for the bottle of sleeping pills. Shaking two out into her hand she walked back into her living room and poured a shot of tequila to wash them down. She sat on the edge of the bed and stared into space for several minutes before climbing back in. Next morning, she didn't remember the dream, the pills, or the tequila, but her head pounded and she felt drained.

Chapter Twenty-Seven

UK 2040s

A winter's afternoon, watery sunlight, wet grass, skeletal trees drooping to catch unwary travelers, but the park at Finsbury Circus was almost deserted as dusk fell. The well-lit windows of the office blocks of international banks overlooked it on all sides. It was a convenient open space at the center of London's financial district, and in the summer, there would have been many more visitors.

Two heavily built men entered the park from opposite sides. One came from the direction of Liverpool Street station, the other from Moorgate Underground, each pulled a wheeled, metal suitcase, tourists heading for a hotel or the airport. The cases were heavy, and they had difficulty maneuvering them over curbs and steps. They met by the bandstand, next to the bowling green, and conferred, one of them held up a phone. Standing together, they began a tirade which lasted several minutes, they took it in turns to raise an admonishing finger as they addressed the camera, before finally throwing it aside.

Working together, they opened the two cases. The first contained, what looked like, a partly dismantled artillery shell with a timer taped to it. The other contained a bucket sized, metal cylinder. As one of them reached to set the timer they both stopped and stood staring, then, eyes bulging, they fell to the ground and lay jerking convulsively for a few moments before lying still. Several tourists approached the bodies but nobody seemed to know what to do.

Two black vans with police markings and blue lights flashing drove up. Four men in dark overalls jumped out of the first vehicle and bundled the bodies into the back. A man and a woman, wearing decontamination suits, climbed out of the second. They repacked the two flight cases, closed the lids, and working together, loaded them into their vehicle. While they worked, uniformed police had appeared, formed a cordon around the scene and moved the onlookers back. The vans drove away together. The police dispersed, leaving no trace of the incident. In one of the flower beds the abandoned phone began to ring.

As Mary guided her host towards the drone wrangler's car, she saw an elongated glistening bubble, slightly larger than man-size, about a hundred meters from the cordon. Her drone was past it before she could get a close look, and when she turned and flew back, there was no sign of it among the onlookers.

Back at Langley, Mary and Abrahams watched the recording of her drone's transmissions. She paused it.

"What's this?" she asked, pointing at the bubble.

"I don't know," said Abrahams. "It could be a stray reflection or aberration, an artefact of the lens perhaps?"

Mary peered at it. "It looks like oil on water, rainbow colors, perhaps you're right." She restarted the clip, and they watched it to the end.

"Fantastic," Abrahams said, looking pleased and rubbing his hands together. "The thing is, no guns, no collateral damage, no massive death toll, and Central London is still intact. That was a redundant Russian MIRV warhead in the first suitcase, jury-rigged for manual detonation; the other contained several kilograms of high level radioactive waste, which would have added insult to the injury of the nuclear explosion."

"It was a close-run thing. The Elizabeth line runs underneath Finsbury Circus" said Mary.

"Yes, in the original incident, a wall of plasma blasted through the miles of London Underground tunnels at supersonic speed, destroying most of Central London's transport infrastructure. The explosion obliterated the financial center and radioactive contamination caused area denial of a huge chunk of Greater London."

"Why didn't the security people arrest the terrorists before they got this far?" asked Mary. "Like they did with the attempt on the Twin Towers?"

"Because the Oversight Committee didn't release the information to the UK Government until this afternoon, there was an, er, failure in the chain of command. We almost had to make our first Retroactive Temporal Adjustment. Our American cousins don't seem concerned about incidents that occur outside the USA. I'm told the PM has made her feelings plain to the President, we're supposed to be equal partners in this technology. The Yanks have assured her it won't happen again."

"Why did we have to kill them, the police could have arrested them?" Mary still found it difficult to cope with her involvement with the killings.

"These days, our masters take a robust approach with terrorists who want to destroy billions of dollars" worth of property, and kill millions of people for the sake of their misguided beliefs," he said. "Personally, I applaud it. Saves the expense of a trial, martyrs, unrest and explanations of how we knew about it beforehand."

"Yes, and bollocks to the rule of law." Mary felt older and more strained. Her hair was still jet black although now she needed to color it, and it had lost some of its shine. The mirror showed fine lines in her face that had not been there a few years ago. She took a small drag of "mist" on her vapourette and held it down while it condensed in her lungs. The drug suffused and relaxed her. She loved the excitement of her missions but found it more and more difficult to come to terms with the ethics.

"If the drone wrangler's car had broken down, we'd have been right in the shit, with a smoking radioactive crater where Central London used to be. What's happened to the 'Special Relationship'?"

Abrahams shrugged, and the screen disappeared.

"I can tell you're not happy," said Patrick that evening in her quarters. He lay on her bed holding a glass of wine. She came out of the bathroom with a towel wrapped around her, drying her hair with another.

"Nightmares, I'm not sleeping well." She poured a glass for herself.

"The spiders?" he asked.

"No, it's my current duties," she said. "I've thought of applying for a transfer back to the UK, but I'm don't know if they'll let me go."

"The sooner you come home the better I'll like it. Anyway, they said your tour would only last two years, it should finish about now."

"My military masters say they've changed the 'mission parameters.' " She sipped her wine. "Let's see how it goes and we can talk on your next visit."

The towel fell to the floor as she walked over to the bed and lay near to him. They looked into each other's eyes, and began to make love, with carefully synchronized movements of their fingers on the Mimic patches they were wearing. She wanted to kiss him, but it was no use, he was virtual to her, as she was virtual to him.

Afterwards, they lay back. HoloSkype was better than cybersex software, she thought as she peeled off her patches, the sharing made it more personal, but even though the link was encryption guaranteed, she still felt spied on. Mary rolled onto her side and closed her eyes.

"Have you heard about Tel Aviv?" Patrick asked.

"No, what about it?" she whispered sleepily.

"It was on the news an hour ago. A dirty bomb, half a million-people killed outright, many more injured, huge damage and contamination."

Chapter Twenty-Eight

In Transit

"You must be more careful where you make your emergences," said Farina. "It was just luck that nobody saw you materialize in Finsbury Circus. There were plenty of private places that would have been suitable."

"I don't think I did badly for my first attempt," said Riley.

"Did you observe the fly drones which landed on the terrorists as they entered the park?"

"Yes, I did, one of them was Mary Lee," he said, wishing that Farina would lighten up a bit. "I'm not sure how, but I could see them, and hear the pilots' comms with their base."

"That's your new implant, Martin, with practice, you will find it can give you all kinds of help. Now let's try again. I want you to move two years downstream and to a different geographical location. As you will be entering a moving vehicle, it would be better if I control your emergence."

"Okay, here goes nothing." Moments later, Riley was sitting in the passenger compartment of a light plane as it cartwheeled across a field, burning fiercely and breaking to pieces. In the seat next to him, a man in flames screamed incoherently and struggled to undo his seat belt. Small white beads ricocheted frantically around the compartment. Moving nozzles sprayed fire retardant foam at the furiously burning interior but they were fighting a losing battle. He glimpsed the pilot ahead of him, also strapped into his seat; his arms flailed lifelessly as the aircraft continued to tumble, flaming pieces breaking off continually. Riley withdrew immediately, but as he did, he was momentarily aware of classical music playing, and a fly drone on the ceiling.

"What the fuck was that," he shouted at Farina? He was shocked rigid by what he'd just witnessed.

"Did you notice the drone?" she asked.

"Yes, Mary Lee was operating it according to my implant. But why did you send me into that? I might have been killed."

"No, if you look back at the data you will see that you never coalesced, you were not in danger."

"Well warn me next time you play a trick like that, or I'll withdraw my cooperation." Riley wasn't sure if he could withdraw his cooperation, or whether it would have any effect if he did, but he was angry, and shaking with reaction to the experience. Suddenly he felt calm. "You've switched that bloody field on, again haven't you?" he said. "I've told you I don't like to be taken over like this, it's brain washing."

"But I hate to see you suffer, Martin, and you do need to be familiar with the recent experiences of the people you have to deal with. I assure you that your next appearance will not be unpleasant."

Chapter Twenty-Nine

USA 2040s

Abrahams had called Mary for a meeting with two English "civil servants" who were over from London for the morning.

"These gentlemen are here to brief you, Mary. This is Mr Brown, and this is Mr Grey."

River Boys, she thought, but couldn't tell which particular flavor they were: MI5 or 6, or perhaps something more exotic. Her gaze slid over the older one, Mr Brown; he was the personification of anonymity. Average height, average build, thinning hair. The younger, Mr Grey, on the other hand, was very easy on the eye, with his lean athletic look, his beautifully tailored suit, and his icy blue eyes. They sat around a table in Abraham's office. Mary poured herself a glass of water and waited.

Mr Grey took the lead, "One of the largest drug cartels in South America has sent its chief accountant over to London for meetings with his 'bankers.' They're actually money launderers, and they've been careful about security. We want the information he's carrying, account numbers mainly, but we need to acquire it clandestinely if it's to have any value. We can't just arrest him and squeeze it out of him; his bosses would change the codes. As part of our plan we need to place a targeting drone aboard the plane that will be taking him from London City Airport to Schiphol, and you get the job, apparently." He looked at Abrahams for confirmation.

Two days later, Mary's host sat on the left epaulette of a young commercial pilot as, flight bag in hand, he escorted his passenger across the tarmac toward the Pilatus PC19, single engine turboprop. They would fly to Amsterdam that afternoon. As she bounced up and down, Mary saw that the plane was at least twenty years old, and looked a little dog eared, but presumably it was still serviceable. The passenger was a Portuguese national, Mary had scanned his passport as the pilot collected it from the company office when he uploaded his flight plan. He was shorter and more heavily built than the slim six-foot pilot. His passport listed his occupation as "accountant" and the photo had shown a moustache but no sign of the small beard he now sported.

"Will you be returning to London today, Capitan?" the passenger asked, making conversation as they walked.

"No Senor, I have to fly another client back tomorrow, so I'll stop overnight in town and probably have to listen to some taxi driver telling me that the airport is three meters below sea level, again. I hear it every time I fly into Schiphol. Bloody Cloggies, obsessed with water, that's why they're all so tall, fear of flooding. It'll be a relief when Dutch law allows driverless taxis like everywhere else in Europe. Would you prefer to sit in the cockpit, Senor?" the pilot asked as they reached the plane.

"A kind offer Capitan, but I have work I must do, and the extra space in the seats behind you will be most useful."

Mary thought the pilot seemed slightly annoyed at the refusal, presumably most passengers would have jumped at the chance to sit next in the right-hand seat. They climbed the steps into the plane. The pilot showed the accountant to his seat, checked the snack box, then walked back down the steps to do a brief pre-flight check around the exterior. He climbed back in, retracted the steps, slammed the door and maneuvered himself into the left-hand front seat. He called the tower to get clearance for take-off.

"Voice ID check please," said the aircraft's artificial intelligence.

"Open the pod bay door, Hal," said the pilot.

"ID confirmed. Good morning, Captain Hodson."

"Pre-flight checks. Report."

"There is a three percent difference in tire pressures between the port and starboard wheels. Debris, possibly bird related, partly obscures the right-hand wing camera. The digital signature for the latest engine compressor cleaning operation is missing. There are further irregularities in the maintenance record, list follows...."

The pilot interrupted. "Are any of these issues flight critical?"

There was, what seemed to Mary, a sulky pause.

"No Captain."

"Good, let's get on with it then." He started the engine, and as it was winding up, spoke over his shoulder to his passenger.

"These AIs are so pernickety. We'd never leave the ground if they had their way. I had one complain that the wastepaper basket in the toilet was full, when there were no passengers on board."

He taxied the plane to the end of the designated runway, rolled it around the circular "frying pan", checked in with air traffic control again, and pushed the throttle forward. They accelerated down the tarmac, lifted away and began the climb to cruising altitude. The pilot busied himself making adjustments and set the radio navigation system to the Schiphol frequency. The plane reached its cruising height after about five minutes.

"AI has control," he said. He took his hands off the control column, leaned back and died a few moments later.

He died quietly; the slight juddering of the plane masked any tremors or convulsions, and his seat harness kept him upright. Practice had perfected the Langley assassination team's technique. Mary had moved to the top of his head to allow targeting, and her sprite had transmitted the conversation between the pilot and his AI to Satan's Electricians in real time, so they knew when to make the hit.

"They want you to look at the display, so they can see the instruments ma'am," her sprite said.

She complied, then turned to watch the passenger working at his virtual keyboard. Presumably he was composing a message to encipher and send to his boss, back in South America.

Meanwhile, the plane's AI kept flying on the set heading. Mary guessed that it couldn't monitor the pilot's vital signs because it was old software that hadn't been upgraded since the plane was built.

Mary knew she should bump out, but she stayed aboard with her host, curious to see what would happen next. She had developed a morbid interest in her work. It was unhealthy, but she'd half convinced herself that it was necessary, to confirm the success of the mission. She crawled out of the dead pilot's short, spiky hair and flew to the dashboard and she looked back at him hanging supine in his straps, eyes closed and mouth open. He'd pissed himself, not unusual under these circumstances. Beyond him the accountant was leaning over his keyboard. She noted his thinning hair; he was using fiber to thicken it rather than paying for restorative treatment. Cheapskate. She sensed the disappointment her host felt when she left the dead pilot. Once they'd started live targeting, she'd been surprised how quickly her hosts knew when the body they were sitting on was alive, and when it became potential maggot food. An hour passed, the accountant continued working. A voice broke the silence.

"*Low fuel, low fuel, low fuel,*" the AI spoke over the public-address system. Mary wondered how long it had been trying to get a response from the pilot, via his sprite. The voice was middle-class, female, English, possibly the pilot's wife or girlfriend.

The accountant looked up and noted that the pilot hadn't moved. He looked at his watch. They should have landed twenty minutes ago.

"What was that Capitan?" he asked. When there was no response, he tapped the pilot on the right shoulder and repeated his question. Still there was no response, he shook his shoulder, gently at first and then with more animation.

"*Choose alternate airfield, choose alternate airfield,*" a chime began to sound regularly.

Mary saw that the accountant was sweating now. He pressed his finger onto the pilot's neck, searching for a pulse, and when he couldn't find one he tried jabbing his finger in again and again.

"Madre de Dios," he said.

Now this will be interesting, Mary thought, feeling a thrill of anticipation. She wondered how he would handle the situation. He might even try to land the plane himself. That would be worth watching.

The yoke in front of the pilot shook noisily as the AI attempted to wake him.

"*Pilot resume manual control, pilot resume manual control,*" the alarm was louder and more insistent.

The accountant became more agitated, and pulled a satellite phone from the inside pocket of his jacket, held it up and said, "Don Roberto." Mary heard the ring tone.

"Ola, who is this?" said a voice. "I am trying to concentrate on a difficult putt."

"It is Matias, Don Roberto. I have a problem."

"Que pasa?"

"Don Roberto, I am flying in a plane and the pilot he is dead, I do not know what to do. We must crash soon. I do not know where we are."

"Don't worry my friend, these planes they have clever computers, they can fly themselves. You do not need a lazy gringo pilot, just relax and let the computer look after you." There was a pause, and Matias heard muttered conversation in the background. "Did you finish the business with our European friends?"

"Si Patron, I have the details of the accounts here. I planned to send an encrypted copy of them to you as soon as I reached Amsterdam."

"Tell them to me now Matias."

"But, Patron, this is bad security, it would be better for you to help me, and let me send the account numbers securely, after I have landed."

"Tell them to me now, Matias, and then we will help you. My personal pilot is here with me, he will speak to your plane's computer, and talk you down to a safe landing. Do not worry my friend, give me the numbers, all will be well."

"Fuel critical, fuel critical," said the AI.

Matias recited the details of a dozen accounts, from memory.

"That is all Patron, what shall I do now?" There was a continuous tone from his hand set. The turbine engine began to wind down, the propeller continued to turn, but more slowly, and the nose of the plane dipped.

"Automatic landing sequence engaged, searching for suitable landing site," the voice of the AI was passionless. The accountant threw away his phone, reached into a side pocket of his jacket and withdrew a set of white Rosary beads. He stared unblinkingly at the back of the pilot's head and began to mutter, while telling them through his fingers.

"Dios te salve, Maria, llena eres de gracia,

el Senor es contigo."

"Mayday, Mayday, Mayday this is BritAir Flight 235 logged for Schiphol."

The AI switched off the alarms and continued to give details of their position and altitude. It began playing a recording of the Flower Duet from the opera Lakme. It was programmed to offer soothing music if turbulence disturbed the composure of its passengers.

"Bendita tu eres entre todas las mujeres,

Y bendito es el fruto de tu vientre Jesus."

Mary was aware of the relative quiet, now that the engine and alarms had stopped. She ought to bump out, her part in the mission had been over as soon as the pilot died. Instead, she took off from the dashboard and let her host perform the tricky maneuver of flipping over, and landing upside down on the cockpit ceiling. She'd practiced doing it herself, it was only a half barrel-roll, after all, but she didn't want to risk missing the excitement. Her all-round vision allowed her to take a professional interest in the AI's attempt to land the aircraft, and to watch the accountant's increasing panic at the same time. The air became more turbulent closer to the ground, and the plane pitched and yawed. The accountant groaned at every jolt. As she watched him experiencing his last few moments of life, her host rubbed its front legs together as if with glee.

"*All passengers check harness. All passengers check harness. Brace, brace, brace.*"

"Santa Maria, Madre de Dios,

ruega por nostoros pecadores,

ahora y en la hora de nuestra muerte."

They should have made a successful landing on the empty farm track near Kiel, that the AI had chosen, but a broken telephone pole severed the starboard wing and spun them around into a rocky outcrop, just before the wheels touched the ground.

The plane cartwheeled and burst into flame as the vapor in the fuel tanks exploded. Mary had tucked her host into a crevice between two sections of the ceiling, but the sections shifted and trapped her. She saw the attempts of the accountant as, enveloped in an excruciating conflagration, he struggled frenziedly to release his harness. Damage to her external microphones meant she couldn't hear his screams. The beads from the broken Rosary flew around the cabin, bouncing off windows and walls as if trying to make their own panic-stricken escapes.

At the back of the passenger compartment Mary glimpsed something rounded, shiny and liquid swelling in one of the seats, but her drone lost vision at that moment, its eyes seared by the heat.

The bird crap on the wing camera lens had obscured the AI's view to the right during landing, it didn't see the broken telegraph pole. As the starboard wing smashed into it, the plane spun around and started to cartwheel. The AI battled to save its craft as it plunged across the rocky field, leaving a trail of flaming debris. It triggered those fire extinguishers over which it still had control, but died as its processor fried in the fireball. Its last conscious act was to eject a capsule, containing all its data and a copy of its processor state, several hundred meters into the air. It fell to earth well away from the flames and lay, flashing, its position also marked by its hi-vis parachute. Unlike Matias, the AI had died confident of resurrection.

As her host crisped and burned Mary was 'back in the room.' She cried out as a series of small convulsions racked her. Ruth was at her side, eager to help, but the software quickly damped the tremors. After a few minutes and a glass of water she was ready to resume life as a human being.

"Fucking Hell, that was intense," she said, still shivering as the shock wore off, "much worse than a simulator."

"You shouldn't do this to yourself, it's not good for you, you'll burnout, or get sick, or both." Ruth had followed Mary's progress throughout the mission using her observer's VR headset.

"Yes, but I love the work," said Mary, knowing the irony would be lost on Ruth.

Ruth removed Mary's visor and gently sponged her face. Mary lay back panting, her eyes closed; Ruth began to unzip Mary's sensuit and to sponge the bare skin of her neck and shoulders. As Ruth peeled the upper part of the suit off, Mary sat up and swung her legs off the couch. She noticed a look of intense disappointment on Ruth's face. Holding the suit about her, she walked towards the changing room. She was lonely, but she wasn't that lonely.

That night Mary's dreams were dark and terrible. In the morning, she couldn't remember their content, but she saw that she'd run out of sleeping tablets. Her mouth was dry and her head ached. She was full of doubts. Was it worth killing an innocent young pilot to get the product that SIS and the CIA wanted? "Just following orders" was no defense for illegal and immoral behavior. Why had she stayed onboard to watch the plane crash and the accountant's death? It was voyeuristic, unhealthy. Sitting in her tiny kitchen, drinking coffee, she drafted a request for a posting back to England with her old squadron, and pinged it to

Abrahams. She didn't care about the consequences, the humdrum world of Royalty Protection would suit her very well and she needed to be with Patrick permanently. She'd had enough of killing, they'd have to find somebody else could do it.

The next day Patrick was in touch. "They've offered me a job at Langley," he said. "It's a two-year secondment as a senior software engineer. They need someone with security clearance to work on your drone control system, I guess they want to keep it in the family. I assume you approve?"

Mary realized that she'd been outmaneuvered; it looked as if she was staying at Langley after all.

Chapter Thirty

USA 2051

Mary watched as Peter Abrahams gestured at the vscreen in front of him. He appeared to be working on one of his pet projects. It was late, the office was empty, he was semi-retired and kept his own hours these days, and apparently this worried the powers that be. She was lodged in a corner near the ceiling, engaged in what was euphemistically called 'routine security' but was in fact spying on friends. Of course, it begged the question, who was spying on her?

A flash of light reflected in one of the office windows distracted her. She suddenly became aware that a figure was standing in the doorway to the main work area. It was covered by a shining multicolored membrane which disappeared after a moment and revealed a casually dressed, middle aged man. He walked into the office and stopped opposite Abrahams.

"Hello, Peter," he said smiling, and extending his hand.

Abrahams shook it automatically, staring speechlessly at the newcomer. Mary saw the apparent solidity of the handshake. Not a hologram then. What was going on?

"Bloody Hell...." exclaimed Abrahams.

"Come on, Peter, you're not that doddery are you, don't you remember me? My name is Martin Riley; I'm the inventor of time travel," he laughed.

Abrahams continued to stare at the newcomer, "I know who you are, Martin, but you died in a car crash forty years ago. How can you be alive, you don't look a day over fifty?"

"Perhaps if you think about it for a while you'll work it out, Peter. Do you mind if I sit down?" He looked around, "Well, it's nice to be back in familiar surroundings, glad to see you're still with the old firm, Peter. You look good for a man in your seventies, the rejuv drugs must be working, or have you led a blameless life?" he laughed again. "Any chance of a drink?"

Whoever he is, he's enjoying this, thought Mary.

She watched as, looking dazed, Abrahams opened a drawer and pulled out a bottle and two glasses. He placed them on the desk, hardly taking his eyes off the visitor.

Riley picked up the bottle and examined the label.

"Real Scotch, the ersatz stuff is good, but knowing it's just a rearrangement of molecules that never went near an oak barrel makes a difference somehow. This'll be the first I didn't make myself for over five years." He poured a finger of whiskey into a glass and raised it towards Mary's corner of the ceiling. "Slangevar," he said smiling directly at her as he downed it in one; he sat back for a moment eyes closed, his face a picture of contentment. "Oh, very smooth, much smoother than my rocket fuel," he said.

Did he know she was there? Mary asked herself.

"Have you come to any conclusions yet, Peter?"

"How can you still be alive?" asked Abrahams sitting on the opposite side of the desk. He looked as puzzled as Mary felt. "Now I think about it, they never recovered your body. We buried an empty coffin."

Riley poured himself another, Abrahams had ignored his, Riley sipped this time.

"I know, I was there, strictly as an observer of course. Farina took me to see it, what a strange experience."

"Farina?"

"She was the one who extracted me from my car, after our employers blew it off the Woodrow Wilson Bridge."

"Extracted, who extracted you, why?"

"Time travelers, they wanted to talk to me about our meddling with the Timestream."

"So where have you been for the last fifty years?"

Good question, thought Mary, if you are who you say you are, where have you been?

"The future, Peter, they took me far into the future. For me, it's only been five years or so. But now they've sent me back to sort out the mess you and I have made, and I need your help to do it. We have to make a Retrospective Temporal Adjustment. We have to realign the Timestream. Millions of lives are at stake; in fact, the whole future of mankind depends on us." He put his feet up on the desk and made a gesture of helplessness, he reached forward to retrieve his glass, and gave a wry smile.

Abrahams looked shocked. "We can't do that, what will happen to us all, what about our families, Martin? If we change the past what will the altered present be like?"

"We'll all still have a life; it's just that it'll be a different life. The Commonwealth has convinced me that we must do this, we've no choice."

"What Commonwealth, the British Commonwealth?"

"No, Peter, the Commonwealth of the future, the world government. Our tamperings have put their whole civilization at risk. We have to undo the damage we've done.

"How far back do we have to go, to make our RTA?"

"About fifty years, apparently it was when we prevented Princess Diana and Dodi Fayed's car crash that the Timestream became seriously distorted."

"I'm sorry, Martin, you were my mentor, you guided my early career, but I can't help you do this. You're asking me to destroy the world as we know it. It's all too much, I can't take it all in, I need time to think."

"Yes, it's not easy. I have something prepared to help you." He stood and walked around behind Abraham's chair and placed his hands on his shoulders. To Mary's amazement they both became momentarily iridescent, then disappeared.

Mary realized that she was out of her depth. A dead man appearing and disappearing, people from the future, it was as bad as when she first tried to get her head around TM. Altering the past was a whole new ball game, she needed time to think. After bumping out, she didn't upload the recording to the registry, but told her sprite to load it into her personal log. She needed to show it to Patrick.

The next day Mary was off duty. Drinking coffee in her lounge, she stared out of the window, took another pull on her vapourette and felt the tension go out of her shoulders.

"You have a visitor ma'am," said her sprite.

"Who is it?" she asked. There was a momentary pause.

Her sprite relayed a voice to her ear. "Hello, Mary, it's Peter Abrahams. Sorry to bother you at home, I need a word in private."

Why am I not surprised, she thought, and went to greet him.

Abrahams sat in an armchair drinking coffee. "The thing is, Mary I need your help. It's complicated."

"Let's take a walk in my garden," she said, "There's a lovely show of fuchsias." They walked on the lawn surrounding the apartment building. Mary didn't grow fuchsias.

Abrahams whispered, "I've had a visit from an old friend, my mentor actually, a man called Martin Riley. You must have heard of him, he invented TM, he used to run the science team at Langley."

"I thought he died in a traffic accident, decades ago," said Mary. "Drove off a bridge into the Potomac didn't he? You told me about him when I first came to Langley."

"Well yes, but apparently he survived. Look, Mary, I know it sounds far-fetched, but he says he was abducted by people from an organization called 'the Commonwealth.' They're the world government of the future. I know it seems crazy but I can prove it."

Mary had already decided to let him off the hook.

"You don't need to," she said, "I was on duty last night, spying on you. The bosses seem to be worried about your 'pet projects' and what other uses you're finding for Temporal Displacement."

"Well, all my ideas are peaceful: mining, manufacturing, medical. The Government only ever seems to be interested in weapons and security. But anyway, did you see Martin Riley arrive?"

"I saw how he came, and how you both left and I've kept the recording to myself. They'll notice eventually, but you're safe just for the moment. So, where did you go?"

"He took me into the future." Abrahams looked at her as if he was expecting a rejoinder but Mary remained silent. "I met a woman called Farina, and they showed me Metrotowers, a necklace of huge memory modules girdling the planet, enormous space vehicles, Earth's rings. It was amazing."

"Did you meet any 'future people,' what were they like?"

"No, I couldn't leave the vehicle; I might have altered the Timestream because I belong here, not there. Farina told me she's some sort of artificial person, although she seemed human. According to her we should never have invented TM. It was a fluke, something they didn't know about until she was researching social history in our era. Our activities over the last few decades have put a severe strain on the Timestream; we've bent it out of shape, and now we have to realign it by reversing our first significant intervention."

"Slow down, Peter, you're gabbling. So, you observed all this from a closed vehicle, you didn't touch any of it. Did this Farina have any special powers?"

"Not as far as I could tell, she seemed completely human."

"Maybe because she is human. Why can't these Commonwealth people do the realigning themselves?" she asked.

"They don't want to interfere with their past, they'd rather leave it to us because they already know that we did it, if you see what I mean. 'If it's not broken don't fix it,' isn't that what they say?" He shrugged but she sensed his fear, his hands were trembling. He hadn't mentioned the massive effect their actions would have on the present. "I realize it sounds unbelievable," Abrahams repeated. He began rubbing his hands together.

"I'm not as surprised as you might expect, Peter" she said. "The thing that originally stretched my credulity was your explanation of TM years ago, when you first recruited me. It's all been downhill since then, just one shocking discovery after another. But I still wonder if this is some sort of hoax."

"Martin needs to talk to you. He says he needs a drone pilot and wants to meet you tomorrow. What I don't understand is why there wasn't a huge explosion as he materialized from the future. The quantum matrix should have tried to neutralize him, like when we do our Temporal Displacements."

"Did you ask him about it?"

"He just fobbed me off, said it was 'too much detail, Peter, let's concentrate on the bigger issues.' "

Abrahams left soon afterwards, she watched as his car drove off, taking him back to the lab. Mary still needed to speak to Patrick; it had been too late when she got home last night, he was asleep, but he'd be back in a couple of hours.

She heard Patrick arrive soon after five o'clock. He sniffed the air in the apartment, "So it's a takeaway tonight, is it?" he asked, smiling as he grabbed her around the waist and kissed her. He saw the fly swat lying on the coffee table and became more serious. "Are you okay?" he asked.

"Sorry, my mind hasn't been on cooking," she gently disengaged. "There's something I want to show you. I recorded this last night. Don't talk, just watch it all the way through, and then we'll talk."

Mary played the recording. Patrick became more intent as it progressed. When it finished he didn't speak but restarted it and watched Riley's arrival in slow motion. He stopped it again where Riley seemed to be toasting Mary's health and then watched the disappearance of the two scientists in ultra-slow mode, reversing and replaying it several times.

"If it wasn't you who'd recorded this, I'd assume it was fake," he said.

She told him about Abraham's visit that afternoon.

"Are you going to report this?"

"What, a man with a message from the far future arrived in Abraham's office, a man who is supposed to have died fifty years ago? I'd be grounded and back in psych eval in a second."

"What about the video file?"

"They'd court-martial me for faking evidence."

"What should we do?" he asked.

"Well, it's a suicide mission if we do what they want. If I go back and change the past, everything will change in the present. We might be dead, we might not be born, we might marry other people. I'm just not doing it."

"But you do it all the time."

"No, don't you see the difference? We make changes in the present that alter things a week or so later. I told you how we prevented the destruction of Central London, for instance. This is different, we'll be changing our past and that will affect our present in unpredictable ways."

"Yes, I can understand that, I wasn't thinking. Sorry."

"They want a meeting; I'll insist that you're included. If I was going to do the mission, I'd need an orderly."

Abrahams had rented a hotel suite. There was no sign of Riley. Mary examined every inch of the rooms and sealed the bottoms of doors and ventilator grills with masking tape. She knew she looked crazy with her fly swat and tape but didn't care.

"We'll suffocate at this rate with no fresh air coming in," complained Abrahams.

"Then it'll encourage everybody to be brief. We can adjourn when we start going blue."

Abrahams was making tea for them all when the wardrobe door opened and Martin Riley stepped out.

"I've always wanted to do that," he said. "I loved CS Lewis when I was a kid." He smiled and then became serious. "Pardon my levity. What's he doing here?" he pointed at Patrick.

"Mary needs him," said Abrahams.

Riley nodded at Mary, "I'm sure Peter has told you who I am," he said.

So, no introductions then, she thought.

"I would've liked to see you materialize," said Patrick. Mary knew he was still suspicious even though he'd seen the recording.

"Best to keep your distance when I arrive," said Riley, "not so dangerous when I leave." He looked around at Mary's security measures. "Let's get on with this while there's still oxygen in the room. Peter has explained the reason for the mission, we have to realign the Timestream and save the future of mankind. It's the most important thing that any of you will ever do."

"How will we do it?" asked Patrick.

"We have to go back and stop SIS from replacing Diana and Dodi's driver in 1997? We need Henri Paul, to be at the wheel, the French police said he was drunk and that was why they crashed. The accident will happen as it did originally, the Timestream will realign, end of story. Pity they weren't wearing their seat belts. Clunk, click and all that." The others looked blank. "Sorry, old TV advert."

"How will we stop the SIS from replacing the driver?" asked Abrahams.

"By stopping their agent from delivering the instructions to his asset at the Ritz," said Riley.

"What instructions?" asked Patrick.

"The instruction to replace the driver," said Riley impatiently.

"So, we'll assassinate this SIS man I suppose." said Mary. "Always such subtlety."

"Yes, your area of expertise, I believe," said Riley.

Mary flinched, "So how are we going to manage it?" she asked.

"By sending a 'packet' upstream into the past," said Abrahams. We need to target it, and that's where you come in."

"I'll take a fly drone in the time capsule and release it in Paris, back in 1997," said Riley. He looked at Mary, "You'll be piloting it."

"I don't see what's in it for us," she said, her dislike of Riley coming to the fore. "If we do what you ask, we sign our own death warrants. We might survive the changes but we'll be different people. The people we are now will no longer exist."

"I was going to appeal to your better natures," said Riley sarcastically, "tell you it's for the good of mankind, but I suspected I wouldn't convince you. However, I have an ace up my sleeve." He reached into a pocket and removed a cylindrical box and tipped the contents onto a coffee table. It was a delicate net of silvery metal threads. He spread it out. "I can copy your brain states and take them forward to the future with me. That way you get the best of both worlds; you'll still have the chance of a life in the new present, but there'll be the certainty of life, as you are now, in the future."

"Nice try," said Mary. "How can a 'brain state' be alive? Are you going to give us new bodies? Will they be clunky robots, or will you grow them for us in tanks? Maybe you'll give us the bodies of erased criminals, if you still have them in your perfect world of the future. How could you prove you've even taken a copy of a brain state? It sounds like snake oil to me."

Riley continued, "The process isn't difficult to understand, it's digital, but at a much higher resolution than is possible in the 21st century. We take the copy, and then move it into the Commonwealth's Tower

Memory. They have copies of people that might be useful to them, scientists, mathematicians, musicians, politicians. They're called 'Incorporeals.' They even have a section for war leaders in case there's ever need of them. Most of them are inactive, but they've made an exception of Sun Tzu, he's active and, I'm told, surprisingly likable, plays a lot of Go. Genghis Khan is left sleeping, he's too dangerous, they're afraid he might take the place over."

Mary was confused, she wasn't sure whether he was joking or not.

"What sort of world do these 'Incorporeals' inhabit?" asked Patrick. "We've been talking about virtual living for decades."

"They make up their own separate environments, like lucid dreaming, but much more real. There's a common meeting area configured as a park with trees and plants and guest houses."

"And fluffy bunny rabbits," said Mary. "Oh, fuck off, with your Tower Memory and your Genghis Khan. It's bollocks; I don't believe a word of it. Prove it."

"I can't," said Riley. "They've taken a copy of me, because I too will disappear when we push the button on this. I'll update my file at the same time as I copy all of you."

"Can you contact this virtual version of yourself?" asked Patrick, still interested despite Mary's derision. "Have you ever spoken to it?"

"No, it's inactive; they don't allow active duplicates, although they keep themselves backed up regularly."

"How regularly?" asked Patrick his professional interest piqued.

"They do it once a month, unless they've done something notable or are planning to do something dangerous. It gives them a different attitude to life; they take more risks, although nobody wants to die early and go to Tower Memory before their time."

"What if we refuse?" asked Mary, she wouldn't be diverted by Riley's 'future' talk.

"Look," said Riley impatiently, "if you don't do it we'll find another pilot. Nobody will believe your story if you blab, and then after the Realignment, as far as you and Patrick are concerned, it's 'game over.' Do I make myself clear?" Mary said nothing. "You two only need to worry about yourselves, my children live in this reality, along with their children, my grandchildren. Don't you think I'm concerned for their welfare?"

"I refuse to kill anybody," said Mary. "Whatever your plan is, I'm not committing another murder, no matter how you try to sell it."

"Look, Mary," said Riley, "we need you to target a particular SIS agent, but I can show you his death certificate. He dies of natural causes, a massive heart attack, two weeks later. We'll take a small part of his life, but it's collateral damage, you're used to the idea in the military. Given the importance of what we're trying to achieve here, two weeks taken from one life is not a big sacrifice. The agent knew the risks when he signed up to the Secret Intelligence Service."

Mary remembered the young pilot in the drug cartel incident. He hadn't deserved to die, he hadn't signed up for military duty, but she'd still gone ahead with the mission.

"Patrick and I need to talk," she said. Riley didn't reply, he stood up and walked to the center of the room.

He paused as an iridescent "skin" enveloped him, moments later he disappeared. There was a pop, as air filled the space he had occupied.

"I find that disappearing trick a convincing argument," said Patrick. "I vote we go ahead."

"Yes," said Mary wearily, "I suppose you're right. We've no choice."

"How are you progressing, Martin?" asked Farina. She was waiting in the time capsule as he slid through the membrane.

He sighed, "I'm having to hold their hands. The drone pilot, Mary Lee, is dragging her feet. Her partner will go along with whatever she decides, he's curious about future technology and that'll help us. Abrahams is on side, we impressed him with our 'brief tour of the future.' Anyway, they can have an hour to talk it over."

"Do they realize that their personal existences will end if they go ahead?"

"I'm not laboring the point with them but I'm sure they do. I've explained Incorporeal living. Anyway, I need a break; that Mary Lee is a pain in the arse."

"Would you like a massage, Martin. Perhaps we could make love?"

"God, you say the nicest things, Farina, and it may be the last opportunity we have."

The chairs reconfigured themselves as a double bed.

Afterwards, he lay and rubbed his temples. "Tell me, Farina, what's it like being a Synthetic?"

"That is a subjective question, Martin, you need to be more specific."

"You eat, you drink, you enjoy making love, and that's a pretty good Turing test. You seem happy. Can you reproduce?"

"No, Martin, we cannot reproduce, and we only eat and drink to make humans more comfortable in our company. It is a form of socialization. My repair and energy needs are more efficiently managed than your own, as are other aspects of my design. I can exist without oxygen for a long period, control the growth of my hair and fingernails or even change my apparent ethnicity." She paused and Riley watched as her hair, skin and eye color began to darken. "Increasing my melanin levels is relatively easy; changing facial features takes hours. I do not suffer moods but I can develop emotional attachments. I have allowed myself a deep attachment to you."

"That's nice of you, Farina, I like you too, but I will disappear soon if the Realignment goes to plan."

"Yes, Martin, and then I will delete the attachment and remember you fondly. Sometimes I will replay our happy times together, but I will not miss you. This is a major difference between us. Estella treated you badly, but you continue to feel an attachment to her. It will take a long time for the attachment to fade. It makes you unhappy because it is an emotion with no positive outcome. Humans dwell on the past even though they cannot change it. It is inefficient, but that is the way you are made." She stroked his face and gave him a sad look. "Poor Martin, you are a slave to your emotions, like all your race. Except the psychopaths, but they are exceptional."

Riley felt patronized, he sensed her sympathy but realized that she was not human, she was a different species. He reached up and held her wrist, something was missing.

"You will not feel a pulse, Martin, my circulatory system is distributed. Like the Tin Man, I do not have a heart."

He paused for a moment. Soon he would need to say goodbye and something had been playing on his mind.

"Farina, er, I've been meaning to ask you something; it's about the incident in the bathroom, after the fight in the 'Bear and Penguin,' do you remember?"

"Yes, Martin, I remember everything."

"Could you delete it if you wanted to? I'm still ashamed of my behavior, I don't know what came over me, I'm so sorry."

"You were angry, Martin, you were scared and hurt and you blamed me for putting you at risk. Your emotions were in turmoil, that was why you threatened to hit me."

He shuddered, he had nearly punched a helpless woman, it didn't matter that she was a Synthetic, it was still wrong.

"I can delete it from my memory, Martin, if that is what you wish, and nobody will ever know it happened except you, but that is the real problem. The incident does not disturb me because you were acting out of character and at the mercy of your emotions. I forgive you, Martin. The greater problem is whether you can forgive yourself."

"I'll be leaving soon, Farina."

"Yes, Martin, I understand the consequences of the Realignment."

"Will we meet again? Will you be able to visit my copy in City Memory?"

"I'm sure we will meet again, Martin."

"You've done so much for me since you rescued me from the Woodrow Wilson Bridge. I wish there was something I could do for you, a friendly gesture to show my appreciation. Is there anything? Flowers, chocolates?"

She laughed, "Well, Martin, I would love a foot massage, it is a slight weakness we Synthetics have, we use it as part of our socializing. It will be another experience I can replay when I remember you."

"I can see that total recall is a big improvement on a photo album," he said.

Chapter Thirty-One

USA 2051

Riley stepped out of the bathroom in the hotel suite again. The other three were still there. Mary lay on one of the beds, her eyes closed. Patrick and Abrahams were drinking tea.

Mary sat up blinking.

"Right, let's get on with it," said Riley, without a greeting or acknowledgement. "We need to make the copies now. The copies won't remember anything after this, but if all goes well there shouldn't be much to remember."

"And our personal data?" asked Patrick.

"Your sprite's data files will be included," said Riley. "Don't worry, you won't lose your digital legacy, all those clips and photos."

Mary sat in a chair and Riley arranged the gold-colored mesh over her head.

"The process takes about ten minutes, it stores the information in the mesh. Here," he handed out meshes to the other two. "I'm not sure whether it's safe to talk or move while the copy's being made. For all I know, one cough and you lose your piano lessons or something, I advise you to sit quietly."

They sat immobile, the meshes on their heads, *like a group under the dryers in a hairdressing salon*, thought Mary. She had an urge to read a magazine and flipped out her vscreen. Riley stared across at her, she felt his silent disapproval. She didn't care, he was brusque and bad mannered. Crossing swords with him had not led to the mutual respect that such confrontations often engender. She couldn't stand the man

One after another the meshes vibrated to signal that the process was complete. Riley collected them and placed them in their cylindrical box.

"How strange to think that I have all four of our lives in my jacket pocket," he said, "such vulnerability." Mary didn't like his self-satisfied smile, and decided to stay on the right side of him while he had it in his power to leave her and Patrick behind. She was finding the idea of a world belonging solely to the two of them very appealing.

"Patrick and I will be together, won't we?" Mary had suddenly pictured them living separate virtual lives.

"Yes," said Riley, "you can share your world with whoever is willing to share theirs with you. You can even combine data to make offspring that inherit traits from both of you, but you need permission. A license to breed." He laughed.

"So, we're backed up," said Patrick. "Why am I still scared?"

Riley did his disappearing act, the other three took a car to the TM lab.

"Hi guys." Doug the technician looked up and smiled as they walked in. He was sitting at a workstation in the Temporal Displacement room wearing a tee shirt sporting the slogan, "Wanted dead or alive – Schrödinger's cat." The tee shirt, like the joke, had worn thin. He was now in his late sixties, Mary was struck by how old and unattractive his grey stubble made him look.

Doug looked from one to the other of the group. Mary remembered that he had a talent for being around when anything important or interesting was happening.

He looked at Abrahams, "Funny thing Doc, there hasn't been a peep from downstream for a couple a days. Either there's a glitch with the software, or something nasty is about to happen." He laughed, then, as his gaze moved beyond Abrahams, he gaped. "Jesus Christ, it's Martin Riley," he said, as the fourth member of the team walked into the laboratory from the direction of the rest room.

"Hello Doug," Riley smiled, "I'm surprised that you can still remember me, you were just a whippersnapper when I went off the Woodrow Wilson Bridge. Not such a long time for me as it's been for you, of course." He looked at the others, "The copies are safe, Farina has installed them." They paused for a moment as the significance sank in, then Mary and Patrick moved towards the drone control room.

Doug sat looking from one to the other. "I need a comfort break," he said.

"In a minute Doug," said Abrahams. "I want you to set up a Temporal Displacement for me, here are the coordinates." Abrahams handed him a note.

Doug began to tap the figures on the vscreen; he kept looking over at Riley as if he couldn't believe his eyes. He stopped. "This is a retroactive adjustment, we're not allowed to do this, who gave you permission?" he looked, from one to the other. "This will cause drastic changes; it's far too risky." He stood up, "I need to report this to my superiors."

Riley walked over and placed a hand on his shoulder. Doug slowly sat back in his chair,

Riley leant down to whisper into his ear. "There's nothing to worry about, you sit and relax, everything will be all right." Doug sat unmoving, staring straight ahead, his eyes blank and unfocused.

"I'd love to know how you did that," said Abrahams as he leaned over Doug and finished setting up the TD.

"It's a neuro suppression field," said Riley smiling and pointing to his temple. "It's all about the implants."

Chapter Thirty-Two

USA 2051

"You have the drone?" asked Abrahams.

Riley held up a transparent box and showed its dark occupant standing head down on one side. "Yes, I have it."

"I assume you'll both be insulated from the quantum matrix when you materialize."

Riley nodded.

Abrahams had finished tapping in the coordinates. Doug sat motionless, blinking occasionally. "It's the quiet ones you have to watch," said Abrahams looking down at his underling. "I used to wonder if there was a CIA spy among us, but I never suspected Doug. With hindsight, it's obvious; he was always there when the team met up for a beer or one of us had a party. He was there, in the places they couldn't easily watch us with their bugs and drones."

The two scientists paused, they turned to look at each other, and then shook hands firmly, both knew that this was 'a moment.'

"Best of luck for the Future," said Abrahams, smiling. Riley nodded, then walked towards the drone control room. Abrahams heard a brief, low conversation between him and Mary. A few moments later, there was a pop, as Riley disappeared into the time capsule. Abrahams turned to look at the vscreens.

Mary finished suiting up and Patrick helped make the final adjustments. She lay on the couch with her head raised. They held hands and looked at each other.

"I love you, Mary," he said. "I wish we'd had a family, brought up kids, retired, grown old, just the usual stuff, we would have been happy. Maybe we still will be." Tears welled in his eyes. Mary nodded several times, her mouth was clamped shut, she couldn't trust herself to speak. They'd said their goodbyes the previous night and she didn't want to prolong the agony. She reached for her visor, put in on and lay back, her tears hidden from Patrick by the visor's reflective surface.

As Mary switched to drone mode, her perceptions changed, her vision became pixelated, still clear but much wider. She no longer had the forward focus of a hunter, now she had the panoramic view of the hunted. She felt her own limbs and body as a ghostly presence at Langley, but her main awareness was of her host's six legs and two wings. Riley had taken it back upstream to 1997, somehow, he was facilitating the connection between host and pilot across fifty years of the Timestream. He released her in the Jardin des Tuileries, in Paris, where the SIS handler would meet his asset.

She knew the direction he'd come from, so she landed on the trunk of a tree near the Orangery in the western corner of the park.

Ah, she thought, here he comes now. He would have covered his distinctive white hair with a hat, if he suspected the meet wasn't safe. It was normal tradecraft. He looked healthy enough, athletic for his age, he didn't walk like a man two weeks away from a massive heart attack. Mary flew to the top of his head, as he passed her, and carefully crawled down through his hair, stopping close to the scalp. She paused for a moment then triggered the targeting signal.

"Target acquired by temporal displacement equipment," whispered the voice of her sprite.

"Goodbye Patrick," she forced the words from the mouth of her Langley self and felt Patrick's ghostly grip on her hand tighten.

"Packet arriving in three, two, one....."

And they were gone.

Chapter Thirty-Three

String Memory 4403

Over a timeless period, Martin Riley became aware, not of his surroundings but of himself. Not of his physical body but of his mind, floating dimensionless and without disturbance from sensory inputs. It was dark, he was nowhere.

He had no way of measuring the passage of time, there was just the slow streaming of his thoughts and memories forming and coalescing. He was relaxed, safe.

A voice spoke to him. It was genderless, accent free, with a pleasant timbre.

"Hello, Doctor Riley, are you comfortable?"

"Yes," he said, although he had no sensation of lips or tongue or breath, "who are you?"

"I am a construct of String Memory; my purpose is to aid your restoration and awakening."

"So, I'm in String Memory. I must be the copy from Langley."

"That is correct. You are conscious and functioning, but you do not have a body or a world yet, you are incorporeal and amorphous. My task is to help you to make a new body and a new environment. We can start now if you wish, there are many possibilities."

"I suppose it would be sensible to begin with something conventional."

"Sound reasoning, Doctor Riley, and you should know that you can alter your appearance later, when you are more experienced, if that is your wish. Which gender would you like to be? I can offer a broad spectrum."

"I'll stick with my previous orientation, one hundred percent male."

"My records show eighty-two percent. I recommend you stay with this at first; you might find one hundred percent difficult to deal with. Please describe the new body you require; I have extensive files which I can show you if it will help."

"I liked my last one, although now I think about it, I'd like straighter teeth, bigger calf muscles and nicer feet."

"I will make a slight modification to your internal body image. What physical age would you prefer?"

"Oh thirty; everything was working well then." He had the familiar sense of an anatomy enclosing him, he had limits.

"What next, Doctor Riley?"

"Light, I'd like to be able to see." He became aware of a diffuse radiance and himself standing naked in it. All around was grey and formless, like the outlook from the time capsule. He moved and stretched, enjoying the sensation of occupying his new body, learning its limits. He stared at his hands and flexed his fingers. "I didn't expect it to be as real as this." He tried walking and jumping.

"All sensory input to the brain is electrical or chemical, Dr Riley. A human being experiences the inputs as external, but they are internal once they enter the nervous system. It is easy to mimic those signals when the 'brain' is a digital compilation, like yours."

"Who was it said, 'Our lives are a fabric of lies?' No never mind, don't look it up, let's concentrate on the job in hand."

"Please describe the world you wish to inhabit. Remember, as with your body, this will be a first attempt, we can change it later."

"I've always wanted to live on a tropical island. Sandy beaches, blue seas, coconut palms, warm weather."

He was standing under a palm tree, on a beach of white sand, with a turquoise sea to his left. Gentle waves broke a few meters out from the strand. He felt relieved to be somewhere familiar.

"I suppose you're going to ask me which eight gramophone records I would like to have with me," he said and laughed. There was silence for several seconds.

"Ah, yes, I see, Dr Riley, an entertainment from your past, most amusing." He guessed, from the pause, that the reference hadn't been easy to find. "You can have as many gramophone records as you like, and a gramophone to play them on if that is your wish." An old-fashioned phonograph with a winding handle and a brass horn materialized on a table in front of him, and then disappeared in a cloud of tiny 3d pixels.

Riley walked, enjoying the gritty feel of the wet sand on the soles of his feet and in between his toes. "Shorts," he said, and there were shorts. "You've forgotten the birds," and there were seagulls wheeling in the sky, parrots squawked in the trees.

"What shall I call you?" he asked.

"What would you like to call me?"

"I'll call you 'Friday,' I'd like you to be female and can you try to be just a little less precise in your speech pattern? Call me Martin. I need a house."

"Okay, Martin, tell me about your new house."

"I'd like it to be Scandinavian style, wooden, with big windows, a veranda, and a log fire for rainy days. Site it over there, about twenty meters back from the sea." The conversation continued as he and Friday constructed Riley's new world.

Several days and many details later Riley asked Friday about the physical world.

"Tolland arranged for your insertions into String Memory. Would you like to see where you're installed? It might give you a better perspective."

Riley nodded, and he was standing in space far above the Earth, looking down on the outer rings, the debris from the Collision. The positions of the Metrotowers were marked but they were too small to see from this distance. Above the equator, and inside the rings, was a line of white spheres, stretching in a long curve around the planet. They were separate but perfectly aligned, and all rotated slowly in synchronization. Perspective diminished them as they disappeared behind the belly of the planet. He thought they looked wonderful. "I've seen these before, but they weren't finished then."

"This is a simulation, Martin; the String still isn't complete, but many of the spheres are in place, you have been installed in one of them. To give you an idea of scale, each is a kilometer in diameter. Eventually there will be fifty thousand of them."

"The rotation is to even out the temperature, as the sun shines on them, I suppose. What's inside them?"

"Fibers, Martin, an uncountable number of interconnected quantum fibers."

"Okay, I've seen enough for now. I'd like to meet up with my companions."

"I'll make the arrangements," said Friday.

"What about Tolland and Farina?"

"You can visit them, as an incorporeal presence, by arrangement."

The next day, Riley had made a camp fire and was standing in the shallows, trying to spear a fish that was avoiding his attentions. "Would you like me to make it slower, Martin," asked Friday. Before he could refuse her offer, he'd speared it.

He lifted it out of the water. "It has to wriggle and bleed a little, Friday, it doesn't even smell fishy."

"Sorry, Martin," she said, "I'll attend to the details. Ah, your companions are ready to meet you. How would you like to be dressed?"

"21st century smart casual, jeans, jacket, brogues."

A doorway appeared ahead of him, a sharp-edged rectangular hole cut in his reality. He looked through it into a pleasant park with trees, shrubs, tables and chairs, a bandstand, strollers, picnickers.

"By convention, Incorporeals appear in human form in this common meeting place. It's not a law, just good manners."

Riley was still holding his spear, he threw it aside.

The door into summer, he thought, as he stepped through. Sitting at a table close by were Mary, Patrick and Peter Abrahams. They turned towards him, smiling. "I don't see any fluffy bunny rabbits, Mary, how about you?"

She blushed, Riley had never seen her do it before, he felt close to her for the first time. He wanted to put his arms around her but suspected that Patrick might misunderstand his intentions. He sat with them.

"Somebody has to start," he said. "I assume we were successful in our mission. Although I suppose it was a foregone conclusion, the Timestream has realigned itself, and all's right with the world. So, what are you doing with yourself, Peter?" he asked.

"I'm cycling around Australia, actually. I don't expect the simulation extends beyond my personal horizon. It wouldn't be worth the processing power to maintain a whole world when I'm its only occupant."

Riley imagined Abrahams cycling slowly around the equator of his grey featureless world at the center of a colorful circular reality about ten kilometers in diameter.

"What about you?" asked Abrahams.

"I live on a desert island," said Riley. "It's very peaceful, just what I need at the moment." He turned to Mary and Patrick.

"We live on a mountain peak," said Patrick. "We've changed one or two physical parameters in our world, the air is denser and gravity is weaker, so we can spend most of our time gliding and soaring on the thermals."

"We have modified bodies with wings and tails," said Mary. "We're what the String calls 'Mythicals.' "

"That makes my world seem very dull. I must try to be more imaginative," said Riley. "Perhaps I'll have a few volcanoes."

"We've populated the plains below our mountain," said Patrick. Mary nudged him as if he was giving too much away.

"You sound like gods, on Mount Olympus," said Abrahams. Mary and Patrick smiled but didn't expand further.

Later, back on his island, Riley had felt pensive for several days. He had walked around the island and slept on the beach wherever he was exploring. There was no need for him to sleep, but he found it comforting to stick to old patterns as his sun rose, moved across the sky, and went down at the end of each day. He was used to a cyclical life.

One morning, he sat staring out to sea, feeling the cold dampness on his buttocks as water soaked through his shorts. The breeze ruffled his hair, but he couldn't feel the sun on his back. He would speak to Friday about that.

He stood and shouted, "My name is Martin Riley and I'm the only one here."

"Can I help you with something, Martin?" asked Friday's disembodied voice.

"Not really, Friday, not right now."

"You seem preoccupied, Martin," said Friday later, as Riley sat above the tide line, occasionally throwing pebbles into the sea.

"Yes," he said. "I've been thinking about what I want to do now."

"Have you come to any conclusions?"

He stood up, "I'd like to do something useful for the Commonwealth. I need to speak to Tolland, arrange it please."

Next day, Tolland appeared on the beach; he had coalesced from a cloud of pixels, dressed in his usual sober business suit. He looked around at the sky and sea, smiled, and ran a hand through his thick Celtic red hair.

"Hello, Martin, I'm glad to see you again. How are you enjoying life as a Discorporeal?"

"I didn't realize Corporeals could come in here, are you a projection?"

"You might think of me as a temporary copy, a ghost. I will share this experience with my original before I am deleted. How can I help?"

"Two things, first, I want a job. I need more than this, messing about living inside my own imagination. I'd like to do something meaningful in the real world."

Tolland nodded, "And the second thing?"

"I want a copy of Estella, made in 1996, just after we won the 'mug punter' bets at Ascot, before the boys were born. For a while after that anything seemed possible. We sang our own song in those days. I want her here, to share this with me." Riley spread his arms as he stood ankle deep in the wet sand.

The ghost froze momentarily, as it communicated with its original, on the home world below.

Epilogue

UK 2015

The writer sat at his usual table, in the lounge bar of the Angel hotel in Halesworth. He had retired to the small Suffolk market town, several years earlier, and was such a regular and undemanding customer, that the staff barely noticed him anymore. When they convened for their morning coffees, acquaintances knew better than to disturb him, sitting in his corner, his gaze directed inwardly, or scribbling in his notebook. A single cafetiere sometimes lasted him the whole morning.

Shoulders hunched, the stranger pushed sideways through the street door and into the warmth. It was cold outside, and he wore a hat and scarf. Pulling his hands from his coat pockets he held them up to his mouth to blow life back into them, as he looked around the dim interior. Groups of chatting retirees, intent on their coffee Americanos and toasted teacakes, occupied the scattering of tables. Coke burned in the fireplace; the low, beamed ceiling was stained yellow from the smoky exhalations of an earlier, less health-conscious generation.

The writer sat alone as usual. The newcomer pulled an empty chair over and sat opposite him. He took off his hat and scarf and pushed them into his coat pockets. There was a pregnant pause before the older man looked up to see who had dared to disturb his muse. He peered steadily over his reading glasses with furrowed brow, a trick he had often used in earlier years to intimidate recalcitrant students. "Do I know you?" he asked evenly.

The intruder pulled a large black notebook from under his arm, and placed it on the table in front of him. This minor territorial claim an assurance that he would not be brow beaten. From a pocket, he withdrew a memory stick, and laid it on top of the notebook.

"My name is Martin Riley, and I invented time travel," he said, "I have a story you may wish to write."

Author's Note

I am disappointed that my publishers have listed this book as a work of fiction. It is almost entirely a work of fact, and only through the medium of self-publishing have I been able to expose the truth. Dr Riley discussed his story with me in 2015, he wanted his scientific achievements to be made public. I have rendered this account from the journal he left with me, and have expanded on the events where Dr Riley's notes were unusually cryptic. He also left a digital copy of drone pilot Mary Lee's logbook, and various other files, including copies of newspaper articles and video clips, it is unfortunate that both the journal and the memory stick disappeared before this book was published.

In the meantime, somewhere out in the gulfs and deeps, the asteroid is rolling and tumbling towards its catastrophic rendezvous with Earth, on Collision Day, the 20th of October 2217. The governments of the world should be preparing for this disaster.

Where I have used the names of real people, or referred to real events, there is no implication that any of the words spoken or the events portrayed occurred in this Timestream. For legal purposes, this book is therefore a work of fiction.

Suffolk 2017

If you have enjoyed reading this book, please consider leaving a short review on Amazon

The Characters

Martin Riley	Inventor of Temporal Messaging
Estella Riley	nee Pearson, wife of Martin Riley
Prof Middleton	Martin's boss at Cambridge
Paul Burnley	Secret Intelligence Service agent
Dr Oakwood	Chief Scientific Adviser to HMG
Robin Buckley	Cabinet Secretary to HMG
Dr Tom	Drone pilots' doctor
Colonel Wilson	Head of Admin for the TM project
Doug	Technician at Langley
Hank and Cliff	Martin and Estella's sons
Phillip Riley	Flying Squad, brother of Martin
Peter Abrahams	Successor to Martin Riley
Farina	Time traveler, Martin's guide
Tolland	Riley's Commonwealth advocate
Mary Lee	Fly drone pilot
Patrick Tighe	Partner to Mary Lee
Maureen Dodds	Mary's orderly at RAF Waddington
Ruth Harbaugh	Mary's orderly at Langley, USA

Acknowledgements

I wish to offer my thanks to the people who helped me in the creation of this book. Most importantly, Martin Riley who loaned me the notes he made during his years as head of the Temporal Adjustment Agency. It is a great shame that he later repossessed them without consulting me. Also, Nicola McDonagh, Edward Wilson, Sheila Ash, Wally Smith, Jack Ley, Tom Corbett and Ann Walton.

Author Page

Roger Ley was born and educated in London and spent some of his formative years in Saudi Arabia. He worked as an engineer in the oilfields of North Africa and the North Sea, before starting a career in higher education. His writing has appeared in The Guardian, The Oldie, Reader's Digest, Best of British and about twenty ezines. His stories have also been broadcast and podcast.

Follow him on:

Facebook	https://www.facebook.com/rogerley2/
Twitter	https://twitter.com/RogerLey1
Blog	http://rogerley.co.uk/
Goodreads	Roger Ley

Also by Roger Ley

DEAD PEOPLE ON FACEBOOK
An Anthology of Speculative Fiction

A collection of stories published in 2018 by various e-zines internationally. A number were broadcast and podcast on the AntipodeanSF Radio Show by Radio Station 2NVR in New South Wales.

The flash fiction stories are a mix of various speculative genres: fantasy, horror, humor and science fiction; there is also a little magic and one romance. These are followed by a ten-part Steampunk novella, 'Steampunk Confederation' featuring secret agents Harry Lampeter and Telford Stephenson, who are in competition for the plans of the new Ironclad warship.

A HORSE IN THE MORNING
Stories from a sometimes unusual life

Norwegian call girls, desert djinns and Berlin roof jumpers are just a sample of the characters that inhabit the pages of this collection of stories, some of which have been published in periodicals including: Reader's Digest, The Guardian and The Oldie, while others appear for the first time. It is the dramatic and amusing memoir of an engineer, teacher, and failed astronaut recounted with quirky British humor.

Both are available on Amazon in print and as Kindle eBooks

Printed in Great Britain
by Amazon